AN
ASTONISHMENT
OF STARS

Kirti Bhadresa

AN ASTONISHMENT OF STARS

stories

Published by ECW Press
665 Gerrard Street East
Toronto, Ontario, Canada M4M 1Y2
416-694-3348 / info@ecwpress.com

Editor for the Press: Jen Sookfong Lee
Copy-editor: Jen Knoch
Cover design by Jess Albert
Cake art by Ayesha Kassam / @aryassweetboutique
Author photo: Azin Ghaffari

This is a work of fiction. Names, characters,
places, and incidents either are the product of
the author's imagination or are used fictitiously,
and any resemblance to actual persons, living or
dead, business establishments, events, or locales is
entirely coincidental.

LIBRARY AND ARCHIVES CANADA CATALOGUING
IN PUBLICATION

Title: An astonishment of stars / Kirti Bhadresa.

Names: Bhadresa, Kirti, author.

Description: Short stories.

Identifiers: Canadiana (print) 20240366638 |
Canadiana (ebook) 20240366646

ISBN 978-1-77041-737-3 (softcover)
ISBN 978-1-77852-278-9 (ePub)
ISBN 978-1-77852-281-9 (PDF)

Subjects: LCGFT: Short stories.

Classification: LCC PS8603.H35 A92 2024 | DDC
C813/.6—dc23

This book is funded in part by the Government of Canada. Ce livre est financé en partie par le gouvernement du
Canada. We acknowledge the support of the Canada Council for the Arts. Nous remercions le Conseil des arts
du Canada de son soutien. We acknowledge the funding support of the Ontario Arts Council (OAC), an agency
of the Government of Ontario. We also acknowledge the support of the Government of Ontario through the
Ontario Book Publishing Tax Credit, and through Ontario Creates.

PRINTED AND BOUND IN CANADA   PRINTING: FRIESENS   5 · 4 3 2 1

Purchase the print edition and receive the ebook free.
For details, go to ecwpress.com/ebook.

Mark,
Ravi,
Nikhil

—

The three best things
that ever happened to me

Table of Contents

PART ONE

Summer Camp   11
Backstage Passes   22
Invasion   46
Lighten Up   57

PART TWO

The Fundraiser   109
Daksha Takes the Cake   119
The Illness   146
Heads Are Going to Roll   170
The Doctors' Lounge   180

PART THREE

Braids   205
The Gossip   226
In a Name   239
The Worrier   253
An Astonishment of Stars   278

Acknowledgements   291

Part One

Summer Camp

CHARA FILES INTO THE DINING HALL BEHIND HER BUNK-mates. She stays at the back of the line, leaves an intentional gap between her and the other kids. The group's junior counsellor, Viola, escorts the group of youngsters toward their designated table. She wears faded cut-offs and a fitted white tank top. *Viola looks fresh and effortlessly glamorous as always*, thinks Chara as she glances down at her own mid-length shorts and the same over-sized T-shirt she wore the day before.

Viola flips her long, straight hair over her tanned shoulder and waves at her teenaged friend across the room. "Morning!" she sings.

Chara waits for Viola to look back to make sure the campers she's been assigned to look after are all still with her. She watches to see if she thinks about them. Like always, Viola doesn't even bother to check on them.

There are several kids like Viola who started going to the camp when they were seven or eight, and now, in high school, have returned as counsellors-in-training, unpaid assistants to the senior staff. But it seems to Chara like all the teens really care about is their own fun time.

Chara considers slipping away from the others. *If I were to stay far enough behind,* she thinks, *no one would notice.* She could turn around and go back to her bunk, where she could tuck into her still-warm sleeping bag and read the books she brought with her from home all day. For once she could have the quiet cabin all to herself. Or she could slip into the office and make a phone call to her parents. Tell them she wants to come home early. Plead. *As if they would listen.*

The ceiling of the dining hall is high. The interior walls and floors are made of pine, which she imagines was sawed from the forest outside. Sound echoes in the open space, so that it's often too loud at mealtimes. There are only a few decorations — a long silver-framed bulletin board covered with tacked on photos of joyful past campers, a thin white cross at the sharp peak of the building above the door. Long tables and benches are also made from planks of yellowish wood, varnished over so many years, decades even, so that their surface is thick with shiny wax. When Chara presses her fingernail into the narrow edge of the table, she can leave a pale crescent indent in the layers. At the spot she has sat for the last nearly two full weeks there is a satisfying series of such marks.

When the kids are all at their tables, the head counsellor Daniel ("Danny!" "Dan!" "D!") claps, a practised, hollow sound he makes with cupped hands. Sometimes he whistles, sharp and high, to get their attention. *As if we're puppies,* Chara thinks. She stands up with all the others then but doesn't even pretend to say the chanty prayer everyone recites together: *Bless this meal. Bless our friends who gather together. Bless our families and our homes. Keep us safe, loving and strong.* As the others say the words in unison, Chara stays quiet.

Daniel makes announcements after that. Two birthdays, friendship awards for the kids who helped organize a scavenger hunt, a warning about making sure to turn off bathroom taps, a reminder to put away oars and life jackets at the end of the day. Danny is effervescent. Charismatic and confident. Charming. He is a camp celebrity, with his flop of sun-bleached hair and golden tan. Everyone loves him. Mostly. Not Chara.

Near the end of the session there is also always an announcement about the museum field trip, which happens on the day before the campers go home. The way Daniel talks about it, the excursion is a reward that they should all be excited about.

"You kids were so awesome this year, we have an extra special surprise trip planned for you," he exaggerates.

"It's the same as every year!" one kid heckles. "Why don't we go somewhere new for a change?"

There is a smattering of applause. "Yeah!" hollers someone near the front.

"Yup, but it's going to be extra special this time."

Several kids groan.

Daniel pauses now and then as he's speaking so the kids stomp their feet, clap or holler to provoke him. He claims that he wants them to be quiet, but Chara can tell he likes the ruckus. Chara has heard that the rest of the year Daniel is in school to become an architect, but she can't imagine him in meetings wearing long pants or sitting at a desk all day. She wonders why the other kids and counsellors like him so much. To her, he's just an ordinary, loud guy.

"I still think it's fun," remarks the girl sitting beside Chara.

Chara replies, "I don't," then continues to make her half-moon marks on the rim of the table.

Daniel finishes his morning talk, like almost every day, by saying how everyone is equal, there is a place for them all, how they ought to treat each other like family. Chara thinks about which few always manage to serve themselves first at mealtimes, who is most wanted on badminton teams, which kids have the confidence to tip their canoes fearlessly into the icy lake in shrieking joy, trusting their life jackets will keep them afloat, and who doesn't. Over the years, Chara has never made a friend among the other campers, which she is aware is partially because of her own unwillingness to give in to the outdoorsy camp experience, the kind of exuberant, groupy togetherness the others seem so keen on.

Everyone moves quickly when the breakfast platters arrive at each table. The room erupts with clatters and scrapes as kids serve themselves.

"Hey, pass the ketchup!"

"You're taking all the bacon! No fair!"

Mealtimes are awkward for her. Chara's family has always been vegetarian. Her parents both grew up that way, and it never occurred to them that they should choose differently when they moved to Canada.

Every year, before the start of camp, Chara's parents encouragingly suggest that she eat everything, not to be like everyone else but out of worry that otherwise she won't have enough to sustain her. This year, Chara tried. She speared a bite-sized piece of white chicken with her fork, slipped it into her mouth and pressed down on it with her molars, hearing, she imagined, the meat squeak against the smooth enamel. Chara bit down twice, then spat the morsel into her paper napkin. A queasy feeling stayed with her even after she brushed. Through the night she kept imagining the sinews lodged between her teeth. After that she couldn't bring herself to try again. The experience made her hate camp even more, which she didn't think was even possible.

At the end of their meals, the kids take their dishes to the grey plastic bins at the front of the room and then leave for their designated activities. Chara lingers. Through the open windows of the dining hall, she hears the kids' feet crunching on the gravel path.

"Can I help now?" Chara asks the kitchen staff. All the kids have a daily job. Chara is the only person who prefers doing hers over anything else. She doesn't like being in the dense forest with its looming trees and finds it upsetting when the others crash through the surface of the still, shallow lake by jumping off the jutting dock, arms and legs windmilling as if to propel their bodies forward, not caring that they can't see past the mirror surface of the water. *Who knows what's lurking under there?* she always thinks.

At home Chara also hardly spends time outside — which is how she likes it. Her school is two blocks from her house. She gets home before everyone else and watches TV or reads a library book until her parents arrive from work. She helps whoever is making dinner and sets the table. Chara likes the familiar clatter of pans in the kitchen at her house, the sizzling sound of onions slipped into nearly smoking oil, the delicate scent of steamed rice, the way they always lay out the same cloth napkins, the glass jug filled with tap water, the unchanging places that they each sit at around the oval table.

After dinner she does her homework in her bedroom. On the weekends if she goes anywhere it's usually to the mall with her best friend, Yuki, for fries, or over to Yuki's house to play video games and watch movies. For most of the summer she is free to do what she wants while her parents work. Except for these dreaded two weeks, which they think will give her real, postcard Canadian experiences. Her mom and dad like to tell her how lucky she is to experience the things that the camp offers. How they wish they had done such things when they were kids too.

In the kitchen at the camp, the cook gives her a navy blue apron to put on over her clothes. Chara winds her hair into a loose knot that will fit into the net she is handed.

"You can cut celery. Careful with that blade," the cook says.

"I will be. My parents let me chop at home too," Chara replies. Plastic-handled knife in hand, Chara relaxes in the hum of routine around her.

Next, Chara takes a spot in a line with two kitchen staff assembling sandwiches. They lay out symmetrical slices of whole wheat bread, spread a thin smear of mayonnaise across the flat surface. Chara flops a square piece of pre-sliced cheese on top of the mayo. The worker beside her adds ham and a leaf of iceberg lettuce, shaking the water off each one before she lays it down. Cool drops land on Chara's bare arms.

The kitchen workers all come from Chile and often slip into quick Spanish around her. The even-tempered head cook instructs the others confidently, keeping them moving with smooth efficiency as the staff cleans up one meal and gets started on the next. They vary the menu enough to keep it from becoming boring by rotating through a series of fairly balanced but inoffensive meals — never too spicy or foreign to the campers. This is not the only kitchen the team works at. Through the winter, they head to heliskiing lodges or a remote oil rig camp. Chara likes when they tell her the stories of these faraway places, though she doesn't actually want to ever visit them.

The radio is almost always on as they work, a staticky rotation of hits. The staff chatter over her head, sometimes talking about Daniel, usually returning to Spanish then too. Chara knows they are gossiping about him though because she hears them say his name, then they laugh or shake their heads.

Now and then, another person in the kitchen compliments her work or jokes affectionately, "Next summer get a job in the kitchen with us, hey." She almost feels like she belongs at camp when she is with them.

For the first couple of days, Daniel noticed her and asked why she wasn't out boating or playing frisbee with the others. "I mean, wouldn't you rather be outside with your friends? Isn't that the point of coming to camp?" he asked Chara.

The head cook insisted, "She's happy here, let her stay."

So Daniel stopped checking in on me, or remembering I'm still here at all, she thinks. *Like he doesn't even see me. Just like Viola.*

The kids board the yellow school bus that takes them to the nearby dinosaur museum. Once there they are introduced to the paleontologist who gives them a tour of the unchanging displays — eerie skeletons lit from below in darkened rooms joined by a maze of carpeted hallways. Through a clear pane of glass they watch working scientists brush clean recently found fossils, putting together full skeletons using tweezers to handle pieces as small as dimes, while the guide tells them what ancient animal each scientist is working on. The trip is the same every year, the tour usually led by the same earnest guide, so that Chara thinks she could pretty much recite the whole thing herself. She stays near the back of the group, watching the kids jostle and giggle in their clusters, even when there's nothing funny happening. *The only good thing about the museum tour is that it means that soon camp will be over,* Chara thinks.

At lunchtime, before getting back on the bus, the kids all sit on the banks of the wide river. Chara pulls her paper lunch bag from her pack, relieved to be spared the dining room ordeal, though they've been told to still stay close to their cabinmates. Viola is nearby, sitting with Daniel and the other older teenagers. Every now and then Viola laughs at something Daniel says or playfully swats his arm.

When they're done eating, some of the younger campers heave heavy rocks into the river, making a loud splash, others skip flat stones across the slow-moving water, competing to see whose goes farthest. A few kids take off their shoes and wade in. Chara shudders, imagining slimy black leeches attaching themselves to their ankles and feet, as she has seen happen before.

Chara moves upstream and sits behind a scrub of bushes. If anyone was actively looking for her, they would find her easily, but it would take them a minute. She faces out to the murky river, finishes her cheese sandwich and drinks from her water bottle, putting the juice box and granola bar back in her pack for later. Chara sees the others clearing up their garbage to take back to camp with them, as they were told to. Through the branches, Chara notices Viola drop the wrapper of her juice box straw. The see-through plastic flutters to the ground, where Viola leaves it as she squashes the rest of her lunch remains into her bag, still talking with her friends.

Chara thinks about how the plastic could end up wedged between pebbles on the beach for years or get carried off down the river, where a young trout might swallow it, dying slowly as the trash twists and knots inside its guts. Everyone else makes sure to take their garbage. They look around to see what they are leaving behind. *Viola should too*, she thinks.

As the other kids all line up to get on the bus she stays where she is. Chara tucks her knees in closer and wraps her arms around her legs to make herself smaller and watches as the group files onto the bus and the folding doors slide shut behind them, thinking again about how much she hates summer camp. Only this time, the awareness calms her.

When the bus starts to roll away she fixes her gaze away from it and stays still. She doesn't want to watch it drive away, feeling like even her glance might make them notice she's missing. Chara hears the vehicle rumble up the hill toward the highway. After the campers are gone, she stands, walks toward the bit of plastic from Viola's juice box. The garbage crackles as she puts it in her pocket. Then she climbs the steep incline to the top of the river valley, holding on to bits of shrub and long grass, feeling the uneven ground through the soft soles of her runners.

At the top of the hill, rolling prairie spreads out in front of her. She starts to walk across it, right through a field of yellowing green. She can see buildings ahead, the curve of the highway. Grasses bite at her ankles and calves, long enough in places to brush along her palms as she hikes. Chara tilts her head and looks up to see a wisp of a cloud shift direction in the clear sky. She walks on, not sure how much time has passed. In the field there is a wide and flat boulder as big as the couch she watches TV from at home. She thinks that, like her, the glacial rock doesn't belong where it ended up.

Chara climbs up onto the top, takes her own juice box from her backpack and pulls the straw off the side. She makes sure to put the wrapper in her pocket with Viola's. The straw is cracked and hisses as she sips, so Chara thinks of snakes, wondering if she should be concerned about them out here, but to her own surprise, she isn't. It might be nice to see one. She'd have a good story to tell Yuki at least. The air is clear and fresh, and the sun warm on her shoulders. In that moment, Chara doesn't feel frightened of anything.

Everyone will panic, she thinks, *when they realize I'm gone. Viola will be in big trouble for not watching out for me and probably won't be able to come back ever again.*

Chara imagines Daniel pacing and lecturing, enraged at the counsellors and other older kids too.

"How could you let such a thing happen? The most important thing is to keep track of the kids!" While he was there on the bus too. "I can't be responsible for every single detail!" she imagines him exclaiming.

She wonders if they will organize a search. *Maybe the kitchen staff will walk the river banks with them, calling out my name.* She hopes they won't overreact when they hear she is missing. *But also, maybe they will worry a little too.*

Chara puts her empty drink container into her bag, climbs down from the rock and carries on toward the buildings in the distance, in the direction she is almost sure will take her home. The field is wide and pathless but she is unafraid. She imagines herself walking up to her house, letting herself in using the key from under the planter on the step by the back door. Maybe there will be leftovers in the fridge to eat, to keep her going until her family gets home. *They'll be so happy to see me. For sure they'll hug me and tell me how much they missed me.*

All alone, far from everyone, Chara lifts her arms and opens her hands to catch the breeze as she walks on, feeling the cool air on her bare skin. She smiles, feeling triumphant. *At the very least,* she thinks, *after this I will never have to go to summer camp again.* Next year Chara knows that her mom and dad won't make her. And the camp organizers probably won't even let her come back, even if her parents wanted her to return. She is, at last, free.

Backstage Passes

S ALINA WAS STRETCHED OUT ON HER BACK, ON HER NARROW bed on her side of the room, facing the white stucco ceiling. She was blowing on her fingernails to dry the polish she had just carefully applied. Between gusts of breath, Salina shook her splayed hands through the air, jazz style. The glass bottle of coral polish was on the bedside table, not yet hidden away in the drawer with the others she had also secretly purchased.

Lakshmi was finishing her math homework on her side of the room, double-checking each answer on a piece of foolscap before moving on to the next problem. She glanced over, irritated by the sound of her sister's exaggerated exhales. *Like she's just being extra loud about it on purpose, for attention,* Lakshmi thought.

"Do you have to keep doing that?" she asked.

"It's almost dry."

Salina twisted her wrists, to admire the smooth shine. The nail polish was a new shade she had picked up from the drugstore on her way home from school that afternoon. Lakshmi looked down at her own fingers gripping her yellow HB pencil and thought briefly how they looked so plain and square compared to Salina's. She had always been the practical one though and usually didn't mind. It was a difference between them that their family openly acknowledged. Their mother often put Salina's artwork on the fridge, but rarely Lakshmi's. Instead, she would attach Lakshmi's science or arithmetic tests, multiple stapled pages that inevitably slid to the bottom of the door, too heavy for the oblong black magnets that held them.

Lakshmi's long hair fell onto the pages in front of her so she paused to re-tuck it behind her ears. She glanced over at her sister again as she swept it back. As soon as they were called down for dinner, Salina would have to use the remover and cotton balls she kept in the same drawer to hurriedly take the varnish off again. *That stuff reeks even worse than the polish,* she thought.

Lakshmi said, "I don't know why you're bothering with that stuff, Sal. It's pointless. You just have to take it off right away. Plus it stinks."

"It's so pretty though," Salina replied, still admiring her hands. "Want me to do yours too?"

"No way."

Lakshmi immediately regretted refusing so quickly. She didn't like the smell and really didn't want to get in trouble if they got caught. And she also didn't like the colour, which seemed way too girly. But usually Lakshmi wanted more of her sister's attention than Salina was willing to offer, so she didn't want to hurt her feelings either. "I have to get my homework done. It's due tomorrow."

"Your choice."

The clock radio, a squat rectangle on the long wooden dresser opposite their beds, was tuned to the pop station. Both girls liked to keep music on in their room. It was a routine they had established when Salina was in junior high, after hearing other kids talk about what they were listening to. She had adjusted the radio dial to the pop station her peers mentioned, 102.3 Radio NOW. They had left it on the same station ever since.

Lakshmi, who was three years younger than Salina, liked the habit for her own reasons. The repetitive ads became comfortingly familiar. There were certain radio hosts she thought were quite funny. But mostly she valued having a shared routine with her older sister. *Especially one that doesn't include wearing coloured formaldehyde.*

Both girls stopped what they were doing when they heard the song by Das through the low-end speaker. It was the first time Lakshmi had ever heard him. Salina dropped her hands so that her palms were resting on her belly. She shut her eyes and kept them closed the whole time the song played. His voice was easy and smooth, in perfect harmony with the guitar. The drumbeat seemed to echo the sound of her own heart so that Lakshmi felt he had climbed through the black plastic of the radio and was singing just to her. Nothing she had heard before sounded like Das's music. While his lyrics were ordinary, the way he crooned them was dizzying.

"I'm living for your love, I'm risin' risin' risin' up above," he sang. "Girl, what you need is what I'm going to be, whatever you need need need, you know I'll be."

The song ended. The announcer came back on. "That's a great song by a new artist on the charts, a musician called Das. That's right D-A-S. The song is called 'Forever Yours.' I think we're going to be hearing a lot more from this guy. This single hit the charts at number thirty-seven, and it's climbing fast."

Salina pronounced, "Das. He's my favourite." She opened her eyes and looked over to Lakshmi, who was still quiet.

Lakshmi, quickly brought back to attention, was annoyed that her sister had claimed him first. "You've never even heard him before."

"Yes, I have," Salina said defensively. "I've heard that song a few times now, I think."

To Lakshmi's irritation, over the next few months Salina's devotion inflated. She doodled Das's name on her school scribblers, plastered the bulletin board on her side of the room with pictures of him she cut out of magazines — *Teen Beat, Sassy, Seventeen* — the ones she bought every Tuesday from the racks at the drugstore, the same place she bought her secret nail polish.

Salina also used her birthday money at the record store to buy an oversized poster, which she tacked to the wall beside her bed. In the picture Das posed with his electric guitar on an otherwise empty stage, a spotlight behind him illuminating his signature long black hair in silhouette. He was wearing a white shirt that glowed in the spotlight. His buttons were mostly undone and his chest was smooth. Das looked directly at the camera. Lakshmi liked to go to sleep facing Salina's side of the room. She imagined the pop star's brown eyes were looking directly at her.

Das never talked about race outright, but with his dark skin and broad features, he was visibly different from the other musicians their friends were fans of — boy bands who looked like they had just stepped off their surfboards, sun-bleached hair swept back in waves. And his sound wasn't bouncy like theirs, instead it was deep and soulful. In his music videos, he remained unchoreographed, often standing alone or walking down abandoned streets, playing a guitar by himself.

When her sister was around, Lakshmi pretended she wasn't that interested in Das's music, but she was secretly a fan too. It soon seemed like everyone was. He became hugely popular, with his songs hitting the top ten as soon as they were released.

But for Lakshmi, his music felt intimate. Just thinking of his lyrics was thrilling. At school, bored at her desk, she could run through the lines of a song in her head and feel awake again. When one of his hits came on in their room, even if it was the seventh time she'd heard the same song that day, it made her want to dance — close her eyes, flail her arms and forget about all of her worries, the ones about her family especially. When Salina wasn't there she took the opportunity to do exactly this. If Lakshmi ever met Das, she imagined him putting an arm around her and telling her that everything was going to be okay, that he could see her life was going to be amazing and people would notice her, know what she was good at. And he would say it all in a way that she could really believe.

One day the sisters heard on the radio that Das was on tour and was stopping in their city. Salina screamed, a high-pitched shriek of excitement, and said, "I knew he'd come! I have to call my friends right now. We have to get tickets!"

"There's no way you're going to be allowed to go," Lakshmi bitingly reminded her sister. *She can't. That would be way too unfair.* She looked over at the poster and imagined Das singing, pointing at the crowd, pointing at her.

Bent over the phone in her hand, Salina had already started dialling. She looked up at Lakshmi. "I'm going. No matter what."

Unlike their friends, Lakshmi and Salina weren't allowed to wear tank tops, go out in the evenings without an adult present, have boys call the house or wear nail polish or makeup, although Salina had also been sneaking lip gloss for months. It was white-ish, frosty and smelled like bubble gum, a gift from one of Salina's friends who couldn't believe she didn't have any of her own. Before she walked in the door coming home from school, Salina wiped it off on the inside of her shirt.

While their friends did lots of fun things together — school dances, sleepovers and late movies — Salina and Lakshmi didn't. There were a lot of rules they were supposed to follow, etiquette that their parents kept in place in an attempt to keep their two daughters innocent, good. Over the years of living in Canada, their parents had mostly made friends who were just like them, all families who maintained a strict environment for their children, and it worked out well. The kids grew up respectful of their parents, excelled in school, became professionals with admirable careers.

Most recently, their mom's best friend's daughter, Nyra, who was only a few years older than Salina, had been accepted to medical school. On a scholarship even. She was dating a man from a family her parents knew well. The two were serious enough that Lakshmi's mom said the youngsters would most likely announce their wedding plans any day. She had already started looking through the department store flyers that came in the mail for potential engagement presents.

"Isn't it wonderful? She's always been a nice girl and now she's on such a path to success," their mom said pointedly. "We can only hope for such good lives for you two. Isn't that what we moved to this country for?" And then, as she was flipping the page of the leaflet from the housewares store, "Oh look at this rice cooker. Or this slow cooker! Wouldn't they love that? Set and go."

Salina rolled her eyes but their mom didn't notice. Lakshmi covered up a giggle by pretending to cough.

"I'd rather die than be stuck in a marriage like them," Salina admitted dramatically to Lakshmi when they were alone again. "Set and go! Can you imagine?"

The girls' father knew what a big fan of Das's music his older daughter was. When his songs came on the radio in the car, Salina, sitting in the front seat, always turned up the volume and hummed along. Their dad's fingers, long and graceful like Salina's, tapped on the steering wheel too.

"You like this fellow, hey? You know, I should play some of my favourites for you too. From when I was young," he remarked one day.

Salina grimaced. Lakshmi hoped he didn't notice. "I'd like to hear your music, Dad," she said, wanting to make up for her sister's visible disdain.

Their dad saw Salina's determination to see Das in concert, however, and maybe even sensed her growing frustration with her parents' expectations. He convinced his wife that Salina should go to the show.

"Remember you used to love going to see musicians play too? Not so long ago."

"That was different," their mom retorted. "It was safer then. I was already a married woman, going with my husband, remember?"

"We have to let her do these things now and then. She can take the train there with her friends, go to the show, and I will be waiting right outside afterwards to drive her home. I think we can compromise sometimes."

"Compromise?" his wife paused at the kitchen counter. She had a damp blue rag in her hand and was wiping the countertops angrily, stopping to scrub at invisible stains as if they were also her enemies. "If we aren't careful, who knows what she will want to do next? Don't blame me if she starts drinking and smoking drugs after this. Remember that it was all your fault." She shook the cloth in her husband's direction.

And then, lips pursed, she said no more. For two days, she didn't speak to any of them. Not even Lakshmi. She made their lunches in silence, handed them the brown paper bags without saying goodbye, prepared dinner and left it on the stove for them to eat without her.

"I hope it's worth it," their dad said as the three of them ate their evening meal. "I hope you appreciate this, Salina. No more trouble after this for a while, okay?"

"It's definitely going to be worth it." Salina stabbed a piece of cooked broccoli with her fork and jammed it into her mouth whole.

Lakshmi put down her utensils. "I'm not hungry anymore. Can I be excused, Dad? I have homework to do."

She picked up her dishes and set them down on the counter beside the sink. As she walked back to their room, Lakshmi saw her mother lying in the centre of the king-sized bed. She was wearing her grey sweatsuit, her arm covering her eyes dramatically. Lakshmi didn't stop to ask her mom if she was okay. There didn't seem to be any point. And Lakshmi really didn't want to be in the middle of it all.

★

Salina and her two best friends got ready for the concert in the bathroom down the hall from the girls' bedroom. Sitting on the beige carpeted floor of the corridor with her back against the wall, Lakshmi tried to listen in. She leaned over and rapped twice on the door, without standing up. "I need in too," she complained.

Salina opened the vinyl door a crack. The cloying scent of aerosol hairspray swelled to the corridor. "Don't ruin this for me," she hissed. "And quit being such a baby."

She shut the door abruptly then Lakshmi heard her laughter rise instantly, as if she hadn't said anything to Lakshmi at all.

The girls came out with their hair curled and sprayed. Salina's was pulled into a high ponytail and fat spirals fell down her back. Suspiciously, Salina already had on her knee-length coat, though their parents didn't seem to notice. Lakshmi didn't point it out either. *But I could,* she considered momentarily, sure that Salina was wearing an outfit their parents would never approve of underneath.

"I'll wait by the main entrance for you after. Here, just in case," their dad said, handing Salina the twenty-dollar bill he had set down on the coffee table. Their mom, still wearing her same grey sweatsuit, didn't seem to care about embarrassing Salina in front of her friends. She only looked away, still not speaking to her daughter, and barely talking to her husband either.

"Maybe you and Sal are alike, Mom," Lakshmi observed later, as she sat on the sofa with her parents watching TV. Her mother kept looking up from their game show to check the clock on the living room wall.

"Both stubborn," agreed her dad.

"I only care about my daughter's future. No one else seems to."

Lakshmi was watching the clock too. *How much time was Sal going to get to be there for, with Das right there in front of her,*

singing all his best songs in real life? Would he look at her? Notice her?
She still couldn't believe no one even considered that she might
want to go too. But then, Lakshmi most likely wouldn't have, not
after seeing how upset their mom was about it all. She would
have said, "I'm fine. I don't want to," even if she didn't mean it.

★

Salina got home late that night. She had on the concert T-shirt
she'd purchased. It smelled stale, like factory, Lakshmi noticed
as Salina leaned over her and whispered, "Are you sleeping?" Her
breath was warm and the ends of her hair itched as they swept
across Lakshmi's cheek.

"No," Lakshmi opened her eyes. "How was it?"

"It was the best night of my life."

"Lucky," Lakshmi admitted. "Is Mom talking to you yet?"

Salina flopped her head down on Lakshmi's pillow so she
was lying beside her. "I don't care anymore. The concert was
totally worth it tonight. It was way more fun than sitting at home
watching TV. There's so much to do out there in the world, Lak.
And I'm not going to be the boring person she wants me to be.
Ever. I'm going to live my own life. For real."

Her words made Lakshmi feel queasy, as if she could actually
feel the fissure in her family widening. She pushed Salina away.
"Go back to your own bed."

"I love you too." Salina kissed the top of her head before
leaving, as if Lakshmi were a small child. After Salina got up,
Lakshmi turned onto her side and shifted so her head was back
on the centre of the pillow. She faced away from her sister and
away from the poster of Das on the wall too. The pillowcase still
smelled like Salina's hairspray.

★

After that night, Salina often tiptoed to the basement and snuck out through the sliding downstairs window late at night. She went down the street to the park to sit there alone, or to the gas station to buy a bag of chips that she savoured on the walk home. Just wanting to see if she could, she confided to Lakshmi.

And after Das's concert she wore what she liked too, tank tops and T-shirts she cut the bottoms off of herself, to make them cropped. Salina didn't bother covering up with her coat anymore as she left the house. If their mom told her to change before school, she would lie on her bed listening to music until her parents realized they couldn't keep her home. A few wins like that and Salina mostly did whatever she wanted. It became a game for her. She kept going further. There were nights she didn't even come home for dinner.

"Don't worry, kid," she told Lakshmi then. "I'm hanging out at Carla's most of the time."

When their parents had friends over, Salina wouldn't even pretend to care. She'd say things like, "I'm not eating that. I'll smell like curry all night. I'll get a burger later," without acknowledging her parents' stunned guests. They were unused to such open rebellion, they didn't see it in their own kids, and never as visitors in their friends' homes.

"Okay, be home in good time," their dad would say in a forced, cheerful way, as if to show their guests they were still in control.

Salina started dating Mike in her last year of high school. One day he was parked outside the building and noticed her come out. He was eighteen and didn't go there but a couple of his younger friends did, and Mike sometimes gave them a lift home. Mike lived in a house with several roommates and worked in a grocery store warehouse, not caring about getting a better job, saying the whole system was fucked anyway. He started work before sunrise and was done early, so he could be there to meet them by three.

Once Mike figured out which door Salina always came out of he parked there every day, keeping his truck idling, so that he filled the air with the rancid smell of burning diesel. Each day, as she went by, he turned off the vehicle and asked her out, loudly, in front of everyone. "Just once," he pleaded.

It must be flattering to have that kind of attention from an older guy, Lakshmi considered. Eventually Salina stopped ignoring him, broke away from the group of friends she always left school with and said yes.

Salina told Lakshmi she thought he was romantic. Even after they started dating, he still waited outside that same door every day. "He doesn't like the idea of me walking," Salina said. Lakshmi didn't ask why Salina was okay with Mike limiting her freedom, keeping her away from her friends, after fighting so hard against their parents. She told herself that Salina would eventually wonder the same thing herself.

From the school, she and Mike usually went to his place. When Salina passed by the bus stop she would wave from the passenger seat of the truck or stick out her tongue at her sister. Later, while Lakshmi and her parents were watching TV before dinner, they'd hear the rattling engine of Mike's truck pull up in front of the house. The slam of the vehicle's door. The turn of the key in the lock as she came in. Then the truck roared off again. Salina looked at her family, who turned toward her, and said, "What?" as if they were staring for no reason, as if they were strangers.

There were more fights too. The worst ones were over grades, after report cards were issued or when concerned teachers called from the school. Salina's art teacher phoned saying Salina hadn't handed in her last three assignments. "It's unlike her," she said. Art was Salina's favourite subject. The teacher remarked, "She's got more talent than some of her peers, but I can't give her a grade for work she doesn't hand in."

"Why are you creating so much trouble for us all? You need to go to college. Make something of your life," their dad said. "Go to art school, if that's the only thing you like."

"I'm not going to college."

"Salina, please. We only want what's best."

"I'm not going to be your perfect Indian daughter. Lakshmi can do that. Look at her. She's an angel."

Lakshmi was pretending to read a paperback on the couch, acting like she wasn't interested in the disagreement but she was curious enough that she didn't actually leave the room. She wrapped the string from the hood of her sweatshirt around her finger, turning the tip purple. The physical discomfort helped her feel less upset by the argument.

"I'm not an angel. I'm just not a jerk," she shot back to her sister, unwinding the string so her nail turned from purple to pink again as the blood rushed back in.

One day Mike's truck engine shut off outside of their house and then two doors slammed shut instead of only one. Their parents hadn't actually met Mike before, and so were still outwardly acting like he didn't exist. He came in with Salina wearing threadbare jeans and a black AC/DC T-shirt. His light hair was messy and it looked like he hadn't shaved for a while. Blondish-brown stubble darkened his face.

"We're just picking up some stuff," Salina said, not introducing him. She was wearing her low-slung Levi's. The loose bottoms were frayed where they dragged on the ground. Despite the chill outside, she was wearing a leopard print tank top so that her bra straps showed and several inches at the curve of her hips were bare. A piece of black ribbon was tied around her throat as a necklace. Her nails were painted dark green and her smudged eyeliner made dark rings around her eyes. Salina's outfit was everything their parents had railed against.

"Hey," Mike said casually. He slouched against the door without taking his shoes off. "I'm Mike."

Lakshmi followed Salina to their bedroom, where she had put the radio on and was packing a duffel bag of clothes. From the dresser drawer she took three neatly folded shirts, the same ones their mom had washed and put there days before. She added a clean pair of jeans from a different drawer, underwear, a hairbrush. Salina put everything into the nylon bag while humming along to the pop song on the radio, as if everything were normal.

"Grab my toothbrush for me, would you?"

"Where are you going?" Lakshmi asked as she handed it to her.

"I'm going to stay at Mike's place for a couple days."

"Mom and Dad will hate that."

"Aw, you'll miss me," she said, reaching over to pat Lakshmi's hair, like she was a pet. Lakshmi pushed Salina's hand away.

"No way. I like having our room to myself."

"Liar. You hate it when I'm not here. Admit it."

Salina put a ball of paired socks into her bag. "Anyway, Das is on tour again, did you hear? Mike says he's going to buy us tickets for my birthday. Maybe we'll even get backstage passes. He says he knows someone. I might get you a shirt too this time. If you're nice to me."

"I'm always nice to you." Lakshmi blinked back tears. *I wish she would say that I could go too. With her.* Then Lakshmi reminded herself that she had always pretended she barely liked Das's music at all. Maybe it was actually her fault Salina didn't think to invite her.

To her sister she said, "Anyway, as if you'll actually get to meet Das."

Salina scooped up her nail polish collection from the drawer of the bedside table, dropped the bottles in so they were loose with her clothes, then zipped the bag shut in a quick swoop.

"You'll see," Salina responded confidently.

Salina barely graduated then got a job at the 7-Eleven by the high school. She was living with Mike by then in the house with the roommates. Lakshmi stopped to say hi to Salina at work one day after school and arrived just as her sister was ending her shift. "Come see my place," she offered.

Outside, the house was unkempt. The paint was peeling on the crooked picket fence surrounding it. The lawn was overgrown and weedy and there was a flag in one of the large main floor windows instead of regular curtains. The front door was wide open even though it seemed like no one else was home. Salina and Mike's bedroom was down the stairs in the basement. The carpet there was dirty-looking, tinged nicotine yellow, and the bed was a mattress on the floor. Their clothes seemed to be mostly piled there too; there was no other furniture to put things away in. Lakshmi couldn't understand why Salina would choose to live in a place like that.

"Well, I guess if you get tired of all this luxury you could come home." Lakshmi tried to say it lightly.

"I'm not coming back, Lak. I told you. It's not the life for me."

"This can't be what you actually want either. You didn't even get tickets to see Das when he was here. And you said Mike was going to get backstage passes."

"Das will be back again. We'll go next time. Mike promised we wouldn't miss another one. He tried. I know he really tried. He loves me, Lak."

"I've got homework to do, Sal. I'd better go." Lakshmi wanted to leave, wished she hadn't seen the house at all. She hugged her sister goodbye from just inside the still-gaping doorway, holding on tighter than she ordinarily would. "I'll see you soon, okay?" She knew that she wouldn't go there again.

One evening their mom set four spots at the table and didn't notice the mistake until they were sitting down to eat. Hands shaking, she gathered the dishes again. She put the clean cutlery on top of the ceramic plate and set the pile on the counter before breaking into a sob.

"I catch myself now and then. Forgetting our Salina isn't here," she said, holding her hands to her face. Lakshmi noticed that she was still trembling. "I keep thinking that it's all because of me. I pushed her away like this. It was all my wrongdoing."

"It's not all your fault, Mom," Lakshmi ventured. But she really wanted to tell her mom that Salina only wanted to make some of her own choices and wanted to feel like she had some freedom. Maybe she would have made better ones if their mom hadn't always just said no, or if she wasn't so concerned about having Salina be like her friends' kids. *It might actually be your fault.* She said, "Maybe she'll come back soon, Mom. Things might get better."

Her dad got up and put the dishes away. He rested his hand on his wife's shoulder. "We can call Sal to say hi, ask her if she can come eat with us, maybe tomorrow."

Salina phoned the house phone one day and said she was going to drop by. Hoping she might stay for a meal their mom started cooking right away. *Out of habit but maybe also out of worry,* Lakshmi thought. *Or even love.*

Their mom had changed since Salina had left the house. She said things like, "I trust you. I know you're not going to take off like your sister." She let Lakshmi go to dances, which she didn't think were actually that fun, and over to her friends' houses for sleepovers, where Lakshmi never actually slept well.

When Salina showed up that afternoon Mike was with her. Their dad was on the couch with his sock feet up on the coffee table watching the news when the couple entered.

"Come, sit down," he offered.

He stood up as they sat and went to re-set the table for five, not four, adjusting the plates on the cotton tablecloth to make an equal space for each of them. He returned to the living room, and nodded cordially toward Mike, as he took his spot on the couch again.

Mike and Salina shared the La-Z-Boy so that she was partially sitting on Mike's lap. From the kitchen, familiar smells became stronger as the onions and garlic fried, and then soon after there was the clang of the lid being replaced on the pan. The aroma faded again. The industrial-strength kitchen fan clicked on, sucking the rest of the lingering scent away. Lakshmi was glad the evening news gave them all something to look at, though she wasn't following the story. On the screen here was a dog with a wagging tail and a cheerful woman in a wheelchair patting its head.

"We should get a dog," Salina said to Mike.

"Only if you take care of it," he retorted.

Lakshmi felt queasy to hear the two making long-term plans together. She was still hoping that their relationship wouldn't last, that her sister might eventually come back home. Then Lakshmi felt more upset that Mike wouldn't want Salina to have a dog, or wouldn't help her take care of it if they got one. As if he didn't really care if she was happy or not. Lakshmi wished she could speak. Stand up for Salina. Instead she felt hot anger rise from her belly into her throat, blocking it. She wished for the courage to shout at him. *If you really cared you would want her to have everything, a dog, if that's what she really wants!* But she was so furious her thoughts were spinning.

At dinnertime Salina and Mike hardly ate any of the several dishes at the centre the table. Over bowls of vanilla ice cream Mike said, "So we've decided to get married."

Salina and Lakshmi's mom made a sound like a sob, a hiccup. She stood up and left the room. Their dad stayed seated but was quiet too. Eventually Mike said, "Well, I guess that's that. They know now," then leaned over to kiss Salina, right in front of them. Lakshmi was stunned by the news. *But he's so gross,* she thought.

Salina's jaw was set, clenched. She was looking down toward her plate, not meeting her sister's eyes. Lakshmi knew that look of determination. Lakshmi wanted to bring up again how Mike never did come through for that second Das show. Instead she bit the inside of her cheek, determined not to cry. There was no point mentioning that now. Sal had decided that she would marry Mike, and so it would happen, regardless of what anyone else said, or how obvious it was that she was making a mistake.

"Well, good luck, I guess," she said apprehensively to the couple.

"Thanks, kid," Salina replied.

Lakshmi noticed that her mom's hands shook so that she could hardly chop vegetables or ladle dahl into bowls. Then her whole body trembled. She got a diagnosis and the right medication to ease the painful and constant quiver of her muscles. After that, there were times she tuned out in the middle of a conversation, as if daydreaming, forgetting what she was talking about. They could see her searching for words as she began to forget the names of everyday things: potato, boot, windowpane, song.

Lakshmi went to university a twenty-minute train ride away, passing the stadium where Das had played all those years ago every day. She lived at home with her parents, though by then they were more like roommates to her. So busy with school and her own life, she only ate meals with her parents now and then.

One day, she heard her mom talking in her bedroom. Lakshmi knocked on the door then opened it wide. "Mom?" Her mother was sitting on the edge of her neatly made bed, facing an empty armchair. She often left clothes for folding or ironing there, but that day there was nothing. Lakshmi knew the way her mother turned and looked at her that, for a moment, she believed there was someone in the chair, the person she was talking to, but also didn't recognize her daughter at all. Her face was slack.

"Come on, Mom. It's dinnertime. Let's make something. I can cook us a grilled cheese. I'll add mango chutney, the way you like it." Lakshmi held out her hand, as if her mother were the child.

★

Mike and Salina moved to a place of their own on the outskirts of the city. It was cheap because it was close to the dump so that whenever the wind blew from the west, the rancid smell of rotting garbage came right into the house.

Lakshmi once went there to visit her sister. A decade had passed by then. Salina still worked at the 7-Eleven, now a manager, and Lakshmi had long finished school and was working as an event planner. Sometimes, Lakshmi helped organize large-venue events with celebrities in attendance, sometimes concerts. Now and then she wondered if she might be the one of them who would actually meet Das. She wondered if Salina had ever considered this too.

From Salina's kitchen window she saw four deer on the stretch of vacant land between the house and the landfill. When she pointed them out Salina shrugged. "Mike figures he could shoot one from the back deck but he'd probably get in trouble for it." Lakshmi couldn't believe Salina could say something so cold. Like it didn't even bother her.

The sisters sat down at the table each cradling a cup of coffee. Salina had on turquoise nail polish. Lakshmi's fingernails were cut short, unvarnished that day, though by then she also liked to get a manicure now and then. The sisters were both wearing faded jeans. Salina had her fleece slippers on too. Her dog, a scruffy mutt no bigger than a cat, was curled up with his chin resting against Salina's foot. It followed her everywhere.

"Drives Mike crazy," Salina told Lakshmi. "He's completely mine. Doesn't go near Mike at all. Bugs him so much, he thinks the dog should like him more even though Mike never walks him or anything." Lakshmi thought that served Mike right.

One of Das's old songs came on the portable radio Salina kept on her counter. Lakshmi got up and turned the dial to make it louder, thinking how she hadn't heard his music for ages. "You used to love this song," she reminded her sister. Lakshmi's socks stuck to the linoleum as she walked back to her side of the table. The dog's nails scraped against the floor as he shifted.

"I still do. I probably still even have my old posters around somewhere. I'm still mad at Mike that we didn't go see him the last time he was in town."

"Do you ever wish you had moved away from here, Sal? Or gone back to school?"

"I wanted to prove Mom and Dad wrong. They thought I had to be a certain kind of person, exactly like all their friends' kids. They thought I couldn't make my own choices." She was pensive for a moment, reaching down to scratch the dog's head. "I won on that, I think. I did what I wanted to do. I didn't come running back to them when life was less than perfect, like they probably thought I would."

Salina didn't see their parents at all by then, even though she lived in the same city. *She doesn't know how their old battles don't matter anymore*, Lakshmi thought. There were flashes, moments when Lakshmi's mom was like her old, strong self. But they were fleeting and becoming less frequent. To her surprise, despite her illness, Lakshmi noticed her mom laughed with the others in the long-term care home, teased the caregivers lightheartedly as she never would have before, when she was so busy keeping to her own strict ideals about how life should be, how everyone should behave. Her mom was dishevelled and forgetful, her hair was often unbrushed and her socks didn't match. At times she didn't remember quite who Lakshmi was, but she hugged her hello and goodbye in a way she never had before. As if her heart remembered love beyond what her mind held on to.

For Lakshmi, it was almost harder to see their dad living alone in their old house, with the friends whose opinions they once so valued barely visiting at all. Lakshmi thought of telling her sister that she should at least go see him. But she decided it wasn't her place.

When Lakshmi went by, she brought him takeout meals, sat on the sofa with him to watch the news, as he still did at the same time every evening. Now and then Lakshmi peeked into the old bedroom, the one the sisters had shared. The walls were bare, the drawers cleared out. She could still feel Salina's presence there though, and the ghost of her own younger self. *The air in the room still smells chemical, still tainted by the stink of that nail polish remover,* Lakshmi thought as she stepped into the bedroom one day and inhaled. She wiped her finger across the dust on the dresser and considered cleaning it off but instead left only the single shining line the width of her finger. As she left the room, Lakshmi shut the door behind her.

Lakshmi, in her forties, came across a photo of Das in a magazine and thought of sending it to Salina, who she hadn't spoken to for a long time. Das had cut his trademark long hair off, shaved his head completely so that he was barely recognizable. By then he had gone through a messy divorce and found out his manager had taken almost all of his money. Cruelly, they called him "washed up" in the byline.

In the photo, Das was sitting on a beach alone. It must have been taken from far away as the image of him was blurry. Instead of sending it to Salina right away, Lakshmi looked up one of his old songs, one called "Stardust Dreams," and played it on her white headphones, the hard plastic plugs tucked into her ears. She closed her eyes and put her hands in the air unselfconsciously as if she were standing in a crowd of fans, swaying, like Salina got to that night so long ago.

Lakshmi loved her carefully decorated apartment, her furniture curated from thrift stores and auctions. At home she could do what she wanted. She made all her own choices. Though she had had a few relationships over the years, in the end, she preferred her independence.

In the living room of her own home, far from her sister, Lakshmi remembered how Salina said all those years ago that seeing Das in concert was the best night of her life. Lakshmi wondered if she was right, if that really was the highlight.

She thought of her own life, how she had done things she wanted to. Though she still worked as an event planner, Lakshmi had set up her own company by then. She set her own hours and decided which jobs to take on. It was work she still enjoyed and was good at. Lakshmi always did pay close attention to the details and wanted others to be happy.

Yet she also didn't become a doctor, a mother or a wife, all the things that her parents once hoped she would do. None of that mattered anymore. Not to them. Not to anyone. Of all the concerts and backstage meetings she helped plan, she hadn't yet met

Das either, though she sometimes imagined inviting Salina if the chance came up. *It would make her so happy I bet*, Lakshmi thought. *Even after all this time.*

After "Stardust Dreams" ended Lakshmi queued up another one of Das's old hits.

I should at least call Sal, she thought, *see how she's doing.*

But in that moment, instead of phoning her sister, Lakshmi kept listening to the music. She searched for that first Das song she and Salina had heard on the radio all those years ago, "Forever Yours." Skipping past several live versions from concerts Das had played all over the world and a different acoustic interpretation by a younger singer, Lakshmi found the original radio version she'd heard with Salina so long ago. She turned up the volume and pressed play.

Invasion

IN THE LAST WEEKS OF HER PREGNANCY, LEYA DEVELOPED A headache that started behind her left eye, radiated vertically over her skull and down the back of her head into her neck. When she said the headache was keeping her up even more than the ache in her hips and the baby pressing hard against her bladder, her doctor blamed hormones or stress and joked that she'd better get used to not sleeping at night.

Leya spent her first day away from her job lying on the sofa, watching *Sex and the City* reruns. She had started her parental leave unexpectedly early because of the headache, and also because she could hardly wait to begin a full year off, away from her work at the NGO: the office politics, the weight of working on projects that sounded meaningful that never seemed to really change anything. Over time she found herself spending her days filling out applications for funding, having long meetings with the other staff and potential supporters, always raising money. The real work, the kind that connected them to others outside their organization, was then assigned to volunteers. After a while it felt pointless.

Soon after the pain in her head began, she also started finding ants in her house. The first one, a black speck small as a splinter, wandered across the bathroom counter as she was braiding her hair. Out of the corner of her eye, Leya saw it move and thought that the headache was distorting her vision.

But when the insect passed behind the faucet, she dropped her hair, squashed the ant with her thumb, then rinsed it down the sink. The baby in her belly shifted.

From the kitchen, the phone rang. It was Nathan, calling from his office.

"I booked us a few days away. Before the baby. Everyone at work thinks it's a good idea."

"When?"

"This week. I'll take care of everything."

Leya felt that she should say that there was so much left to complete at home, but she felt a weariness come over her, making the words feel like too much effort. Nathan was the kind of guy who got things done. When they needed a fence built he organized a group of friends to come over on a Saturday, ordered pizza, rented equipment and filled a cooler with beer ahead of time. They had the whole thing constructed in a day. Just last month he'd re-painted the entire living room in a single afternoon.

But every time he brought up the baby, saying he liked a certain name, or so-and-so had a rocking chair they were giving away, Leya could only say, "Not yet, I'm not ready," and he would look at her with worried eyes and exhale.

"Okay. Tell me when."

She still had the feeling of the baby not quite being real. As though if she really acknowledged that they were about to fit a new human into their house, she might jinx the whole thing, cause something to go terribly wrong. She had continued, throughout the entire pregnancy, to be surprised when people noticed her growing belly, asked her how far along she was. It felt as if the pregnancy were still private, happening only between her and her own body, and she could hardly imagine there being an actual person, a combination of herself and Nathan, a complete human that she was about to bring into the world and share with others.

Pregnant, she felt awkward and embarrassed, unused to herself. Nathan, unlike Leya, moved with ease through the world, in his life before her and now, with her. Leya could feel his concern over her lack of desire to plan and prepare, and yet she could hardly participate, not even to ease his worry.

With the phone pressed to her ear, she considered that planning a weekend trip was Nathan's way of taking action, feeling productive somehow. She pictured him calling from his grey cubicle, talking in a low tone so the others around him couldn't hear, even though he talked through the idea with them first. So she said, "Sure, it'll be great." Pressing the hang-up button, Leya felt her headache shift from behind her left eye into the bridge of her nose. She rubbed it between her index finger and thumb.

Over the next two hours, she discovered three more ants. After killing each one, she thought that she should have found a piece of paper and taken each little thing outside, but instead she found herself squashing all three, instinctively, as she had the first. She rolled out the vacuum and sucked up the tiny carcasses with the open end of the grey hose, and then took a nap on the sofa in the afternoon sunshine. Sleeping dreamlessly through the baby's hiccups and kicks, curled around her own belly like a cat.

★

It was late afternoon when they made their way in their blue Subaru to the resort in the mountains. The hotel sprawled luxuriously, stoically, as though it had always been there, rising from the grey rock and green forest like magic, like in a fairy tale.

They spent three nights at the hotel, sipping lemonade near the windows in the lounge, looking out at the pale blue lake and the sharp grey peaks that surrounded it, eating heavy meals they could barely afford and Leya couldn't finish, the food kicked back up into her throat by the baby's busy feet.

As a child, when Leya had regularly come to this same hotel for her father's annual conferences, her family was often the only dark-skinned one and the hotel seemed sparsely visited, the lobby quiet and often empty. She felt embarrassed then, especially of her parents who didn't notice how they stood out, though they were regularly asked where they came from. These days the hotel was busier, especially in the summertime, with wealthy tourists from all over the world. No one cared about her and Nathan or their mismatched skin tones. Much of the staff were from countries in Asia or Africa, their rolling accents warm in her ears.

The couple didn't go out hiking or stay up late huddled close together under the night sky, appreciating the quiet away from the city as they would have in the past. Instead they spent evenings and mornings in their cramped room, watching old movies, pressing the mute button through the ads. Leya and Nathan caught glimpses of the late summer sunset through the window and turned off the bedside lamps before eleven. The headache shifted again, this time circling both Leya's left and right eyes, as though she were wearing goggles.

On the drive home they both kept their windows cracked so that the air whistled around them and it was hard to hear each other. The road was familiar and the drive easy in the summertime. Nathan drove with one hand on the wheel and the other on Leya's knee. She tried to keep it very still, lest he see her movement as a kind of rejection. She considered asking him what he was thinking about, but instead looked out toward the shimmering mirage that the sunlight made on the smooth road in front of them, the shadows of dark green forest on either side.

When they got home, Leya slid her silver key into the lock and opened the door. She kicked off her black flip-flops and beelined for the bathroom, then back to the kitchen for a drink. Over the rushing sound from the tap she heard the front door squeak shut, the *thunk* as Nathan dropped their bags on the floor.

"Nate, we have ants."

She had started pouring a glass of water, which was overflowing into the enamel sink. Nathan reached around her to turn off the faucet and looked over to the countertop, where Leya was watching several bugs hurry away from her shadow in different directions. He looked down and saw another on the floor. He squished the ant with the toe of his sneaker, then pulled a tissue from the box on the counter and wiped the dead insect off his shoe. He folded the soft paper in half and used the other side to dab away the ones on the counter. Leya dumped the contents of the over-full glass down the drain without drinking it.

The ants were all over the kitchen. As if sensing the house had been left untended, they had invaded. Nathan got the vacuum out and went around sucking them off the countertops and floors, without killing them first. Leya, on her hands and knees, washed the floors with a mixture of soapy water and vinegar, the best way, according to the internet, to wash away all traces of scent that each ant left for the next one. The acrid smell made her gag; her belly hung so low that it nearly touched the floor.

They threw out the rice and a nearly full bag of flour. When he opened the white plastic bucket of honey that they kept on the bottom shelf of the open pantry, Nathan saw it was nearly black with the insects, as though someone had spilled a bag of ground pepper into gold. The lid had been left open a crack, wasn't sealed all the way around, and so the hungry ants had, one by one, made their way toward it, then into it. Stuck and engorged, they were unable to bring the sweet treasure back to their queen. Nathan slammed the lid down hard and took the bucket out to the trash, trapping the live ants inside.

They stayed up late that night, washing and vacuuming. Leya wondered again if they were ready for parenthood.

Stepping out of the shower the next day, Nathan at work and the house quiet, Leya looked down at the expanding white lightning bolts stretching across her brown skin and reached for the coconut oil. Rubbing it into her belly she hummed a tune that her mother also used to sing to her. She wasn't sure the baby could even hear her voice over the internal clanging of her body. A memory came to her then, sharp as worry, of her mother's childhood home in the coastal Kenyan city of Mombasa. The last time they'd visited was when Leya was a teenager, before her grandparents died and the rest of the family moved away, evacuating, as most of the South Asians did at that time, and transferring their money to more stable British banks. They left in a single generation, as they had arrived, only decades before.

Leya's family had moved from India to East Africa, then on to England, the US or Canada, her home. Clusters of the family followed each other. She used to think they were travellers, adventurers, but wonders now if they were, in fact, only opportunists, moving for jobs and money, setting down roots that reached scarcely below the surface but no deeper, driven by a need more basic than adventure, and always loyal to the sprawling British empire, to a belief in that crumbling hierarchy.

When she was a child, Leya and her two brothers argued all the time, but on those long overseas vacations when they visited the family still in Kenya, they became allies, sleeping in the same row of narrow beds their mom once slept in beside her sisters. As teenagers, they talked about things they missed. The siblings complained.

"I just wish we could be home for a normal Christmas, with a tree and stockings, even the Santa stuff."

"Marlow invited me to go skiing with him and his family for a whole weekend. I could be nice and cool on the hill right now instead of dying in this heat."

"Who cares about skiing? I just want to go home and play regular video games. I can't believe we have all these relatives here and none of them even have a Nintendo. And the TV sucks."

"Isn't it weird that Indian people actually eat Indian food all the time? Don't they ever get sick of it? I'd do pretty much anything for a pizza."

The siblings spent afternoons sprawled on their grandparents' ornate wooden furniture watching an old fan agitate the heavy heat around them. In the evenings they visited one relative or another, crowded into small cars with the windows closed despite the heat, down potholed streets dotted with palms, the road busy with honking cars, pedestrians. At relatives' houses they watched TV with groups of cousins, ate elaborately spiced meals that were consistent, if not identical, at each house. The kind of food Leya craved now.

Leya got dressed and called her mom on speaker. "Oh good, you're home. I'm coming over."

Leya's parents lived in the same house in the suburbs that they had bought when Leya was only four. It was comfortably similar to the others in their cul-de-sac, all with pale shades of vinyl siding that had faded over the years, though the lawns were still neatly trimmed, the trees pruned.

Inside, the house was clean and dated, living room walls lined not with purchased art, but with photos of the family through the years. Leya and her brothers on a beach, laughing. The family in front of an artificial wooden bookcase filled with fake books in a studio photo, school pictures. Leya alone, wearing a sari and elaborate yellow-gold earrings, heavy black eyeliner. Down the hallway and along the stairway to the basement were pictures that she and her brothers had drawn as children, yellow suns and red flowers, green strips along the bottom for grass. They were set in plain frames and dusted every two weeks.

As she let herself in, her mother greeted her with a call from the kitchen. "I'm here! Come in." Her mom was at the sink. She dried her hands on a dishcloth before pressing them on either side of Leya's belly, then rubbed her daughter's shoulders. "I'll make tea."

Sitting at the same spot at the dining room table where she had sat as a child, her spot, Leya told her mom, "While we were away the house got infested, hundreds of ants, all after a bucket of honey we didn't close all the way. It could have been worse, at least they aren't really big bugs, cockroaches or anything, but still, it was disgusting. We cleaned and cleaned, but we're keeping the traps out, in case. In case they come back."

Was she testing her mom, she wondered as she was talking, expecting her to also wonder if Leya was really ready for motherhood?

Leya's mom faced the window, in the same spot she, too, had always sat. Her face, Leya noticed in the bright light, had aged around her eyes and mouth. Her hair was still dyed brownish black, no grey showing. She laced her fingers on the flowered tablecloth and listened to her daughter without fidgeting.

As Leya finished telling her about the ants, her mom said, "Do you want to come and stay here?"

Leya considered temporarily moving into the room that used to be hers but that now contained only a narrow desk with a desktop computer and a printer, a double bed with a department store comforter on it. She imagined crawling into the bed and sleeping for hours, letting her mom cook for her. She rubbed at the headache, now lodged between her eyebrows, took a sip of her sweet, milky tea, and contemplated staying, if only for a nap.

Thinking of how easy it would be to linger, to never leave, and the impossibility of it she said, "I'd better go home."

The mid-afternoon drive back to the inner city took about half an hour. There were only a few other cars on the street at this time, though the cafés and restaurants she passed were busy. Paused at a red light, Leya looked up at the white lines of contrails criss-crossing the blue sky. Her head felt as though she were wearing a too-small helmet. Her arms reached far for the steering wheel, like two narrow bridges over her round middle. A song she remembered from high school came on the radio. A slow dance that Nathan might sway and sing along to, as a joke. She might have smiled if he were there.

At home, Leya kept her flip-flops on, in case there were still some ants left. She washed her hands and pulled a glass jar of dry red lentils from the cupboard. The house was quiet; squares of sunshine from the windows patterned the floor.

She pulled an enamel pot from a shelf and put it on the stove, added a glug of oil, found an onion, and cut it into narrow strips on a wooden board. The onion made her eyes water, and she felt the pressure in her head loosen, as though someone had pulled upward on the top of her skull and then let go. She added the slices of onion to the pot. As they browned, she chopped a carrot, took spices from a rack and added them without measuring to the sizzling mixture. The carrots, the lentils, water from the kettle, a bit of salt. *What else?* There was a bag of wilting spinach in the fridge, and she added that too, altering her mother's recipe but only a little. She hummed to herself again and to the baby as she worked, stirring until the lentils were soft and fat.

She tore a piece of paper from a pad she found in the junk drawer and scribbled on it with plastic pens until she found one that worked well, then set the paper and pen down on the table. She got a clean bowl from the dishwasher and filled it from the steaming pot on the stove, pulled a single spoon from the cutlery drawer.

As she put the bowl of soup down and eased into the chair in front of it, she looked out toward her compact backyard, crowded with the green of summertime. Kicking off her flip-flops at last, Leya then stretched her arms upward, rotated her neck in a slow circle, one way then the other. She ate a spoonful from her bowl. Then picked up the pen and titled a list in blue ink: "Things a Baby Needs."

An erratic mosquito bashed against the screen door in front of her, attempting escape. Down the street, a humming lawnmower coughed and sputtered to a stop; a bike bell rang four times. The baby's foot pushed into her ribcage. With the pen still poised in her hand, Leya used her elbow to push down on her belly, until the pressing weight eased, and so became tolerable again.

Lighten Up

WHEN NAINA FIRST NOTICED HER AUNT COULD LEVI-tate, she had already been worried for weeks about Shanti's frailty, the way her eyes would become unfocused as she gazed vacantly into the distance. She seemed almost transparent at those times, a gossamer of a person barely tethered to earth. Maybe it was inevitable that she would eventually begin to phys-ically lift upward, but Naina was afraid. She felt, then, that it was her job to keep her aunt's body fixed to the ground.

Months earlier, she had arrived in the city, the one her aunt happened to live in too. There were no distant cousins to meet her at the airport, no old friends of her parents to hug her and offer to make her dinner, which she felt fine about. Naina had waved down a taxi and, from the back seat, gave the driver the address to her new apartment just off campus. She had only seen the furnished second-storey suite in photos on the university's accommodation website and so felt more at ease when the driver said, "That's a good location. Close to everything, but quiet enough."

When Naina got there she looked around the unremarkable studio and said, "Well, this will do." Her navy cotton dress was rumpled and smelled like airplane, but she decided not to change, or even unpack. *Those things can wait,* she thought. Instead, she grabbed her grey backpack and left to find the music building.

Naina crossed the campus in the shade of evenly spaced trees. Leaves swished and chattered above her. With sprawling lawns between brick buildings, the grounds were beautiful, cinematically picturesque. But Naina kept her head down. She only paused to look at her map, too intent on locating the practice rooms to get distracted by her surroundings.

Working hard was the most important thing to Naina. Getting her master's degree and practising until she wasn't just good but among the best was the only way she could eventually earn enough to be financially independent in her field. As her parents often reminded her, if she was going to choose such a difficult career, she had to be exceptional. And playing the piano was the only thing Naina really wanted to do.

She said hello to the security guard on the main floor, who took his time giving her directions. "No one's been up there for a while. You'll see, it's pretty dead this time of year."

Naina followed his directions to the floor where the practice rooms were located. Each one had plain white walls and wide-plank wood floors, a large window so that, in the late afternoon, sunlight came into the room in uniform lines through the half-open blinds. There was a gleaming baby grand piano with a matching bench at the centre of each, a few black metal music stands, and several folding chairs leaning against the walls. Naina turned the blinds to let more light into the first room, then went right to the instrument. She played a single note quietly, listened closely to its echo, then more boldly went through all the major scales, moved on to the minors, banged out a few emphatic chord sequences. After that Naina moved to the next room. She took her time in each of the six spaces, knocking on the door before entering each one, just in case, then played unselfconsciously.

The Sherlock-Manning in the room at the end of the hall was the best one, she determined a couple of hours later: mellow but clear. Naina felt more prepared to live in a new city now that she had found the right keyboard. On the chart beside the door, she jotted her name down in blue ink in the same time slots for each day. Hers was the only one on the list so far.

Now, with two weeks left before the start of school, there was time for Naina to relax between her practice times, explore the city, and meet her estranged aunt. She texted her from the broad steps of the music building.

"I'm here! Unpacking tonight. Would love to meet if you're still up for it. Maybe dinner tomorrow?"

The aunt, Shanti, was the relative the family never saw and hardly spoke about. When they did it was disapprovingly. Everyone said she was unreliable, uncaring. They said she had abandoned her siblings and aging parents, even as they got older and needed more support. Shanti only ever thought of herself, they complained. Naina wondered if the other family members were jealous. Especially her own mother. It seemed the family most valued not thinking of themselves as individuals at all. No one could ever say that they felt like spending time alone, that they didn't feel like having a meal that was offered to them. It was inconceivable to openly disagree with an elder even if you knew they were wrong. To Naina, especially as she got older, this disregard of family members' individuality seemed like no way to live, though she would never tell them so. Naina wanted to decide for herself what she thought of Shanti now that she was living nearby.

Shanti replied hours later. By then Naina was back in her apartment, freshly showered and putting her clothes away in the utilitarian dresser beside the single bed.

"Just seeing your message now! Wonderful! 6 p.m. tomorrow? Trattoria on 4th? Very close to you! I hardly check my messages so try calling me if you get lost."

"I'm sure I'll find it no problem. See you there!" Naina looked up the restaurant right away. It seemed nice but not fancy, based on the reviews. She raked through the outfits she'd just finished hanging in her closet to decide what to wear.

Naina put on the clothes she had laid out on her bed, her beige linen shorts and sleeveless white blouse, brushed her hair, and then pinned her bangs back. She considered putting on con-cealer or a bit of blush but imagined it melting off her face in the heat. Instead she applied her favourite muted lip gloss and a sweep of mascara. Then she looked up the route on her phone one more time just to be sure.

Trattoria was also in the collegiate neighbourhood that was tucked into the inner curve of the broad river. Naina liked the liveliness of the community near the campus. Murals deco-rated the sides of buildings. Galleries and storefronts displayed student works in their windows. Tattered posters advertising live music and plays covered utility poles, leaving glittering lines of silver staples on their rough surfaces.

The intense warmth from the sun radiated down and then reflected back up again from the concrete. Naina paused, stepped off to the edge of the sidewalk so people could move around her easily. She checked the map on her phone once again and tried to discreetly wipe the sweat off her forehead with the back of her arm.

By 5:47 Naina was seated inside the restaurant, at a small round table beside an open window. Her fingers twitched, drumming one by one on the checkered tablecloth, as if she were practising a very basic five-note scale repeatedly. It was an old nervous habit. Her hands were strong from so many years of playing, her nails cut aggressively short so they wouldn't click on the keys. They made no sound as they tapped on the table either.

Naina put one hand over the other to still herself. From outside she felt a slight breeze on her bare arms, like a sigh. Realizing she had been holding her breath, Naina exhaled too. She had definitely arrived early but now her aunt was late. Maybe everyone was right about Shanti, Naina considered, and she really was unreliable. Perhaps Shanti wouldn't show up at all.

Naina surveyed the sidewalk. The pavement was bustling with mostly young people strolling or sitting on wooden benches. They lingered outside busy cafés, idle in the waning summer before the start of classes. She wondered at their ease then tapped her fingertips in sequence on the tablecloth again.

Waiting there, she realized that she couldn't actually remember ever sitting in a restaurant by herself before. Naina had grown up in a large extended family. Through her undergrad she had lived with her parents and had an uncomplicated boyfriend, Paul. She met him during the first week of university, and they had spent most of their spare time together. They found a group of similarly diligent friends. The crew studied together at the same long table in the library, played games of darts or trivia at the pub on campus. After graduation, the circle dissolved. Everyone moved on to grad school or jobs in other cities. She and Paul drifted apart from each other too. Eventually Naina told him that she wanted to leave town for her master's, that she needed an adventure. They broke up that same day.

She gestured to the waiter to order herself a glass of wine. *If Shanti doesn't show, I could still have a drink, maybe something to eat. This,* Naina realized, opening the menu in front of her, *is an opportunity to become more independent.*

The waiter had just put her Riesling down when Naina saw her aunt walking down the street toward her. Despite being late, Shanti didn't seem hurried. She was wearing layers of clothing — a pair of patterned tights under a skirt that flowed past her knees, a long draping shirt and a thin cardigan. A saffron scarf looped around her neck, despite the summery weather. The strap of a fabric purse, almost large enough to be a tote bag, crossed her body.

Naina recognized Shanti right away. She was obviously different from Naina's mother, who would never have left the house in such a strange assortment of clothing. And yet, Naina noticed, the two looked alike with their white-streaked hair and squarish faces, the strong set of their jaws. Watching her colourful aunt from afar, Naina felt dull in her plain outfit. *Maybe I should have worn something a little more interesting.*

Spotting Naina, Shanti waved and hurried her pace.

"How lovely," she said as Naina stood up to hug her. "I'm so glad you're here." Shanti pulled the strap of her bag over her head and set it down on the floor beside her chair. She nodded toward Naina's wine glass. "Good idea. Maybe I'll join you."

But when the server arrived, Shanti smiled up at him. "I'll have ice water please. I'd love to toast my niece, but as I get older it goes right to my head."

For dinner, Naina ordered the bolognese, Shanti ordered a kale salad, the small one, which hardly seemed to be enough for dinner. When Naina went out for meals with other family members, they ordered appetizers and each had a full plate to themselves, which they shared around the table. But when their food arrived, Shanti hardly touched her salad and then shook her head when Naina offered her a bite of her pasta.

"How is it?" Naina gestured toward the bowl of greens.

"Oh fine, only I ate earlier." It seemed odd to Naina that her aunt would eat before meeting for dinner. As the waiter took the barely touched salad away, along with the emptied pasta plate and wine glass, Naina decided her aunt was nervous to meet her and wasn't hungry, and so she didn't think any more about it.

Outside the restaurant, the street was still busy but some of the younger people, students, Naina assumed, were more dressed up, ready for the evening. A group of women walked by wearing spaghetti-strap dresses, tinging the air with their candy-shop blend of perfumes as they passed. A more casually dressed couple strolled by licking ice cream from waffle cones, both wearing flip-flops. Naina liked the sound of the two of them, the flap of their feet in comfortable unison. A bar on the corner thumped techno through their outdoor speakers to beckon people in. Even then Naina didn't miss having her friends with her and didn't wish she was part of a romantic couple. *Not yet,* she reminded herself.

"Are you in a hurry or do you have time for a walk?" Shanti asked.

"I was hoping you could show me around."

The two weaved around the evening crowd on the main road and then onto the quieter residential streets toward the river. They walked close to each other. Shanti was a similar height to Naina's mother; aunt and niece walked comfortably. It was as if they had been doing the exact route together for years.

"I wasn't sure what it would be like, to meet you like this. I haven't seen you since you were a baby," Shanti said as they paused on a bridge, looking toward the twisting current below.

"It's strange, isn't it? Like we don't know each other well but we should." Naina shivered. It was cool by then, the daytime heat pushed away by a chillier evening wind.

"Here, take this." Shanti set her bag down and unlooped the scarf from around her neck.

Naina wrapped the wide fabric around her shoulders so it was more like a shawl. It was finely woven and soft on her skin. "Thanks. I'll give it back to you next time."

"Keep it. I'd like you to. You'll need something light in the evenings here. Even in the summer it gets cool as the sun goes down."

They were quiet then, still looking toward the water that shimmered like diamonds in the waning light. "There are beautiful paths there, along the other side of the river. I could show you if you have time tomorrow," Shanti offered. "And a good stationary store if you need anything for school. There are all kinds of little spots you might like. I can show you my yoga studio one day too if you're interested."

"That's a great idea. There's nothing I'd rather do." The idea of spending time with Shanti didn't feel like pressure at all. With her, Naina felt the reassurance of being with a family member, but strangely without any of the weight of expectation she felt at home: the way her mom always wanted her company as she made dinner or went shopping for new clothes, or how her parents assumed she would accompany them every time a relative invited them over for tea.

Naina wondered about the yoga studio though. Her other Desi friends, as well as her cousins, had almost all quit practising at popular studios out of silent protest over the appropriation of their culture. It was uncomfortable, upsetting to be led in a class by an instructor who had only completed a short course in the discipline, but then behaved like a spiritual authority. Naina wondered what kind of studio Shanti would go to, after growing up in a family that practised yoga and meditation so ritually it was entrenched in their daily lives. Already, she could sense that Shanti was different from most people she knew. Judged things differently. Or possibly was not judgmental at all.

Over the next weeks Naina practiced piano every morning, mostly scales and chords, experimenting with the minor seventh, the primary scale of Indian music. She was planning to explore the links between classical piano and Hindustani rāgas through her master's program.

It was difficult, some said impossible, to achieve a clean translation of the sounds. The harmony of South Asian classical music was usually made by fretless stringed instruments. The separation of discrete tones on the piano made the more subtle sounds nearly unplayable on the Western instrument. Stretches of harmony that held notes together in Indian music disappeared on the piano. And yet, Naina found there was magic in trying to adjust to the lack of nuance on the keys, combining sounds and pitches to create a compromise between her two cultures, even if it was an uncomfortable one.

Naina also walked with Shanti every afternoon. They often chatted about Shanti's upbringing as they hiked. It was hard for Naina to believe she and her mother had grown up in the same family. Shanti didn't seem to know how the rest of the family perceived her, and, when Naina asked about the distance between them, Shanti only said that they had drifted apart and made no mention of hard feelings. Naina kept quiet. She didn't say how the others actually felt. At first she thought that she didn't want to hurt Shanti's feelings but then admired the way Shanti didn't overthink the way she was perceived either. It seemed as though Shanti just didn't worry about it.

"Growing up, our dad cared most that we had a good spiritual life. Everything else was secondary. As a child, before coming to Canada, I thought I might grow up to be a real sādhvi," Shanti told her. "I loved the simplicity of devotion, the feeling of walking home from temple after our prayers. Everything felt so peaceful then."

"Your life seems peaceful now."

"That's because you're meeting me at the right time. I found my way back to what matters most to me. Before, I was always looking for happiness in the wrong places. My relationships, my work, nice clothes, parties, owning objects. For years all these things mattered so much. I'm learning now as I get older. Letting go."

Naina considered her own feelings about religion. Growing up they went to temple for pujas as a family, but it felt more like a social gathering than a spiritual one, a place to meet. After praying, the adults would gossip while the children ran and played, and then everyone ate together. The only thing that felt like prayer to Naina now was when she was sitting alone at a piano. Then, the most essential part of her — every sorrow, worry, joy — made more sense. Each tone echoed some fragment of her. The notes that emerged through her hands held meaning; when she was deeply into her practice, each sound felt holy.

★

Shanti was a fast walker. Naina often paused like she was looking out at the scenery or was appreciating the architecture of a modern building as a way to sneak in breaks. Sometimes she asked Shanti a question to keep her talking and slow her down, not wanting to admit she could hardly keep up. In fact, it sometimes seemed as if Shanti was barely touching the ground at all. She moved so effortlessly, never got hungry, and rarely even thirsty.

By the time she got back to her apartment, Naina was usually ravenous. She made a trip to the grocery store down the street and filled her small freezer with ready-made meals that she could heat up in the microwave and eat standing up at the counter. Naina would then slip her shoes back on and walk, for the second time in the same day, to her practice room.

More and more students went to the music building as the beginning of school neared. Others signed up for the rooms too. From the hallways there was the squeak of violins, thumps of drums. The voice students practised casually in the hallways, trilling scales down the corridors. Professors stopped by to pick up their mail and organize their offices. They nodded hello to Naina as they passed by.

But at night the music building was almost empty, like the first day Naina went there. In the practice rooms she liked to open a window to feel the cool evening air spill into the small space, knowing that within minutes she would be sweating from the labour of practising. Playing at night felt different. She didn't care if improvised notes clashed or if her harmonies weren't melodic. There was no one nearby to judge her skill. Sometimes Naina even turned the light off so that she could see only the silhouette of her own hands, bold and quick in the near-dark.

One day Naina woke up to clouds, silver skies that darkened more by mid-morning. By the time she was at school it was raining. Hard. The sound was so clamorous on the windows and streets she paused to listen to the rushing deluge of it as it washed the dusty city clean. By early afternoon the sky was clear and the air was crisp. The rain had left pools of water on the sidewalks that she hopped over on her way to meet Shanti. Naina smiled at a child who was wearing yellow boots and jumping right into the centre of the puddles, landing on both feet, squealing joyfully.

Shanti and Naina met at a bench in front of Trattoria. From there they continued through the neighbourhood, on the same route they'd been taking for days, toward the picturesque unpaved trails that ran parallel to the river. That day there were sections of the path too mucky to cross easily, despite the warm sun shining down on them again.

"I'll go first," Naina offered at a particularly wide puddle. Naina took three long quick strides across. She called back to her aunt. "It seems fine, you won't sink in too much. It's not deep." On the other side, she wiped her feet on the damp grass beside the trail. "It's pretty sticky though." She turned her feet to look at the bottoms of her sneakers. They were still caked with thick mud.

"How are yours?" Naina looked toward Shanti, who had navigated the puddle behind her.

Both women looked down at the soles of Shanti's shoes. "Well, they seem to be fine." Several blades of grass stuck to the rubber, and they were a little dirty, but there was strangely no mud on them at all.

Naina frowned. "Well, what's your secret?"

"Secret? I don't have a secret. I went same as you. More carefully, I suppose," she teased.

"But you can't even see your footprints." Naina pointed to her own patterned marks across the black muck.

"It's all the yoga I do. I'm light-footed. Let's carry on, Naina. We can cut back through here to the sidewalks again. It will be less messy."

Naina, unnerved, nodded. She felt as though her aunt had tricked her in a way she couldn't make sense of. There was a vacant look on Shanti's face too, one that made Naina feel inexplicably excluded, as if she were a child again and there was an adult secret she wasn't let in on. Or she had been shown a magic trick she couldn't work out. Shanti didn't respond to Naina's upset. *Or perhaps doesn't even notice it,* Naina thought. And then, feeling petulant, as if she really were a kid, *Or maybe she doesn't even care.*

"I think I'd better get back to work." Naina missed her piano then, and longed to return to the predictability of it. At least there, things made sense.

★

She knew that Shanti had studied interior design after art school as a way to make a living. But when Naina first saw her condo, she understood that Shanti was also skilled at it. Her home was on the third floor of a walk-up. It was bright and quiet, a feeling that seemed carefully curated. The clean lines of her sleek furniture were softened by colourful textiles. The entire space was painted cool white and crowded with artwork, yet the walls didn't feel cluttered. Shanti's work, Naina surmised. She took her time examining each piece, noticing the similarities in colour and depth between them. In most, there was a human form — a child, a woman, young, then bent as if aging. The figures traversed multicoloured landscapes, scenes made up of vivid shades — blues and greens like sky and earth, pink for mountains, gold flecks like stars. The light in each work radiated out from the centre. The paintings seemed to all come together like a story. *Or a complex harmony,* Naina thought. *Like a piece of music.*

"I keep my work around me like old friends," Shanti said as Naina looked around. "Each one is a part of me."

It was the most distinctive home Naina had ever been in. It was also the first home she'd ever visited where a person lived alone — without a family, a partner or a roommate. Naina didn't know it was possible to have your residence become an extension of your whole self. And she loved it.

Shanti filled a kettle and put it on the stove, gestured for Naina to come sit on a barstool across the stone counter from her. "Let's go to my yoga studio today too. We'll have tea first." Naina watched her aunt fill the kettle with tap water, and put it back on the stove to boil. From a metal canister she scooped dried leaves into a teapot. Shanti took two small hand-thrown ceramic cups from a shelf as the kettle murmured, wiped the pottery clean with a sand-coloured dish towel. The kettle whistled, and Shanti poured the steaming water into the pot, infusing the air with the fresh scent of mint. Her movements were careful. Shanti turned back to Naina.

"Now you've seen my art. One day I'd love to hear you play." Shanti hadn't asked Naina about her music before. In fact, she rarely asked any questions. Instead she simply welcomed whatever information Naina offered.

"You can come with me while I practise one day," Naina suggested. It was rare for her to make such an offer. Her practice time felt private to her, sacred even. But it was easy to make an exception for Shanti. Naina knew she wouldn't criticize, and most likely wouldn't expect anything of her at all. Shanti would appreciate just being there.

Naina reached for the handle of the teapot. "Should I pour?"

"Not yet, Naina. It needs a minute to steep. There's no hurry."

The yoga studio Shanti frequented was a short walk from her home. It was in a detached single-storey building that had once been a hardware store. From the outside the structure was unremarkable. There was a gravel parking lot in front and patches of dry grass around the sides and back. Naina wouldn't have noticed it if not for the large hand-painted sign outside, a white background with letters painted green, the shade of springtime leaves. "Humble Hearts Yoga Studio and Wellness Centre."

There was the mark of an om above it, which irritated Naina; she always disliked seeing the religious symbol used so casually. Below the letters there was a continuous line painting of a cross-legged meditator in the same deep colour as the lettering. It was unsettling to Naina that Shanti would frequent a place like this — a business that hand-plucked elements of a culture, their culture, like the om symbol out front, to create a space that, she could tell already, was most comfortable to privileged white people. Naina knew this without having to walk in the door. She'd seen it enough times before.

"We're arriving between classes so we won't disrupt anyone," said Shanti. She clearly knew the schedule well.

There was a stunning transformation from the rough exterior of the studio to the finished interior. Inside, polished floors and pale walls pulled in the sunlight that flooded through the large windows covered only by sheer curtains. Even Naina found it beautiful, despite her reservations. Her frustration eased.

A young woman was behind a minimalist reception desk. Her brown hair was worked into dreadlocks and pulled up into a top knot. She played with a rope that had fallen loose as she chatted. Her feet were bare, Naina noticed, with tan lines across the tops of them. The woman was on the phone but playfully blew Shanti a kiss.

"I helped Zane with the design before it opened. We update it now and then, swap things out with the seasons," Shanti explained to Naina. The sound of the bamboo water fountain near the entrance soothed people as they came in, so that they could symbolically wash away the worries they brought in from the outside world, she told her. The bench seating around the perimeter invited people to linger. Large cushions and a few lush plants on wooden shelves added to the welcoming feeling. "We tried to think of the details," Shanti said.

"Oh, and this is Zane." A man emerged from a back room. He was tall and broad, with thinning hair. His feet were bare too. As Naina glanced down, the sight of his long toes felt slightly obscene. She tried not to giggle.

"And you must be the niece." Zane held out his hand to Naina.

"This space is really lovely," Naina said shaking his. A snicker still pushed at the corners of her mouth.

"I couldn't have done it without Shanti. The universe brought her into my life for a reason." He let go of Naina's hand and looked at Shanti in a way that made Naina take a small step backward, as if to give them some privacy. She hated the way he said the word universe, as if it started with a capital U. The amusement she felt a moment earlier turned back to annoyance.

"Oh, stop it," Shanti said flirtatiously. Naina looked around the room again, intentionally away from them.

A decade earlier, Shanti had told her, Zane had quit his job selling kitchen appliances to restaurant owners and started on what he called his spiritual path. He put his house on the market, moved to an apartment, and invested his savings in the inner-city building. Zane did most of the renovation work himself.

"My life's meaning became clear to me here," Zane told her. "I hope you feel at home here too."

"Thanks," she said awkwardly.

Zane didn't seem to notice her discomfort before he nodded and turned away to take a call on his mobile phone.

"Ready to carry on?" Naina asked her aunt then. She waited for Shanti to respond. "Should we go?" she asked again.

Shanti's eyes seemed unfocused, as if she were daydreaming. Her arms were loose at her sides. Zane's voice was low; he was a distance away from them. But otherwise the room was quiet. Naina moved closer to Shanti and cleared her throat.

The office phone rang again. The receptionist answered. Zane was still talking too, saying something about branded water bottles. The water fountain trickled melodically. Naina touched Shanti's arm, said her name. This gesture seemed enough to rouse her. Shanti's gaze broke and her eyes seemed to focus on the room again.

"Okay, Naina, let's go." Shanti spoke slowly. She seemed befuddled, as if waking from a nap. Shanti smiled affectionately at Naina. "Now you've seen everything. You must be hungry; we can get you something to eat."

Zane paused his call. "Great meeting you, Naina. Come to a class one day soon! First one's on me."

"Maybe." Naina knew she wouldn't. "Thanks again," she added, to sound more polite.

"Namaste!" the receptionist called out. She pressed her hands together as if praying in their direction.

"Bye," Naina responded pointedly. She didn't understand how Shanti could enjoy being in this place that was clearly profiting from the culture she grew up in. Naina felt prickling heat rush through her as she pushed open the door, overcome by anger and resentment, fury crushing her chest so that she could hardly breathe. She was outraged by the ease of it, the way the receptionist used the word Namaste so casually, and so incorrectly. But also so confidently.

Outside the sun was bright. Shanti took her arm and held it loosely. Naina's rage faded as they walked away from the studio. She told herself that she was making a big deal about nothing. Maybe she needed to be more tolerant, like Shanti. Maybe she had to learn to be more easygoing. Lighten up. Her aunt seemed to move through the world so simply, so comfortably. Naina wished, sometimes, that she could do the same. Again she just yearned to be alone, back in a practice room. Playing something loud and dramatic, pounding on the keys as if she were shouting, but without needing to know the precise words to express why she was so upset, without needing any words at all.

★

Shanti was always late and usually Naina didn't mind. She often brought her books or sheet music with her to study. But one day Naina cancelled a practice time to arrive at a café when planned, and Shanti still wasn't there twenty minutes later. If it had been anyone else, Naina would have texted to see where they were, but she knew Shanti wouldn't respond to a message for ages. When Naina was about to take out her phone and try calling, Shanti arrived. It turned out she had only come from the yoga studio just minutes away.

Her aunt kissed her hello, without acknowledging the time, then announced excitedly, "I came up with an idea. A wonderful plan to take that ugly parking lot around the studio and make it into a beautiful garden. I could see it all clearly. The flowers, the stone pathways weaving through the garden beds. I was standing outside just feeling it. All that potential. It will become a place people can gather. I only have to convince Zane." She pulled a notebook out of her bag and opened it to a sketch. "I drew this. It's a rough plan but it gives you the idea."

To Naina, the monochromatic drawing looked like scribbles, but her irritation dissipated seeing Shanti so inspired. Naina knew how that felt, losing track of time in a rush of creative energy.

Her aunt continued. "You know, I've spent so much of my life helping people decorate interior spaces. I'd never thought of working outside before. I wish I had earlier." Then, "Oh I must be so late. Am I?"

"It's fine," Naina said. "Can I order you something?"

"Only tea. Non-caffeinated please."

"I know." Naina wished she could get Shanti something more substantial. "A muffin?" she pushed.

"You get what you like for yourself," Shanti replied. Her pencil was in her hand and she was already sketching again.

Naina had started her classes and still practised for hours every day. She was still working on writing music to bridge her two cultures. Now and then she invited Shanti to come with her to the university, and her aunt sketched or wrote in a notebook as Naina played. It was comfortable to have her there. The Indian sounds she was trying to recreate were more familiar to Shanti so she was able to offer suggestions, intuitive ones rooted in a life-time of experience, not in formal musical training like Naina had.

"Often the rhythm of our music is repetitive, Naina, but the speed changes — fast, steady and then completely unhurried all in one song. Just when you think it's slowed down so much that it will end soon, the song speeds up again. That's what I always found. It is almost uncomfortable at times. That's the point of it, I think. You need to let the discomfort last longer, to get to the heart of it. To let go of wanting to control it."

"I'll try that." As Naina played, she considered how she tried to hurry through uncomfortable feelings both in her music and in her own life, through difficult bars of music and conflicts with her family, even in her relationship with Paul, who she had left because their relationship began to feel too familiar to her, too settled. She hadn't even considered that Paul might have craved an adventure too, or may have been willing to move with her.

Shanti could fill the gaps in Naina's knowledge with other information that couldn't be found online or in books. Shanti told her stories about certain songs, or family memories associated with a rāga — happy recollections and, occasionally, sad ones. She once said, "Your grandfather loved music, didn't he? He did when I was young. He would be especially proud if he heard you play now." Naina felt herself increasingly connecting to her own project in a way that was less scholarly and more spiritual.

Shanti's final design for the garden was, by then, elegantly rendered. The completed images had precise lines, unlike the rough sketches she had first shown Naina, and were brought to life in careful watercolour. Zane agreed to the entire project and was especially enthusiastic that Shanti had included a broad platform in her plan. The deck could be large enough for a class of twenty, she proposed, and they could add a permanent awning for shelter from the sun or rain.

"I could see him doing the math in his head, how much money it could bring in with all that visibility, plus the extra practice space," Shanti told Naina jokingly as the two stood side by side in the parking lot one afternoon, talking through the nearly finished plan. "Of course, that made him agree."

Naina was impressed by Shanti's capacity to imagine it all in such detail. She nodded. "It will be great." Naina sounded more sure than she felt.

"I do think people will love it. Zane will do most of the building work himself. He said that he'd like to work with his hands again."

"You'll get to work together too." Naina was curious about the relationship between her aunt and Zane.

"Yes, it's nice to have another project with him. But don't think you're off the hook. I need your opinions too."

Shanti was holding her notes and sketches tucked against her chest, like a schoolgirl would clutch her textbooks. She was gesturing toward an area along the chain-link fence at the edge of the property.

"From there the path will curve this way. Can you picture it?" Shanti asked. "I see it so clearly," she responded to her own question and then was quiet.

Still imagining, Naina thought, as she tried to do the same. With the stillness between them, the noises around seemed to become louder. Far off a siren sounded, long and repetitive. Cars slowed at the intersection and then sped up again, engines humming. Naina heard the ordinary afternoon rhythms of the city like they were new, like they were musical. Her fingers twitched as though pressing gently down on sequential piano keys. She thought that she would like to get back to work, feeling inspired by the everyday cadence around her.

Her aunt's sleeve brushed against hers. Naina noticed the featherlike touch of the fabric, and then Shanti seemed to get slightly taller, as if she had adjusted her posture. Naina perceived the change the way she might notice a fly land on her arm, like a slight and vague itch, a tickle. She looked down, thinking perhaps she had sunk down into the grass. But the dry turf was firmly set beneath her.

Instead, Shanti was lifting. Her feet pointed downward in her sneakers as if she were standing on her toes. Then she rose even more, so that it seemed she was hovering off the ground. Shanti's feet quivered as she lifted from the earth. As she levitated, all the detailed individual sounds around them seemed to blur into an indistinct high-pitched humming sound, like TV static. As Naina watched, her heart jackhammered.

She put her arm around Shanti. *Stay calm*, Naina told herself. *She won't float away. I won't let her.* Shanti began to lower back down to the ground. Naina pressed down more.

Shanti's shoulder felt frail. Bony. She dressed in so many layers Naina hadn't noticed how slight she actually was. Her aunt sighed then, making a slight wheezing sound as she released her breath. When Shanti's soles were flat on the earth again, Naina took her hand off her shoulder and held her aunt's hand instead. Shanti's fingers were dry and cool.

It felt impossible, unreal, to see Shanti actually resist the pull of gravity. But Naina knew right then that she hadn't imagined it at all.

★

Through winter the neighbourhood was much quieter, so unlike the buzz of the streets in summertime. Soon after the first snowfall the humans, like bears, seemed to go into hibernation. There were fewer people outside and those who remained were hurried, rushing from one warm destination to the next. Naina and Shanti stopped going for long walks.

Instead, Naina went to Shanti's home on Saturday afternoons or in the evenings. She took her research books and laptop, her sheet music. She was still focused on piano interpretations of Hindu rāgas, and Shanti was still often helpful.

Most days, working alone with only her piano, her pages and pages of notes, Naina felt profoundly exhausted and discouraged, as if she had spent a day doing physical labour but still hadn't built anything functional. She only wanted to eat and sleep when she wasn't at school. But when she was with Shanti, she felt confident about her project again. As if what she was working on really mattered. Because it mattered to Shanti too.

As Naina worked, Shanti brought her tea or dainty snacks: a small bowl of nuts, a plate with two store-bought biscuits, neatly cut carrots or celery sticks. Her aunt handing her food felt like a performance. Shanti ate so little that it seemed as if she had lost her sense of how much others would consider a regular portion, so the snacks felt more like a child's offerings at a pretend party.

Shanti drank tea or warm water with a squeeze of lemon. She ate only things like a handful of raw spinach or vegetables, thinly sliced. She ate so slowly Naina could hardly watch.

It got dark by early evening at that time of year, so Naina's route home was lit by streetlamps; the bare trees overhead loomed like ghosts. Now and then a star glimmered through the cold city lights, one bright enough to be seen when she glanced upwards, like a pinprick in the night sky.

Naina often stopped at a burger place on the way home, stepping out of the frigid air into the glowing warmth of the old-fashioned fast food joint. She ordered a hamburger with cheese and extra onions, and ate sitting at the same table near the door. Each time the door opened cold air rushed at her.

Naina pulled her mittens off and set them down on the table but didn't bother taking off her heavy coat or toque for the meal. As she bit through the soft bread, the crisp lettuce, the onions sweet and pungent, she felt carnal, like she was back in her body again after being with Shanti who was so spiritual. When she was done she crushed the grease-stained paper wrapper into a ball, tossed it in the garbage, then carried on home. Once, as she finished a late evening meal, Naina realized that eating on her own in public had, already, become no big deal.

The city hesitatingly awakened in springtime. Cafés brought out a few tables and left chairs stacked nearby for people to pull out if it felt warm enough. Naina bought a new pair of ankle boots on a whim one dreary spring day. They were functional and comfortable to walk in, but they had a swirly pattern etched into the leather that looked like comic book clouds. *Or like the spiralling movement of a symphony,* she thought, as she picked them up in the store and ran her finger along the tiny stitches. She bought them in burgundy instead of dark brown or black, as she usually wore.

Naina felt pleased when Shanti noticed them. "Your boots are very chic. They suit you."

That spring Zane hired a crew with a Bobcat to do the hardest labour in the garden. He and Shanti also led the volunteers who signed up for the project, mostly long-time studio members. She directed the creative vision, while he led the actual construction: lifting hefty river stones and arranging them into pathways, building raised beds from planks of smoothly cut cedar that smelled, to Naina, like the incense her mother burned at home, the same kind Shanti also lit to purify her apartment. Naina went by to join the work crew when she could, after classes or on the weekend, wearing jeans and her puffy jacket, her old runners. She took a pair of too-large work gloves from a stack in the corner and tried to be careful, as always, not to injure her hands.

Naina helped smooth soil into garden beds with a metal rake. She liked the rotting, earthy scent of the darker compost as they added it to the grey soil. The construction crew was pleasant to be with, straightforward and chatty. She regularly reminded herself, when she heard the other volunteers fall into their annoying hippie talk, that she was there for Shanti, not because she was supporting Zane or his business. The physical work felt good, but Naina still wasn't trying to make friends, even at school. As the months had passed, she had only become more and more comfortable being by herself.

Zane built the platform at the centre of the garden. He was determined to make it circular which meant using a saw for the rough cuts and then hand-sanding the edges into perfectly smooth curves. With great care he measured each section so precisely and even kept the distance between screws consistent. He whistled a dad-like aimless tune as he worked, wore hiking boots and an old college sweater. To Naina, he seemed more at ease, more genuine, when he was outside working than when he was inside, playing the part of a yogi. She liked him better then.

One day, when Naina arrived, Shanti and Zane were standing near the platform. They stood so close that from a distance their silhouette was of one form, motionless. Shanti's head rested on Zane's chest and his arm was around her. The embrace was intimate, easy, with the comfort of familiar lovers. Naina noticed how Zane seemed so relaxed. His shoulders low, his body still. She had never seen him like that before. Usually he was moving, talking, making phone calls, arranging schedules for his business, telling cheesy jokes, schmoozing clients.

Naina decided to leave, let them have that quiet moment together without intruding, but Shanti noticed her. Her aunt broke away from Zane, raised her arm and waved her over. Zane took a step back as Naina approached. She apologized. "Sorry. I'm early."

"Never mind that," Shanti said. "I'm glad you're here." She seemed genuine but Naina saw a different, downhearted look on Zane's face.

"Shanti just said that she was expecting you. I'd better get to work too."

Later, as they walked back to Shanti's apartment together, Naina asked her about the closeness between her and Zane. "He used to talk about his feelings with me but he always wanted too much. He really wants a real girlfriend he can cook meals with, a wife to share a home with. I can't imagine any of that anymore. Deep down, I've always wanted to be free."

Pausing to take a sip of her tea, she added, "You understand, Naina. Or one day you will. If you truly choose yourself it's almost impossible to be with a man too I've found. It seems to me that usually in romantic relationships, one person ends up wanting more and more from the other."

Naina nodded and put her own cup back down on the counter. She looked toward the ceiling and sighed. "I know what you mean." When she picked up her cup again she noticed the light had already shifted; the afternoon was swiftly easing into evening. "I'd better go. I want to get in one more practice session tonight while there's no one else around."

Soon the garden was ready to plant. Shanti and Zane worked together to transplant the perennials they had purchased in black plastic trays from the nursery. They filled every space between with annuals the same colours as Shanti's first full-colour drawings: brash scarlet and vibrant yellow, tiny cobalt flowers that were more restrained. They purchased lavender plants that scented the air. The garden beds were divided by meandering paths that ultimately led to the circular platform. There was a pond to hold rainwater, with a wooden bench handmade by Zane beside it. In the middle of the bustling city, bordered by a street busy with car and pedestrian traffic, the garden felt like an oasis. It made the studio stand out too, in a way it hadn't when Naina first went there.

"This might be your masterpiece," Naina told her aunt. The colours and lines also reminded her of Shanti's condo artwork, brought to life. "It's phenomenal."

"If I've completed my masterpiece, Naina, perhaps my work is done," Shanti responded thoughtfully. Her face was flushed. Over the months of work she had been efficient and busy, but now she seemed slower again.

Naina was distressed by her aunt's weighty comment. Her fingers tapped again, this time against her own thigh. "Or imagine this could be your new line of work. A new career."

"I feel tired, Naina. Like I need to rest, let go for a while."

Naina reached for Shanti's arm, held on, feeling bone. "Let's go then. I'll walk you home."

Shanti did slow down. Though she was still often at the yoga studio, she didn't take classes anymore. Instead, she was weeding, or sitting on the bench in the garden with her sketchbook, so that Naina thought, *She seems, all of a sudden, elderly.*

One day, in the middle of her piano practice, Naina got a call from Shanti. "Naina, come quickly," her aunt whispered into the phone. "I need your help, I'm at the studio."

"Are you okay?"

"It's not me. I'm fine. Just come."

"I'll be right there."

When she arrived, Naina saw Shanti squatting down on the pathway, peering under a recently planted bush.

A black bird quivered under the branches. "What happened?" Naina crouched down too.

"One wing seems to be broken," Shanti murmured. The bird, as if in response, flapped the good wing while the other stayed at its side. Its pebble eye watched them as its body twitched, afraid.

"I'll call someone." Naina looked up the number for the vet clinic she often passed in the neighbourhood. The receptionist there calmly suggested they take the bird to a place that specialized in wildlife rehabilitation. She put her on hold then got the vet on the line, who told Naina how to transport the bird. Shanti had stood up and was humming an old familiar lullaby, one that Naina had almost forgotten, but then remembered from her own childhood. The tune was distracting, and Naina found herself thinking she would like to try to work out its composition on her keyboard.

Shanti looks so small, not only thin but shrunken, Naina thought, with the phone still held to her ear, watching her aunt, who had moved a distance away. Still humming, Shanti continued to deadhead flowers, gathering them in her hands. The woman kept giving instructions through the phone line as Naina watched Shanti's fists open. Dried petals from her hands dropped to the ground.

As the vet continued to talk, Shanti began to lift, up onto her toes so that she looked like a dancer rising en pointe, with only the tips of her toes touching the earth. Naina hung up as quickly as she could and calmly slid her phone back into her pocket. As she had done before, she put her arm around her aunt and pressed down, so that Shanti's feet settled fully again.

"Okay," Naina said in a hushed way so as not to startle Shanti. She tried bringing Shanti back to the present moment with her voice. "I know where we need to go. What to do. The vet told me. Let's find you a place to sit down first." She led her toward the bench.

Naina found an old apple box in a stack for recycling. The scarf around her neck was the same one Shanti had given her, but she took it off, knowing her aunt wouldn't mind if she used it for the bird.

"I'm not going to hurt you," she promised as she kneeled down beside it with the crate. "We're trying to help you." Naina took a deep breath as she dropped the fabric on top of its body. Through the cloth, she could see that it was flapping its good wing furiously. She stayed calm as she wrapped the scarf around its body, trying not to lose her cool. When she held the bird firmly in the bundle of cloth, it finally went still, as the vet said it would.

"I've got you," she told it. She gingerly placed it into the box, then Naina loosened the scarf before putting the lid on.

Zane gave Naina the key to his Prius. "Don't rush back, I'm totally happy to pick up the car later from Shanti's," he said.

It occurred to Naina that Zane wanted a reason to see Shanti again, away from the studio, though she also noticed that he hadn't offered to help them either. As if he cared about Shanti, but wasn't putting much effort into something that mattered only to her, like trying to save an ordinary bird. *After all, there's nothing in the small bird's life that would benefit you or your business,* she thought cynically.

"Here, I'll give you my number in case you need the car back sooner," she offered.

Naina drove. Beside her Shanti held onto the apple box, her thin hand resting on top of it. From inside there was an occasional scratching sound of claws against the cardboard, but the bird was mostly still.

The wildlife sanctuary was tucked into parkland at the edge of the city near the foothills, set into a dense patch of forest. *The air feels cooler here than it does downtown*, Naina noticed as she walked the soft path to the entrance carrying the box. Shanti was a step behind her. In front of the door she paused.

"You go ahead, Naina. It will be better if I wait outside."

"Okay, I won't be long hopefully. I'll let you know what they say."

The woman who worked there led Naina, still holding onto the box, down a short hallway into a room that looked clinical. A man was there, working on a computer. His black hair was cut short and he was wearing a white lab coat over his blue dress shirt and jeans.

"Well, what do we have here?" he asked, turning to face them. He took the box. Naina liked his voice, his gentle accent.

"We found a bird. Well, my aunt did. It seems injured. Hopefully you can help." Her words were choppy.

He pulled off the lid. Inside, the bird was still loosely wrapped in the scarf. "This is beautiful. I mean the scarf. Not the bird. This one has definitely seen better days." He laughed at his own joke.

"It was a gift so I hope it's not totally wrecked," Naina said. "The scarf, I mean. Not the bird." The vet chuckled.

His touch was graceful, she noticed. Unwrapping the bird and then handing the scarf to Naina, he said, "Well, I'd definitely wash it before you wear it again, but it's probably fine."

The man was confident too. He held the bird gently, cupping his hand around its body. "Don't worry. I trained for this."

"I'm not worried."

After a while he said, "Well I think this little one is going to be fine. Come look?" he moved his seat over to make room for her. "It's a starling. Probably terrified to be on its own. They aren't often found by themselves like that."

Naina moved closer so that she was leaning over him.

"But see the way the wing moves? I can tell it's not broken. It should be okay once it's hydrated and rested for a week or so. It should heal completely. We can release it here after that and hope it will find a flock to fit into. We'll do our best. I promise."

"Thanks," Naina said. "My aunt will be happy. She's the one who found it."

He looked at Naina then, as if seeing her for the first time. "I'm Okoro by the way."

Naina was so close to him that she could smell his soap, a familiar drugstore brand. The bird in his hands was still calm.

"Naina," she told him.

"It's cool that you brought this one in for us. Some people get panicky about these things, or pretend they don't notice when they see an injured animal. Especially one like this, I bet he was good at hiding too. You know, we're always looking for volunteers if you ever want to come back again."

Was he asking her out? Naina wondered. Maybe it wouldn't be so bad if he was. She'd been single for a while. Maybe it was time to consider dating again.

Driving home, Naina had a good, optimistic feeling. The bird was going to be okay, and she had signed up to help at the sanctuary every second Saturday. It might be nice to think about something besides music now and then. Another volunteer who was there every weekend had offered her a ride back to the remote spot, so maybe she was finally making friends again too.

An Astonishment of Stars

The car wheels crunched as she pulled up in front of Shanti's building.

"You can come in if you'd like to," Shanti said, hesitating. She was just being polite, Naina realized.

"Sure, I'd love to wash my hands," she replied nevertheless.

Naina hadn't been to Shanti's apartment for a while. The climb up the stairs left her winded. Shanti was still breathing evenly, as if she had taken an elevator up. She unlocked the door with a copper-coloured key, jiggling it in the lock before it took. As the door swung open, Naina noticed a pile of odd objects beside it: a small pot nested inside a larger one, a vase that looked handmade, a fuzzy blanket.

"Just a few things I'd like to give away. If I set things out behind the building they get taken so quickly. Others must need all these objects much more than I do," Shanti explained.

It seems strange to be donating things you've spent years gathering. Looking around the room, Naina felt the absence of the vase on the open shelf where it used to be. The spot was left bare.

"Let's go get dinner," Naina suggested, feeling worried.

"Oh, it's been such a long day. I think I'll rest for a while now. Zane will be by soon enough for the car."

There were half-moon circles like bruises under Shanti's eyes. Perhaps from the strain of the afternoon. "You look tired," Naina said to Shanti, an observation her own mother often annoyingly made to her too.

"These days I don't feel like I need to sleep. My mind wanders until morning."

"And you never eat either." Naina realized that she had never directly said this before. Now she said it again. "I hardly see you eat anything. Ever. I don't get it. You need to sleep and eat." She tried not to sound angry.

"I don't feel hungry. I'm listening to my body. I'll eat when I need to. I'll rest when I need to."

"I mean, that's fine." Naina tried to keep her voice even. "But to survive you need to eat. Maybe your body doesn't actually know what's best. Maybe if you ate more you'd be hungry more and then you could sleep. Aren't you the one who believes everything is connected?"

Naina heard herself sounding even more like the rest of their family then. Judgmental. Bossy. Her voice getting louder. She didn't like the way it felt, but she couldn't stop herself.

"Yes, maybe." Shanti nodded blankly.

"Nothing good can come of starving yourself." Naina's voice rose as she tried to startle her aunt back into the conversation. Keep her engaged. Shanti looked directly at her then.

Her aunt sat down on a chair, pulled her legs up so she was sitting cross-legged. "You know, Naina, when I was much younger, about your age, living alone for the first time, I went with my friends to a fair. We rode on the Ferris wheel and I remember when it got to the top and started to come down again. For that moment, right at the peak, I felt like I was flying. My body was starting to descend but another part of me was still lifting upward, separating. All my life I've missed that feeling. I went on that ride over and over for that moment, when I got to feel like I weighed nothing at all."

She leaned back as if imagining a wide sky was above her, not only the plain white ceiling. "Part of me has always wanted to float away like that. I haven't thought of it for years, but that was perhaps best feeling of my life. Like the peace I had as a child after our prayers. It's all I long for now."

Naina could imagine it, like how it felt when she was playing music, lifting herself off the bench as she pounded heavily down onto the keys. She sighed. "Okay, but you still need to eat."

"I will. Later."

When she hugged Shanti goodbye, Naina felt like she was hugging a child. Her aunt was so skinny, Naina's hands easily reached around her slight body to touch her own elbows. Her frustration turned to sorrow. Naina felt powerless, unable to help.

"I'll take that vase if you don't want it. It reminds me of you. I'd hate for it to end up with a stranger."

Shanti handed it to her. "It's yours then." The vase was rough and solid. Cradling it in the crook of her arm was reassuring as Naina made her way back to her apartment, down now-familiar streets.

One Saturday afternoon at the wildlife sanctuary, Naina was sitting on a stool waiting for Okoro to finish up so they could leave. Sarah, the other volunteer, had left early that day so he had offered her a ride home instead. Each animal's cage was clean and Naina had filled up all the water bowls as Okoro fed them. He was doing one last check as Naina was rotating a half circle one way, then pushing herself back the other, lifting her feet as she spun.

"This bunny doesn't want to eat," Okoro said, noticing the untouched stack of straw in its cage.

"Does that happen often?" Naina stopped rotating. "That they don't eat like that?"

"All the time, especially if they feel bad." He had opened the hole in the top of the cage and was stroking the rabbit. On his hand he wore a purple medical glove.

"I mean when they aren't physically injured anymore. Do they ever stop eating for no real reason?"

"Sometimes. It's like they don't want to get better. They don't live for long after that. It can be hard to watch." He looked away from the bunny, up toward her. "And I guess logically, it's hard to make sense of it."

"Do they seem scared?"

"It's the opposite, from what I've seen. It's more like they get really calm. First they stop eating, then they stop drinking. One day we find them. Gone. It actually seems kind of peaceful." Okoro gently closed the lid on the bunny cage.

"Gone. Like dead?"

"Of course. They don't just disappear," he chuckled. How could he know why she was so serious?

Okoro continued, "When it happens it feels sad to be the one who couldn't save them. It doesn't seem like the worst way to go for the animal though." He stopped talking for a moment. "Anyway, what's up? You have a lot on your mind today." He tugged the glove off and dropped it into the garbage bin.

"It's my aunt. She never really eats. She gets skinnier and skinnier. I feel like she might just drift away. It's like there's nothing holding her here. Not even me." Naina felt embarrassed for being so direct. *Don't cry,* she thought. At least she hadn't actually told him about Shanti levitating.

Okoro nodded. He moved closer to her and she thought he might kiss her but instead he leaned back so he was half sitting on the counter beside her. He was such a good listener. There was so much about him that was attractive. She stood up.

"Let's go. Is it awful that I'm hungry now?" She tried to laugh off the seriousness of the moment.

"Maybe we can stop for something to eat."

"I happen to know a place that makes a great burger," Naina offered without thinking. A moment later, she wondered about giving away a private experience, her meals on her own at the fast food joint by Shanti's place, a habit that she might have wanted to keep to herself.

"I'm in. Let's go." It felt too late then for her to say that she wanted to go somewhere different instead. Part of her didn't want to share her private dinner spot, but then she considered that sharing things might be good for her too. Maybe she was now spending too much time alone and had become too accustomed to it.

In the car, back in the city, they stopped at a red light and he glanced over at her. "This is going to sound super strange but when you said you imagined your aunt drifting away I was thinking of this article I read a while ago. A journalist had put together a list of these instances of people actually drifting upward. But like, levitating. It sounds bizarre but who knows, maybe it happens."

It was dusk by then. The traffic light still glowed red in front of them. The turn signal was on and the consistent clicking sound steadied Naina, like a metronome.

"Yeah, that does seem pretty unlikely," Naina bluffed.

"Maybe. Growing up we always went to church. I heard about Christian saints who did pretty wild supernatural things. When I was a kid I took it all so literally so I believed in it. I guess part of me still does."

"When I was a kid we used to travel to India and I remember seeing yogis levitate," Naina added. "But that was a total fake. A trick for tourists. I knew that even then."

"You're smarter than me then, I guess," Okoro said. "I really don't know what I believe." He made the left turn so that the clicking signal turned off and the continuous sound was gone again. The rest of the way into the heart of the city Naina looked out her window. In comfortable quiet, they hardly spoke.

★

The last time Naina saw her aunt levitate was in Shanti's nearly empty apartment. Naina hardly went there anymore. Ever since Shanti had begun giving things away it felt less and less like a home — the increasingly empty bookshelves, the lack of dishes in the cupboards. There were no knick-knacks left. The hand-carved wooden utensil container on the kitchen counter was gone. No incense holders or beeswax candles decorated the bathroom counter. Shanti's lip balms and hand lotion had been cleared away too. Only a single bar of soap perched at the edge of the enamel sink, not on a dish anymore.

When Naina had called Shanti from her practice room earlier that morning, she hadn't answered. Naina tried three times in a row then decided to check on her. The route she took went past the yoga studio. In the garden, early autumn yellows and reds were fading to withered mustards and browns. Once-green leaves had decayed into frail, dying ones. Some still clung to their branches, while the others had already fallen to the ground. Naina walked faster.

As another resident emerged, Naina slipped into the building, saying hello as if she lived there. She ran up the stairs, out of breath by the time she was at the top. Naina knocked on Shanti's door several times, but when there was no answer she turned the handle to let herself in, thinking, *It's probably open*. She regularly reminded Shanti that she needed to lock up even when she was home.

"You're way too trusting," Naina would tell her, seeing her leave the deadbolt unturned.

"Or you could try being more trusting, Naina," Shanti always retorted.

That day, as Naina creaked the door open she called out, "Hello? Are you home?"

To her relief, Shanti was in fact there, sitting on the floor in the centre of the living room. Her phone was on the kitchen counter, a stark rectangle on the cleared-off space. Shanti was looking out toward the patio door. *Meditating*, Naina thought. Her calm pose was much like the line drawing on the sign at the yoga studio. Naina looked around the room.

Almost everything was gone, as if Shanti was getting ready to move out. Even the rugs had been donated. All that remained were the built-in bookshelves, the sofa, the two-person dining table and chairs. The remaining furniture seemed soulless on the exposed wood floor.

Naina looked back towards Shanti. "Hello?" she said again.

"Oh dear, I didn't hear you." Shanti's voice sounded rough, as if she hadn't spoken for a long time. She cleared her throat. "Help me up?" Shanti held out her hand. As Naina pulled her to standing, she noticed that Shanti felt so light that Naina almost fell backwards. She reached for the arm of the sofa behind her to steady herself. Naina thought of the bird they had rescued that day, how, as she lifted it, the animal seemed to weigh nothing at all. *As if it were made of air.*

"I'll get you a drink of water," Naina offered. She wasn't sure what else she should do. The relief she had felt a moment earlier was gone again.

There was a lone tumbler in the cupboard that she filled with tepid water from the tap. Naina was about to ask Shanti if she could check the ringer on her phone, make sure it was on, when she noticed her aunt was daydreaming again. Tuning out. And then, trembling, Shanti began to lift off the ground, her toes again pointed downward. Naina turned off the tap. She gripped the glass in her hand, grateful to be holding on to something tangible. Naina realized she was afraid. She used to think she knew what would happen next, knew what to expect from the people around her. With Shanti, she didn't.

Naina wondered then what would happen if she didn't try to push Shanti back down. All her life she had heard that her aunt was unreliable and uncaring, but with her, Naina had felt what it was like to be truly seen for the first time. Her aunt expected nothing from her, didn't anticipate what she would do next or what she should achieve. It occurred to Naina that acceptance might be the truest act of love. Like Okoro said, maybe she was only thinking about her own pain, her own loss. Maybe she was keeping Shanti connected to the earth when she didn't want to be.

She let Shanti be then, and only watched. Her aunt stayed close to the ground, not rising any higher than a hand's width. Her arms lifted slightly away from her body. An airplane buzzed overhead, then it faded. The sounds of traffic disappeared too, as if all movement outside had paused. Still holding the glass of water, she watched Shanti, and Naina began to feel as calm as her aunt appeared to be. The dark, sad feeling of worry she had a moment before eased.

She was startled when Shanti said her name. "Naina?"

"Yes. I'm here."

"A glass of water would be nice. Thank you." Shanti's feet settled again, first her toes and then her heels. Then her arms lowered too, as if in slow motion. Naina's hands trembled as she carried the glass over.

They didn't talk about what happened after; both sat together for a long time on the bare wood floor. The afternoon softened into evening, clouds shifted unhurriedly, shadows elongated. When the streetlights came on, Naina felt her stomach growl. It was time for her to leave. "I'll check on you tomorrow," she promised her aunt.

"You can if you want to, Naina. It's up to you," Shanti responded as Naina hugged her goodbye.

★

When Zane's name came up on her phone, not long after that day in the condo, Naina knew.

"It's terrible. I don't know what happened. Why." His words tangled incoherently. He was sobbing. "No one knows. I don't know. Her heart."

"What are you saying? Slow down, Zane, I don't know what you're saying."

"She's gone, Naina. I'm sorry. I found her, in the garden. But not in time. It was too late. They say her heart stopped. No reason. There was nothing we could do. I should have been there. I was too late. Oh god. Oh my god."

Don't fall apart, Naina told herself. *Go.*

"I'm coming," she said, then hung up quickly.

Naina left the plate with her half-eaten sandwich on the table. After, she wouldn't remember putting on her winter coat or grabbing her keys. She didn't wait until it was safe to cross streets. The sound of a car blaring its horn would come back to her when she relived that moment for weeks after, that same screeching F-sharp, over and over.

She hoped Zane was wrong. Maybe it was a terrible joke. But by the time she got there, the paramedics had covered Shanti with a cotton sheet pale as the overcast sky. As she walked toward Shanti's body, Naina covered her ears with her hands, not wanting to hear anything at all. First she wanted to see Shanti for herself.

A paramedic lowered the cloth so that she could see Shanti's face then stepped away. Zane stayed back too, though she sensed him watching her as he sat down on the edge of the cedar platform he had built. He slouched, his body curved inward, into the shape of sorrow.

Shanti's skin had changed colour, reminding Naina of the blue god, Krishna. When she was growing up, there was a statue of Krishna on the table beside the front door of her family home. The figure was draped in orange-and-ruby-coloured fabric from his waist down. In his graceful hands he held a flute, so that it looked as if he was lifting the instrument toward his lips. The god's skin was tinted sapphire. His expression serene, eyes closed. As a child, Naina had found him comforting. Now, looking at Shanti was comforting too. Her eyes were also closed. She didn't look peaceful exactly, but more like she was completely absent, as if her soul had lifted away and her body was no longer necessary. Emptied.

The word *forever* came to Naina like a thud then. She would never see her aunt again.

Naina pressed her flushed cheek against Shanti's. In the frigid air Naina's breath plumed like smoke around them both. "Please," she whispered to her dead aunt. As if the word so ingrained in her for her whole life could bring her what she most wanted now. What was it that she wanted? Only more time. "Please," she said again.

Zane approached Naina when the white coroner's van pulled up, and Naina kissed her aunt's cold forehead, not hurrying. She lifted the sheet and placed it down over Shanti's face, aware that she was being watched but she didn't care. Naina stayed on her knees beside Shanti a moment longer, before standing up and letting them carry her away. *They're lifting her so easily,* she thought. *As if she doesn't weigh anything.*

Naina walked away without comforting Zane, having nothing to say. She walked home still bewildered. When she got there, Naina slid her old sandwich into the garbage, finding it hard to believe that she had so recently been doing something so ordinary as eating lunch. She slid down to the carpeted floor and pulled her phone from her pocket to call her mother, who sobbed. "But I hadn't seen her for so long. I wish I'd at least said goodbye. My sister." Before they hung up, her mother said she would tell the rest of the family. After she put down the phone, Naina wept too.

Naina's mother held a small ceremony at their home for Shanti. Naina didn't go, saying she would take care of things at Shanti's apartment and start the school semester as planned. The instructors from the studio held a celebration of her life, open to all the regulars, and asked Naina to come too. Naina agreed, knowing her aunt would have liked it.

She took her time walking there. The wind was chilly. It made her cheeks tingle as she walked into it. Naina thought of the day she ran, panicked, after Zane's call, and how walking to the same place now felt like there was no hurry at all. As if the pressing air was also telling her to slow down.

People sat cross-legged in a circle and told stories about Shanti. Times they spent with her, conversations they had. Almost everyone mentioned the garden.

Naina shook her head when she was asked to speak. She didn't know what to say, she told them, and would rather listen. They nodded. If they were disappointed they didn't show it, which Naina appreciated.

Friends sitting side by side held hands. There was the sound of people sniffing, exhales of despair. A box of tissues was passed around the room, and people used them to dab at their tears, crumpling them after so that they littered the floor like white flowers. Zane made a speech, during which he broke down several times.

"Shanti was so much more to me than a friend," Zane said. "The first day we met, I felt as though a missing piece of my soul had been put in place. I would give anything to have had her here, with me, for longer." He paused to wipe the tears from his face. "And yet, I think the most valuable lesson I learned from her was about letting go. She didn't grip onto material things. She was selfless. And she didn't want to be held on to." Those words made him cry again so that he could hardly finish speaking. He looked around the room. "Shanti was a saint. I believe that. She blessed us all with her presence in our lives, her true heart."

Naina felt sorry for being so disparaging about Zane all along. Though she thought that Zane was wrong when he said Shanti was selfless. Rather she knew herself so well. Better than anyone Naina had ever met before. Naina began to cry too. Someone handed her a tissue, without asking if she wanted one. "Thank you," she whispered.

Alone again after the ceremony, Naina had a flash of memory from her childhood.

"Here take these," her mother had said to eight-year-old Naina as they hurried from their car across a freshly mown lawn. It was summertime. They were walking across the park, going to an outdoor family birthday party, a picnic. Her mother was carrying a blue cooler with handles on either end.

"Hold on tight, Naina," her mother reminded her.

It was hard to grasp so many thin strings. Naina tried to adjust them to get a better grip. As she did, one began to slip away.

"Come on," her mother urged her without looking back. "We're late."

The string of the yellow balloon separated from the others. Naina reached for it while holding on to the rest but the end of the twine was already above her. She thought of shouting to her mother, asking for help, but she was well ahead of Naina by then, walking quickly toward the gathering of relatives. In the time that it took her to glance at her mom the balloon had drifted impossibly far away, moving steadily upward on a slant that seemed to lead directly into the sun.

Naina stopped to watch it getting smaller until it was only a dot, and then, like that, she couldn't see it at all. The sky was vivid blue with only a smattering of cloud. Pure summer light shone bright in her eyes as she squinted, searching for it still.

Her mother called her name.

"I'm coming." Running to catch up, she held tight to the rest of the strings, all damp in her sweating hand. The cluster of balloons bobbed as if trying to rise, as if, Naina worried, they might take her skyward with them. Her family wouldn't notice one was missing, she hoped. And they didn't. No one at the party looked upward at all.

★

Shanti's will was in a sealed business envelope that she had given to Zane soon after she and Naina had first met. She had written it by hand, her penmanship neat, and Zane had witnessed it. The will left Naina her apartment, which contained almost all that remained of her possessions. By the end, she had given away all of her savings and cleared out almost everything except her sofa, which was far too heavy to take down the stairs on her own.

In Shanti's closet there were also a few articles of clothing, including a heavy duffel coat, a long dress, another scarf much like the one she had given Naina, and a pair of loose grey linen pants with a matching long-sleeve top, the outfit Shanti had worn most often in those last months.

Her bed was gone. Shanti had taken to sleeping on the floor of her otherwise-empty bedroom. Throughout the apartment there were rectangular patches on the wall where the art used to be, where the paint hadn't faded.

The place didn't smell like anything at all. There was no trace left of the incense that Shanti often lit, no scents from lingering spices. Those seasonings, along with Shanti's collection of herbal teas, had been cleared out too. *It was like no one had ever lived there at all,* Naina thought.

In the hallway linen closet, Naina found Shanti's old paintings. "They're here!" she cheered out loud. Shanti hadn't given the most important objects away. Naina was jubilant, like she had found lost treasure. Her eyes tingled, so that she thought she might cry again. But this time, from happiness.

At the front of the stack was the final plan for the garden. It had been professionally mounted, protected by glass. The image looked how it did in real life, at the peak of summertime, like it was a vision and not only an idea. Naina put her arms around it and hugged it to her, resting her chin on the smooth frame.

Naina hung all the pictures back on the wall, exactly where they used to be, judging the locations by matching them to the rectangles of unfaded paint. But mostly she remembered the story they told. In sequence, like a familiar song. She was able to simply push nails back into the same places without a hammer. The one of the garden seemed to be meant for Zane, but Naina sat with it for a long time, her arms crossed around it again, trying to decide if it should be part of the story at the condo, or if she should take it to the studio.

★

Okoro texted that evening and she invited him over.

"Bring something to eat?" she messaged. "So hungry." He arrived with a large margherita pizza and a six-pack of pilsner, and he seemed slightly winded from climbing the stairs. They each sat at an end of the sofa, the soft dough bending in their hands, the box between them.

Okoro asked, "Music?" She nodded and took another bite. He started a playlist he had on his phone, an electronic rhythm without lyrics. The steady sound gave the living room a more lived-in, warmer feeling.

"I don't think I'll sell it. The condo I mean. I think I'm going to live here." Naina looked around, trying to see the space objectively. The decision seemed more clear since she had hung the paintings back up in their places.

"I thought you would," Okoro replied.

"It feels right. To have a place of my own. A real home."

"It's life-changing for you. Hey, let's go furniture shopping?" he suggested. "I could drive."

"Maybe," Naina replied, popping open another beer can. She

realized how easy it would be to furnish the place with him. She could let Okoro help choose and then he would feel more at home too, and then eventually, she knew, they would end up in some kind of relationship. One she wasn't sure she really wanted. "Or maybe I'll leave it like this for a while. Not forever. But a while longer. All I really need here is a piano. A good upright would be fine."

"Well, I'll help you bring that in then," Okoro said. "I mean, if you want me to."

"Maybe," she said again.

They finished the pizza and drank the rest of the beer warm, not bothering to put it in the fridge. The music was a steady presence between them. Okoro had put his phone down beside him on the armrest and was watching her. He was so gentle, the sort of person who would never really make the first move, Naina realized. It looked like Okoro wanted to ask her a question but then sighed and leaned back so he was looking up at the ceiling. "I like you, you know," he said. It surprised her, that he said it so plainly.

She laughed. "God, we're not teenagers." She tapped her fingers on the arm of the sofa.

He shrugged. "Well, it's true. I'm saying it so it doesn't feel strange having that feeling hovering around all the time. I wanted to say it. I don't think I've ever met anyone like you."

"I think you're really great. But I don't know."

"You don't have to," he said. "It's okay. I'm not asking for anything. I'm just saying how I feel."

Naina's head felt fuzzy from the beer, her belly warm and full from the pizza. She leaned back too. Outside it began to sleet. Fat, wet flakes spattered unevenly against the closed patio door before melting together, running into larger droplets in a way that reminded her of her own work, bringing parts of her identity together, however awkwardly.

★

When Naina woke up she noticed the music was no longer playing. The pizza box was closed and placed on the kitchen counter, the empty cans beside it in a neat cluster. Okoro had moved to the floor and gone to sleep there. His arm bent in a way that looked uncomfortable under his head, propping it up. He had pulled his hands into his sleeves in a way that made her think he must be cold.

The wool coat in Shanti's room, her room, slid off the wooden hanger easily. Naina took it down, held it to her face for a moment to inhale what was left of Shanti there, and then carried it back to the living room, where she placed it over Okoro like a blanket. She took a cushion from the sofa and put it beside his head. "Here," she whispered.

It was satisfying when he moved so that his head was partway on it, at least. Naina hoped he would get more comfortable on his own. Looking down at him in the faint glow from outside she had a strange vision, as if she could see him at every age. A child, the adult he was now, an old man, vulnerable at every point in his life. She could imagine him moving through time in a way that made her think of a song, an easy legato piece that shifted smoothly, in sequence. She considered lying down on the floor beside him, putting her head on the cushion too. But she stretched out on the sofa again instead. There was no hurry, she thought. She was, she realized, really sleepy.

Maybe, Naina thought drowsily, *I could go help in Shanti's garden. I could weed, or rake leaves.* It might be a way to remember her aunt, in a way she would like. Yes, she would stop by and ask Zane what might be needed. She didn't need to go into Humble Hearts, but she could lend a hand outside. Maybe she'd see if Okoro wanted to come too, then wondered what he would think of Zane.

She thought of the vase she had taken from Shanti's give-away pile. It was at her old place. *I could bring it back when I bring my clothes over*, Naina considered, her thoughts blurry. Or she could just give it away, as Shanti had intended. Let it go. Finally put it out in the alley for someone, a stranger, who might need it more. Maybe another student just starting out on their own, someone who didn't own anything beautiful yet.

Okoro shifted without waking so that his head was fully on the square cushion she had put beside him. Naina yawned. Warm air rushed in from the vents, then the system clicked off again. The night was quiet, the space cozy in the dark. Naina curled up on her side. Okoro's even breathing was a soft whistle. *Maybe*, she thought drowsily, *Shanti is watching over me, from someplace higher above, beyond the city lights or between the stars.* Naina felt safe then, so that she knew she would be fine, and possibly even happy. With that, her thoughts melted, faded away, and Naina drifted back to sleep.

Part Two

The Fundraiser

THE OLD DOG MABEL WAS FIFTEEN YEARS OLD. SHE WAS A medium-sized tawny mutt with loose jowls, weepy eyes and a waning appetite. When she was young she barked to be fed, then inhaled a bowl of kibble in seconds, but over the years that had changed. Lately, she only ate individual pellets of hard food from the palm of Teja's hand, one at a time, with lots of encouragement.

"Good girl," Teja said to Mabel each time she ate a piece or two.

The vet said Mabel's teeth were still fine for crunching, but as she aged, eating wasn't exciting to her anymore. Mabel would stare indifferently across the room at her filled enamel dish, drooping eyes shining, body sprawled across the floor, without standing up, without bothering to make her way over to the bowl. She ate from her peoples' hands as if she was just doing them a favour.

That morning, Mabel finally finished her meal then went back to sleep. Teja washed the dog food dust from her hands and was making herself a second coffee when the doorbell sounded. She left her mug on the counter and peered through the gap between the living room curtains, hoping it was just a delivery.

Evelyn, another parent from the school, wearing her workout clothes, stood on the cedar front deck. She saw the movement as Teja looked out and waved toward the window. *Even Evelyn's wave is energetic*, Teja noticed. Evelyn lifted a familiar green jacket into the air. Teja motioned that she'd be right there. On her way to the door she glanced at herself in the hall mirror then pulled her loose T-shirt down over her bum, feeling caught off guard. Her black sweatpants were flecked with dog hair, which she tried to sweep off with her hands. She ran her fingers through her hair. *I should have brushed it this morning, or at least tied it up*, she thought. Mabel followed Teja wearily.

"I know," she said to the tired pooch.

"Oh hi," exclaimed Evelyn brightly, as if surprised to see Teja at her own house. The spring air was cold on Teja's bare feet. Evelyn's cheeks were rosy. When Teja was a child, she wished she had fairer skin so her face would flush pink like that in the cold. "I recognized Ron's coat on a bench outside the school this morning and thought I would drop it off before heading out for my run. You're so close by."

Evelyn's workout clothes were also upbeat. Her pants had a neon band down the side, and her windbreaker matched, with a stripe in the same shade of hot pink. Distracted by the '80s hues of the outfit, Teja took a moment to register Evelyn's easy shortening of her son's name to Ron.

"Great, thanks. Ronak's always so hot, I bet he took it off the minute he left the house." She emphasized her son's name, to make a point, but then told herself she shouldn't make a big deal about it, especially as Evelyn was doing them a favour.

"I thought after I should have taken it into the school, but I guess you could get it back to him before recess if you wanted."

"He'll be fine without. I've got a full day's work to get done here." Teja thought of her cooling coffee.

"You know, you can buy iron-on labels through the school. In case he loses things again. We use them on everything. Our kids can be so forgetful." Evelyn looked as if she'd like to stay and chat. She peered in as if Teja might ask her to come inside.

"Good idea." Teja rested her hand on the doorknob. Behind Evelyn a white plastic shopping bag ballooned in the breeze, lifting and then falling again as it travelled down the sidewalk past the house. Teja watched it for a moment and then noticed Evelyn looking at her, as if waiting for her to say more. Teja smiled again.

"Oh, you have a philodendron," said Evelyn, pointing to the plant on the shelf behind her.

"Is that what it's called?"

The plant was one Teja had picked up from the flower section of the grocery store, before Ronak was born. A maternal feeling had come over her then. She had wanted to prove she could take care of something, anything, even a plant. The dark green vine now spread across the wall and toward the ceiling, sprouting heart-shaped leaves. She didn't know what the plant was called, but over the years she had kept it alive, sensing when it needed watering by when its leaves started to pucker. Mostly, the plant thrived with benign neglect. Teja let it be, so it grew as it wanted to.

Mabel quivered with the effort of standing for so long and leaned against Teja's leg, sliding down toward the tile floor until she was lying down again, her legs awkwardly splayed. She was panting. Her breath warmed Teja's toes.

"Well, as long as you know that it's poisonous," said Evelyn. "I mean to pets. I'd hate for your dog to get a hold of it. Deadly, even."

Teja didn't know that, but thought, with irritation, about how she could hardly get the old dog to eat. They had tried all different kinds of food — the kind from the grocery store and the expensive specialty brands. None of them increased Mabel's appetite. Teja couldn't imagine why Mabel would bother to eat a houseplant.

"Huh. I didn't know that. I'll keep an eye on it." Teja shifted her hand, still resting on the doorknob.

"Well, better keep on," said Evelyn at last. "I guess I'll see you at the school for the fundraiser pickup tomorrow?"

"Definitely." Teja lifted the jacket that Evelyn had handed to her. "Thanks again."

Before Evelyn was at the end of the walkway, Teja had closed the door and picked up her phone from where she had left it, beside her now room-temperature cup of coffee. Of course, the fundraiser. She had put off ordering for so long she had missed the deadline. Teja phoned the school right away, sitting on the floor beside Mabel as she made the call, scratching between the dog's ears with her free hand.

"Helen, hi, it's Teja, Ronak's mom. I'm so sorry, it looks like I missed the fundraiser cut-off date. Any way you could still add me to the list?"

"Let me check my numbers." She sounded unsurprised. Helen, nearing retirement, had been a school administrator for ages, and never sounded hurried or flustered. She could hear Helen inhale and exhale through the phone line instead of putting her on hold, then the sound of pages turning. "It's your lucky day. We have two cases of the pork left that no one claimed. Can I put you down for those?"

Gross, Teja thought. "Sure. Thanks, Helen. I'll take both."

Teja didn't mind most of the school fundraisers, though she wished there weren't quite so many. Some were annoying, but the sausage one was the worst. She wasn't a strict vegetarian but grew up in a family that was, and she still only ate meat occasionally. The first time she had bought the sausages she had read the list of ingredients on the side of the box and couldn't bring herself to eat them after that, and so abandoned the case in the basement freezer.

There were other money-making events for the school throughout the year that she didn't mind: a bucket of cookie dough, hoodies with the school logo on them, herbal tea. Others, like the Christmas tree decorations or wine-tasting evenings, and this sausage one, weren't organized with families like hers in mind. They were made for people who celebrated Christmas, drank alcohol, ate meat. But it felt to Teja like she was the only person who wasn't into any of these things.

Every year, standing in the lineup to pick up their sausage order, other parents said how they easily went through a box or two. Usually Teja bought one and kept it in the freezer until it was long past its expiry, feeling guilty every time she opened the door to pull out a bag of frozen peas or the bucket of ice cream. Once, she had tried to donate the meat to the food bank but was told they didn't accept frozen goods. She wished she could give the money to the school directly but understood that the display was important — having her name on the list, joining the garrulous lineup of parents outside the school on the pickup date.

Teja wanted to show she also cared if the school had enough money for field trips and laptops. So she made the purchase. Lined up. Brought the box home. Every time. And eventually, on garbage day soon after their expiry date, Teja slipped out early in the morning and quietly disposed of the entire box into the black bin in the alley.

Teja ran into Evelyn again weeks later, both waiting to meet their kids after school. With time in the empty yard before the bell, the two stepped out of their vehicles to talk outside on the shadeless asphalt. In the bright sunlight both women left their sunglasses on.

"We're having a potluck this weekend to celebrate the end of the school year," said Evelyn. "Why don't you and Ron come by?"

Teja wondered again why her son's name was being shortened to Ron, a name that didn't suit him at all, and couldn't think of a good reason not to say yes to the invitation. "I think Ronak and I are free. What should I bring?" She tried to emphasize his name again, without being obvious about it.

"Nothing fancy. It's mostly an outdoor party so maybe something picnicky." Evelyn didn't seem to notice Teja's pointed use of her son's full name.

Teja thought of her favourite chickpea salad with lots of garlic, red onion, and a big squeeze of lemon.

"Something the kids will like," Evelyn added. Teja quickly understood. Nothing spicy or unfamiliar. In Teja's family the children always ate what the adults did. She thought of the two boxes of sausages in the freezer, still unopened, and, luckily, not yet expired.

★

The day of the potluck was clear and warm. Using the most basic instructions on the internet, Teja set a pot of water on the stove. She eased the pallid sausages into the water while trying not to look too closely at them, then opened all the windows and put on the hood fan as she boiled them for half an hour. When the timer sounded she sliced one open with a paring knife to make sure it wasn't pink inside, then piled them into a plain glass bowl. Ronak looked skeptically at the pepper-flecked, now white-ish meat. "Are they supposed to look like that?" *His voice is uneven, getting deeper already*, Teja noticed.

"I'm sure they're fine," she said. In fact, the sausages looked nothing like the picture on the internet. They didn't brown on the outside and, in fact, the boiling water only blanched them. She quickly double-checked the recipe and saw that after boiling them, she was supposed to sear the outside too. *But,* she thought, *they are cooked through and definitely safe to eat. What difference could that last step actually make? It's probably better to skip it and arrive on time.* She changed out of her T-shirt and cut-offs and put on her sleeveless orange dress, one she had bought just for the day.

When they got to the party. Evelyn met them at the door and took the covered bowl from her. "Oh wow," she said, then put it near the back of the long table. Teja followed behind her and took the plastic wrap off, balled it up and put it in her purse. Everyone ate paper plates full of food — corn dogs and mini-pizzas, tater tots and spoonfuls of a bulbous retro marshmallow salad — but avoided Teja's greyish offerings.

The party felt awkward to Teja but she reminded herself that it was important for her to be there, to chat with the other parents about the decisions made at the last parent council meeting, the amount of homework the kids were bringing home (too much or not enough, depending which parent was talking), hear about which teachers were moving to other schools or going on maternity leave. Ronak was having fun, which was the most important thing, she thought. The kids didn't play tag like they would have a couple of years earlier, instead they ate plates full of food and played video games, then took turns shooting hoops on the driveway.

At the end of the party, Teja's glass bowl was still full. She would have thrown away the contents right there if she didn't think it would look bad, so instead she covered them again with the wrinkled plastic wrap from her purse. It was greasy and felt wet so the plastic no longer stuck to the sides like it was supposed to. Teja carried the bowl all the way home with Ronak a step behind her. She tried to hold down the edges of the sliding plastic and turned her face to not inhale the smell.

Mabel was asleep when they arrived. The dog didn't wake up until after they were in the house and taking off their shoes. Finally noticing them, she thumped her tail on the floor. She groaned as she stood up, sniffed the air as she approached them. Mabel lifted her nose toward the glass bowl. Ronak kneeled down to pet her head.

"Maybe she wants a sausage, Mom," he said.

Teja was picking up a fallen leaf from her philodendron plant. She'd become more careful about it, just in case. The dead foliage still held between her fingers. She remembered the ingredient list on the side of the box of sausages then considered Mabel's age and appetite. "I mean, I guess it can't do her any harm, right?"

Ronak lifted a corner of the slidey plastic and took a sausage out. He held it hesitantly, as if it were a living thing. Mabel's tail thumped louder as she took the sausage gently from him. She looked up at Ronak, her shining eyes glazed blue with cataracts, then carried the sausage over to her bed. She set the meat down gingerly, licked it before taking the first nibble, and ate the rest in small bites.

They gave Mabel two cooked sausages a day until the first box was gone. Then they cooked the second box too, now remembering to brown the outside. The old dog ate each one with the same slow, loving attention, so that they didn't need to feed her by hand anymore.

Instead of sleeping on her bed most of the time, she found patches of sunshine around the house to snooze in, or stayed outside, half watching for squirrels as she dozed, as if the change in her diet had brought back Mabel's younger spirit, her interest in the things she used to love.

Teja regretted the years she had thrown the sausages away without thinking of her dog. If Mabel lived for another year she wouldn't even mind placing an order again, Teja considered as she sipped her still-warm coffee and checked her work emails on her laptop. Mabel slept on the floor at her feet, her body twitching as she dreamed.

It occurred to Teja that she should invite Evelyn over one morning while the kids were at school. She could make them tea and a snack that she liked, ondhwa or farsi puris. Or maybe she'd pick up a coffee cake from her favourite bakery.

She also thought that she should tell Evelyn plainly that she preferred people called Ronak by his full name, that it was her grandfather's name and she had loved her grandfather dearly. *There have to be ways to belong and also be myself,* Teja thought. *And to show Ronak that he can do the same.*

Teja picked up her phone and dialled Evelyn's number.

As the phone rang, Teja leaned down to pet Mabel. "You're a good dog," Teja whispered to Mabel, "a very, very good girl." The pooch stretched out on the rug, made a contented sound, like a happy sigh.

A chirpy voicemail greeting kicked in: "Hey, I can't take your call but leave me a message and I'll get right back to you! Promise!"

Teja inhaled, readying herself to leave an equally cheerful message for Evelyn. "Hi! Teja here! Just wondering if you might be free for a coffee next week. I'd love to have you over, let me know when you're available! You can call me back or I'll see you at the school later. Or text me if that's easiest. Okay, hope you have a great day!"

She hung up the phone, noticed Mabel looking up at her quizzically, perhaps wondering about Teja's unusually enthusiastic tone. Teja shrugged. "I'm trying," she said to the dog.

Daksha Takes the Cake

DAKSHA ARRIVED AT THE DINER WEARING HER FADED jeans and favourite teal sweatshirt, her hair pulled back into a quick bun. The laces of her sneakers were still untied, hastily tucked in so she wouldn't trip on them. Though they pressed uncomfortably into the soles of her feet Daksha didn't stop to tie them until she was sitting down, pen and notebook in front of her, ready to get to work. She never felt like she had enough time on the weekends.

In those days, during the week, for money Daksha did whatever came to her through the WorkFirst temp agency. Usually she was assigned data entry jobs, which meant spending eight hours entering numbers into spreadsheets and hardly speaking to anyone, or the opposite, customer service, which meant talking on the phone all day while feigning a cheerful attitude. But at least these allowed her to dedicate her weekends to her creative calling: novel writing.

There was a lunch counter that faced the kitchen, a row of cherry red booths along the window, and retro tables with matching chrome and vinyl chairs running down the centre. A fig tree held court from a large ceramic pot in one corner; a sprawling jade plant welcomed customers near the entrance. From the kitchen wafted the comforting smell of fresh coffee, the brown-butter scent of pancakes cooking on the grill.

On weekends, the diner was bustling. There was always music on in the background. It was a playlist that was hard to hear, drowned out by the clatter of dishes and the racket of voices: groups of friends, families with exuberant kids, the occasional crying baby. Daksha noticed all this excitement peripherally, only barely heard the rise and fall of voices around her. The hubbub blurred as she focused on the minutiae of her invented sentences.

She had some confidence in her writing since she had published two lengthy murder mystery stories online. The few people who read them seemed to really like them.

"Lots of twists and turns! I couldn't stop reading until I found out how the bodies ended up in the dumpsters!"

"The setting was so creepy I slept with every light on in my house for three nights after finishing this. And I still can't stop thinking about the ending! Terrifying!"

Daksha appreciated the way the easygoing diner employees didn't mind that she paid for one coffee and nodded her head for refills at least twice after that. It didn't seem to bother them that she sat alone, taking up a whole table instead of a spot at the counter because she liked to look out the window as she paused to think of her next line. Black ballpoint still held in her hand like a divining rod, Daksha waited for clarity, insight into her invented characters, and what they might do next. She ordered food too. Toast with peanut butter and jam, or a plain bagel. The cheapest things on the menu.

Daksha was usually the first customer to arrive in the morning and she was still there, bent over the page, when the rush slowed after lunch. It felt like a different space after the peak time, when it was quieter. The diner still hummed with the lingering energy of all those people, like an emptied living room after a house party. She could actually hear the music that was piping through the speakers in the ceiling then: a compilation of pop songs interspersed with hip hop and soul. Daksha liked how her writing voice shifted through the hours, she noticed that her creative rhythm recalibrated to match the sounds around her. By the time the restaurant closed in the late afternoon, she was one of the last customers left, still scribbling down some last few words.

One day as she was paying, Daksha noticed a generic Help Wanted sign posted beside the cash register. The server behind the counter was the one who was almost always there. Her dyed hair — green, blue or fuchsia, depending on the month — pulled into a '50s style ponytail or elaborate-looking French braid. Today, her hair was lavender, a colour that made Daksha think of springtime, Easter bunnies and pastel-tinted eggs. She wore a flowered scarf as a headband to hold loose strands off her face. The colour, the vibrancy, ended at her neck, where her standard all-black diner uniform took over.

Seeing Daksha looking at the sign, the smiling woman said, "It's a pretty decent place to work if you know someone who's looking. The hours aren't bad, and the manager's not a creep or anything." Then she added, "My name's Brenda, by the way."

Daksha told Brenda her name too. "Maybe I'll apply."

"You should," Brenda encouraged. "The boss isn't in today, but he usually is at about this time."

"I'll come back tomorrow."

"I can let him know to expect you."

The manager interviewed Daksha right after she passed him her resumé the next day. "Well, I see you don't have a lot of experience. But Brenda says you're friendly enough. And smart."

Daksha wondered if Brenda assumed she was intelligent because she had seen her writing in her notebook. "I'm a quick learner," she agreed with the boss, feeling awkward for praising herself. But she really wanted the job. "And I already know the menu."

"No harm giving it a shot," he offered. "You can start Thursday. Get a couple days in before the weekend, when it gets really busy."

A few weeks later, in the quiet after the lunchtime rush, Brenda, who had by then become her co-worker and good friend, told Daksha about the baking show she'd started watching.

"So then I decided to look up how much the winners make and it was unbelievable."

Sitting at the end of the lunch counter on her break Daksha almost choked on her iced tea when Brenda told her the amount. "You're kidding," she coughed. "Just for baking?"

"Look it up yourself. You'll see." Brenda pulled out her phone. "Last year's winner posted this picture this morning." She turned the phone toward Daksha.

The photo was of a petite woman standing triumphantly beside a multi-tiered cake. It was frosted in gradient shades of pink and stood taller than her. And the kitchen the woman stood in was magazine perfect: bright and spacious with tall cupboards and a contemporary white backsplash. The shining countertop looked like real marble. "Special cake for a special someone!!!" said the caption under the picture. Daksha found the multiple sequential exclamation marks tacky and the wording irritatingly vague.

"Look at her house though. It's pretty much a mansion."

"I mean, that's just the kitchen," Daksha ventured.

Brenda gave her an exasperated look, clearly trying to enjoy the glimpse into a celebrity baker's life of luxury. "Anyway, that could be you one day. All you have to do is learn to bake."

Her remark was casual, but it made Daksha look more closely at the picture still in Brenda's hand. It was a really nice kitchen. Not that Daksha wanted a fancy house, but an income boost would be nice.

"Or you. That could be you," she offered.

"Nah, I like my life the way it is. You're the ambitious one."

It was slow in the restaurant. She knew Brenda wouldn't mind if she took longer on her break, so Daksha looked up the past champions right then.

Brenda was right. First they took home fifteen thousand dollars just for winning. Then they became celebrities, earning money from writing cookbooks, or for cameos on other TV shows on major networks. One winner was in an online ad for a fancy grocery store, strolling down an aisle with a nearly empty cart, saying how Sunshine Market was the only place he shopped for his family. She watched the commercial and wondered how much that guy got paid for that thirty-second promotion.

"I mean, how hard could it be?" Daksha pondered aloud. She considered how she had barely turned on her own oven in months. And she hadn't even made cookies since she was a teenager.

She turned to Brenda, who was wiping down the lunch counter, making slow circles with a damp cloth. "Don't lots of people do it all the time?"

"Do what?" Her friend had moved on from their conversation.

"Bake."

Brenda paused, cloth in hand. "I think it's way harder than it seems to get really good though."

Daksha took those words as a challenge.

She chose a basic cake recipe online, then stopped for ingredients on her way home: flour, eggs, baking powder, a carton of milk, the smallest bottle of vanilla she could find. Plus butter and icing sugar for frosting. Daksha dropped a set of plastic measuring cups into the shopping basket too. At home she added everything into a mixing bowl in the order directed, following the instructions exactly. She scraped the batter into a round pan. In the heated oven the cream-coloured paste expanded to the top of the tin. The finished cake was slightly brown at the edges when she pulled it out of the oven after thirty minutes, as the recipe said to, but it was pale near the centre. And it sagged in the middle too, unlike the plump yellow one on the website.

She read the recipe for buttercream and made it as well, while the cake cooled. Daksha smeared the icing across the top and sides using a regular table knife from her cutlery drawer, then ate a big slice standing up over the sink.

It was dark out by then. Daksha licked the icing off her fingers and listened to the familiar rattle of the hot water pipes as the people in the apartment below hers washed their dishes. She heard voices in the hallway. A deep voice murmured something, a woman laughed in response. A door clicked open and then closed again.

The cake itself is bland, gummy at the centre. The sweetness of the frosting is too much, sharp on my teeth, Daksha mused. Crumbs were smeared through it so the texture was also a bit off-putting. *Grainy,* she thought, as she licked it off her finger. She contemplated the ingredients on the website again, and said out loud, "Could be better."

Daksha sent a photo of the rest of the cake to Brenda who hearted it, then sent a message back, "You're nearly there!" followed by a yellow laughing-crying face.

The next day at work, near the end of her shift, Daksha noticed a small branch had broken off the jade plant by the door. She picked it up and put it into a filled glass, placed it on the window ledge. The oval leaves stayed at the top, shining thick and green, with plenty of room for new roots to grow downward. Daylight filtered in through the glass, shimmering. Daksha felt optimistic then too, as though such a small act could be a new beginning for her too.

She decided then to keep baking. To try. To get good enough to enter a competition. Daksha pictured herself sitting at an oversized antique wooden desk, the kind real authors had. Writing every day, gazing out to a picturesque scene through a large window for inspiration. She imagined not having to rush to a different job, but living comfortably off her winnings. Daksha pet a plump leaf with the tip of her finger, like it might bring her luck. The plant bobbed at her touch, the movement fragmenting the sunlight shining through the water that held everything afloat.

★

After that Daksha approached the challenge of learning to bake as she might start a new novel. To begin, she researched. Daksha watched reruns of all the past seasons of the baking show on her laptop when she was at home, jotted notes about recipes and the contestants, their weaknesses and strengths, considering them like characters in a book. Many were overconfident, trying to achieve too much in the given time, she noticed.

One thought he could trash a whole pie shell, start again from scratch and still finish. "What are you doing? Just use what you've got!" Daksha bellowed, as if she were a sports fan hollering at players on a television screen. Of course, the contestant's finished crust was raw. *Way too optimistic,* she thought. Daksha felt sorry for him but agreed with the judges that he had really messed up, or at least made some pretty regrettable choices under pressure.

Daksha began listening to podcasts on her walks to and from work and when she was out doing errands: Flour Power, Knead to Know, Pie Me. She signed out every book on baking she could from the library, plus there were online resources — blogs, recipe websites, video tutorials. Daksha even read the long explanations that came before the recipes, the ones that she would have ordinarily scrolled right through, bothered at times by the slips of grammar and obvious virtue signalling. She still didn't think that making everything from scratch actually made you a better person, or meant that your entire life was idyllic, as a lot of online cooks seemed to imply.

"Why buy mayonnaise when you can make your own?" one influencer rhetorically implored. "Is there any better way to tell your family that you love them?"

At the diner, Daksha lingered when the baker was in, queried the pastry chef when he dropped off his pies and cakes.

"European butter only," he casually told her, "for the higher fat content." When no one was watching, she liked to lean over a fresh croissant to inhale its essence, memorize it.

She bought an apron from the thrift store to wear as she worked on her recipes. The apron was heavy cotton, with red flowers on a sage background. *Cheerful,* she thought each time she slipped it on.

Alone in her queen-sized bed every night, Daksha hardly slept. Half-awake she considered edible flowers, imagined piping meringue into heart shapes to fill with strawberries. Or a clementine curd. Both. Combined into something celebratory. A collage of colours and textures came together in her mind in layers, as if she were an artist, a sculptor.

Brenda enjoyed talking through Daksha's baking adventures as they worked. She cooked a lot at home and knew more about flavour combinations than Daksha did. But Brenda sometimes had strange advice.

"Oh, I add cream cheese to almost everything, it really smooths out the other ingredients," she once told Daksha. Daksha pretty much only ate cream cheese on bagels, and even then she liked just a bit of it. Thinking of the pasty texture then, she could hardly imagine how it would be good on *everything,* then decided she should be more open-minded. In those days, Daksha was willing to try out any advice.

"I have loads of tips," Brenda said. "I have great cake recipe that uses vinegar to make the cake rise, and no eggs at all. You can use a hairdryer to smooth out lumpy icing. My mom baked all the time and taught me all kinds of things."

With all her research, Daksha was really learning that baking, like writing, wasn't as simple as it appeared. Everyone had their own opinions. There was a lot to learn, and it was hard to figure out which advice she should take and what she should ignore. She was learning that it took a lot of work for the end result to seem both effortless and refined.

From online videos Daksha figured out how to make flaky pastry by encasing butter in dough. She banged it into a square with the side of the rolling pin, flattened and tucked repeatedly to make perfectly sealed layers, enjoying that this was called a book fold. Making delicate pastries required unexpected force, and so she found her hands ached some mornings, her arms burned as though she'd been working out. She sought out European butter too, though cost-wise it was a real splurge.

Daksha kept checking the jade stem she had placed on the window ledge at the diner. At first, the roots were white nubs, barely visible. Another week later they were almost a centimetre long. She carefully swaddled the plant in a damp paper towel and placed it at the top of her backpack to carry home. From the same box store where she'd bought her first cake ingredients, Daksha purchased a small bag of soil and a plain terracotta pot about as wide as the shelf in her kitchen.

Back at her apartment she scooped the speckled soil into the pot a bit at a time, using a soup spoon. The dirt was dry, floury. She dug a pit in the centre, pushing the excess to the sides with the back of then spoon. Then Daksha positioned the plant in the hole, careful not to touch the curled roots with her fingers as she buried them. When she was done, Daksha watered it from the glass she'd been drinking from, as if adding wet ingredients to dry. She judged the right amount by poking her finger in, just past her knuckle, until it felt uniformly damp, as an online video had instructed.

From then on, Daksha gave the young plant a drizzle now and then as she was washing her mixing bowls and spatulas. Over time she found that she didn't need to touch the soil to know if it needed water. Instead, she could tell just by looking at the pucker of the soon-plentiful leaves — in the same way that she could by then judge if the rise of a yeasted bread dough was sufficient or determine the doneness of a baked cake just by looking at the colour of its surface. The plant grew, her confidence increased, and her bakes got better too. Her jade was thriving.

It took several drafts to complete the application form for the *Rising Stars Baking Show*, to tell her own story as compellingly as she could. She created her character as she would a fictional one: colourful, funny, possibly a bit misunderstood. As she was drafting each answer she found herself looking at her jade. The plant was still flourishing. The day before the deadline, Daksha poured herself a glass of wine, then submitted the final version of her online application, feeling hopeful.

With new equipment from the fancier kitchen store — two pans, a whisk and a set of rubber spatulas — Daksha kept working, starting as soon as she got home from the diner until late at night. While the oven was on she had time to write, so she brainstormed other character descriptions and made plot notes for a book too. It was satisfying to be so focused, and she had real momentum as she worked toward multiple creative goals. Daksha didn't need to leave her home to write anymore either.

It turned out the view from her kitchen table, her feet bare and her apron still on, was as inspiring as the hubbub of the diner.

She started working on a short story titled "A Danish to Die for." Another murder mystery, the plot at first centred on a young tourist who travelled to Europe on her own. Sitting in a café in Copenhagen, the protagonist witnesses an elderly man take a bite of a pastry, then collapse on the floor, dead.

Daksha abandoned the tourist as the main character, then rewrote each scene from the perspective of the baker who made the pastry, then she tried the perspective of the café owner. After that she wrote the story again, from the point of view of the man who was eating, up to the moment he collapsed. This scenario gave her the opportunity to describe, in detail, the experience of biting through crisply laminated layers of pastry, right down into the sweet tang of the jammy insides. Writing and re-writing the scene with the pastry several times, Daksha found herself fixated on getting the description of the baked good right, which wasn't necessarily that important to the plot, she periodically reminded herself. But it felt like she was really getting to use her newly gained learnings.

Daksha put her pen down each time her alarm sounded and took a break to sample her finished goods. Almost always, she ate over the kitchen sink, not wanting to wash an extra plate. Then, using her same plastic Bic, she jotted notes on old-fashioned recipe cards before putting her cooled creations away in Ziploc bags. She left scones and muffins for her neighbours in the mornings, attached notes to the packages: wordy descriptions of the contents jotted in thin script followed by a quickly drawn doodle — a flower, a heart or a smiling sun — then went to work at the diner after only a few hours of sleep. But she hardly felt tired in those days. Instead, she felt energized, inspired. Ideas for both stories and baking constantly bouncing through her mind like Ping-Pong balls.

★

When Brenda said she thought Daksha should post photos on social media like other bakers, she did that too, and deleted the older pictures as she got better. Gathering followers, she traded recipes with strangers and felt like she was making friends.

"I'm going to make these rolls too!" one person replied.

"I love the colours. So classy!" a follower noted about the cupcakes she made to celebrate Brenda's birthday. Each cupcake was frosted white with a buttercream apple blossom piped on top. Others liked that comment and some posted birthday messages to Brenda too. "What a lucky friend Brenda is!" wrote ComfyCook99. Brenda saw that message and responded, "The Luckiest!"

One time seven people asked for her sugar cookie recipe and so she sent each one of them the link to the website she found it on, along with a few modifications. "Double the vanilla," she encouraged. "You won't regret it."

Daksha posted a photo of apple muffins she made, along with the hint to add ginger. One person did, and said "My family loved the zing of it. I'll definitely make these again!"

Now and then Daksha slipped in updates on her social media account about her novel-in-progress, which earned fewer likes but some words of encouragement too.

"These mocha cupcakes are just the inspiration I needed to finish writing a crucial coffee-shop scene today!" she captioned a photo.

"Multi-talented!" wrote back one person within minutes, as if implying that baking mattered as much to Daksha as storytelling. Daksha, feeling offended, wondered then if she had gone too far. Baking was, after all, still just a way to keep writing. She didn't want people to think that it actually mattered to her as much as being an author did.

Daksha put her phone down on the table in front of her then, upside down so she could see just the case and the circles of camera lenses, but not the screen. In her mind she summoned again that writing desk she had always dreamed of. Herself, sitting there looking out the window toward a luscious garden, or a thicket of trees. Yes, she needed money for that dream to happen. And yet, since she'd been baking she'd been writing more too. And it didn't seem to matter as much where she was sitting, whether it was at an oversized desk or her ordinary table.

The next day, Daksha had a day off from the diner. She only wrote. She wore her flannel pyjama pants and an old T-shirt all day and worked at her kitchen table without turning the oven on once. Daylight moved from one side of the room to the other as the time passed.

When evening arrived, Daksha took a photo of her cold cup of tea, her notebook and pen arranged on her kitchen table. She posted the picture online along with the caption "Took a whole day to complete a final round of edits on this short story!"

Hardly anyone liked the post compared to her ones about baking. But Brenda posted a comment, "Happy Writing! Can't wait to read this one!" even though Brenda had once admitted that she didn't like to read at all. She responded to her friend with a double heart emoji and sighed.

Right after Daksha got a call from the show, saying that they'd like her to come in and bake for them, as a tryout, she called Brenda.

"You've got this," her friend reassured.

Daksha was confident on the day of the evaluation. After all, she knew the easygoing, friendly character she had created for her application so well that she should be able to play the part easily. She wowed the evaluators, who observed as she put together raspberry lemon cupcakes in their industrial kitchen, with the pre-measured ingredients she had brought from home. Then she mixed together a loaf of her rosemary pear bread, which had become one of her specialties.

"We admire Daksha's determination and creativity," she noticed one judge jot on their feedback form, and Daksha mused that those were good qualities for a writer too.

"That bread of yours was perfectly tender," another told her directly. "And look at that crumb," he said jabbing at a slice with his thick index finger.

For the final in-person interview for the baking show, Daksha didn't need to make anything. She used concealer to cover the dark circles under her eyes. They had appeared since she'd been sleeping so little. Daksha arrived just before the scheduled time and was shown into an ordinary conference room with a long table — six people who worked for the broadcaster already settled around it, and one empty chair, intended for her, where she sat.

A psychologist perched at the end, making notes. The woman smiled and said, "I'm here because the producers want to know how you might react to being on camera for twelve hours a day. We need to make sure you can handle the pressure." Daksha assured them that she could. She wasn't a crier, a shouter. She got along with most people. She didn't say that she had also learned, from a young age, to keep her feelings to herself.

In the end, Daksha attributed the show's interest to her other skills, specifically her ability to create a lively and believable protagonist, more than her baking. She still wasn't convinced her actual cooking skills really stood out. The interviewers laughed at her jokes and nodded as they scribbled notes on the papers in front of them. They asked her again about her childhood and what it was like to travel so far from her birth country to Canada when she was so young. In fact, Daksha didn't remember any of that, but didn't want to disappoint the encouraging faces lined up in front of her: comfortable white people of a certain age who were used to stories of immigration, arrival, success. *What's the harm,* she thought, and she told them a few stories she had heard from her parents about the hardships they went through when they first emigrated.

One interviewer said, "Don't be afraid to really highlight your background in your bakes too," so Daksha kept to herself the fact that she hardly ate spicy food anymore.

Instead, she considered how she might work in the flavours the interviewers imagined and responded enthusiastically, bobbing her head in agreement. Of course, she could fuse her heritage with her baking skills in a compelling way, she told them. *This is my chance*, Daksha reminded herself. The psychologist shook her hand before she left and said she thought Daksha would do well on the show. The next morning, they called and offered her a spot.

After that, Daksha worked on adding an Indian spin to her recipes. She developed a recipe for masala cupcakes, simmering black tea and spices — cinnamon, clove, star anise — in whole milk to be added to the batter, so that the cupcakes were delicately spiced like the sweetened tea she had as a child at her grandparents' house. Then she perfected a recipe for mango cream cheese tarts, remembering how her mother spoke of the fruits she ate fresh as a child from the tree in her garden. She thought she could tell the judges that story too.

The tarts were of course Brenda's favourites. "I told you, always add cream cheese!" she exclaimed after taking a bite, making them both laugh.

Daksha used turmeric in plain icing to tint it to the hue of summer flowers, topped cardamom cupcakes with toasted coconut and practised piping elaborate henna-like designs onto biscuits. Decorating them was calming, she found, like doodling in the margins of her notebook when she was coming up with story ideas.

She took the biscuits into the diner for Brenda who now thought Daksha was really onto something. "Okay, these are actually amazing," Brenda said. "Like, professional." She hugged her friend.

Daksha occasionally felt uncomfortable developing recipes that were so purposefully exoticized, but kept her mind on the end goal: to make enough money to write full time. That's what mattered. For most of her life, people judged her based on her background. They assumed she ate spicy food, would be married by thirty, practiced Hinduism and did sun salutations daily. Now she realized her ethnicity was an asset and those preconceived ideas about her could push her ahead of the other candidates, if she was willing to work them in her favour, into her baking. *It depends*, she weighed, *how badly do I want to win?*

At that time, nothing seemed more important.

★

The night before the competition, Daksha dreamed she was turning into an ancient tree. As if she had become her jade plant but had grown so much that she had reached the height of a gnarled oak. In her dream her body mutated and twisted hideously, monstrously, her fingertips swelling into bulging green orbs. She looked down at her tree body and saw that it was creviced and grey, a moss-like disease growing on her belly-trunk, her skin thickening into gnarled bark. Her feet grew roots that reached far down into the earth and her arms moved with aching slowness. She felt, for the first time, afraid. *Maybe entering the contest, baking in front of the world, is too ambitious, too much*, Daksha thought, trying to get back to sleep again.

The next morning she put on the knee-length denim skirt and the carefully ironed white button-down she had left hanging on the metal hanger on the back of her bedroom door. She slipped her feet into her canvas runners then tied a scarf around her neck, a colourful one Brenda had given her, for luck. Makeup and hair crews were ready at the studio so there wasn't anything more for her to do except gaze into the mirror at her regular skin, her ordinary human length arms and legs. *I'm fine. I'm going to be just fine*, she tried to convince her reflection.

Daksha noticed before leaving that her windowsill plant had grown another new branch, two offshoots and several new leaves. Its centre stem was wider too. Sturdier. Healthy. There was nothing hideous about it, and the plant looked nothing like what she had become in her dream. She took its steady growth as a good sign.

"Well, wish me luck," she said, nodding to its leaves. As she left home with her tight throat and queasy stomach, she wondered, again, if she had taken on more than she was ready for.

The set was inside a giant white tent with a row of sharp peaks like perfectly whipped meringue. It was centred in a large field surrounded by manicured hedges. The grass was radiant green and a bird chirped nearby, idyllically. It was as vivid in real life as it looked in the episodes she'd streamed at home.

Daksha put on the cream-coloured apron provided, her name embroidered in bold burgundy letters across her chest. It fit differently than her own apron at home did. Production already swirled around her like hungry, meowing cats. She felt the seriousness of the situation then. Of the eleven other competitors she counted one Black woman, an Asian man, and a person wearing a hijab, her, and one dark-skinned camera operator. Daksha wondered if the other bakers had also been encouraged to draw from their backgrounds for their recipes.

It was hot. She wished they could have set up someplace with air conditioning. Instead ceiling fans just stirred the air like slow-moving whisks. In front of her was a large butcher block counter, a stainless cooktop with an oven below it, a narrow sink and a standing mixer. There was a drawer that held mashers and spatulas, wooden spoons and a shelf with all the pans she might need. For the first day she'd brought her own toasted spice mix in a small jar, planning to include the blend into the finale.

James, the baker at the station behind hers, made a whistling noise. Not a shrill one, but the pull of air being sucked in between his teeth, a nervous sound. When Daksha turned to look at him, he said, "Good luck, then." He was sturdy looking with reddish hair, a tattoo of a vine twisted up his forearm. She tried to picture herself back in her own small fourth-floor kitchen to steady herself.

"Get set . . . Go!" said the exuberant host at the front of the room.

Daksha said, "Good luck to you too," then was startled by the instant cacophony around her. The clatter of bowls, the whirring of mixers, so different from the meditational quiet she was used to in her own kitchen. It rattled her through the next round, the technical test, so that the raspberry filling of her handheld pies was too runny. It wasn't cooked down enough, she realized, which might have been okay if the mistake hadn't made the bottom crust soggy.

James seemed genuinely sorry when he said, "Better luck next round, right?"

The final challenge was to make petits fours, the kind of dainty French cakes one could find in a Parisian bakery, which they had been advised to practise ahead of time. More than halfway through the round, as she was leaning over cakes that hadn't risen as they did at home, as if they were underbaked, Daksha felt something damp on her face. She wiped at her cheek with the back of her hand, thinking it was sweat. But there was a tremor in her fingertips too. Then her nose started to run. Daksha thought, stunned, *I'm crying. Now.*

James said, "Hey, you okay there?"

Realizing how she was losing time and losing resolve, Daksha just felt more overwhelmed. James left his own nearly completed miniature cakes on the counter, came around and said, "Do you need a hand?"

The production crew noticed as James approached and slid toward them. Daksha glanced at the timer and sidestepped the video camera that still watched her closely, hungry for such depth of feeling. The videographer followed as she splashed her face with cold water at the sink at the back of the room, making her mascara smear so she looked tired, she noticed, as she checked her face in the round mirror beside the sink. Daksha realized that she was, in fact, very, very tired.

She didn't finish on time after that. Her hands shook as she iced. Her still-gummy cakes looked amateur, incomplete without the fondant roses she had planned but never got to. Daksha thought of her social media friends, of Brenda, watching her as the judges evaluated the cake, shook their heads. One said, "What a shame. The flavours aren't bad but your execution is a disaster."

Maybe the psychologist was wrong, Daksha thought. *Maybe the character I created for myself is fatally flawed.* The plot, the one where she ended up winning the competition and then spent the rest of her life writing books at that majestic, imaginary desk suddenly seemed impossible.

To her relief, Daksha was the first one out of the competition. As she shook everyone's hands, the only one who seemed authentically sad to say goodbye was James. Weeks later she looked him up and saw he too had months' worth of bakes posted on social media — pies topped with elaborately woven pastry, simply frosted cakes tinted using natural food colourings photographed against muted backgrounds. She sent a message to thank him for being so nice to her, and a response from him popped up on her screen that same day.

"It wasn't the same after you left," he replied, in a way that was so open she felt almost embarrassed for him.

"I was only there for one day."

"That was the best day."

Daksha liked how he didn't even pretend to be cool and it occurred to her that he was a really genuine person.

In the week that followed, Daksha went to work at the diner like always. After the show aired, the manager gave her a raise to thank her for the free publicity. Lots of people had watched that first episode, it turned out, and recognized her, then told their friends who came in too. These fans of the show often tipped her extra. "Oh, the poor thing," she heard one customer say.

At work, Brenda would sometimes stop what she was doing, cleaning tables or restocking the fridges, look at her and say admiringly, "I still can't believe you did that."

Daksha re-read her notebooks crammed with the excerpts that had come to her while she was waiting for the oven timer to sound, then kept writing in the evenings and on her days off. Occasionally James stopped by with a fast food burger or take-out from his favourite Indian restaurant. On warm days they ate together on her narrow balcony, facing the weeping willow in front of her apartment.

"I still think the best part about the whole thing was meeting you," James said one day.

"Not making it to the semifinals?"

James had in fact become quite famous from his near-win. He was in two commercials after that: one for flour where he kneaded dough in a kitchen at sunrise, pinkish light coming in through the window beside him. By morning, a finished loaf of bread, plump and bronze, was on a wooden cutting board. The ad ended with James slicing into it with a serrated knife. Another was for a brand of paper towel. James magically appeared as other home chefs spilled milk, dropped an egg, or had a pot on the stove dramatically overflow. Each time, James handed them a piece of paper towel to mop up the mistake before it turned into a disaster. "Every great cook sometimes makes a mess. QuickClean Towels help you mop up fast so you can get back to making your masterpiece," he said looking right into the camera.

One day James took a picture of him and Daksha side by side and posted it online. A lot of people liked it. They said things like "How cute!" followed by several hearts, as if they were already a couple. *People probably look for that kind of storyline*, Daksha thought.

The first time they kissed, his lips tasted sweet, as she had imagined. They were on her balcony again that day and she was leaning against the metal railing. Daksha pulled him in closer toward her. When a group of teens from the sidewalk below shouted that they should get a room they laughed and went inside. He didn't leave her apartment for two days. James brought over a carry-on sized suitcase with some clothes and left a spare toothbrush. He read the first draft of her new novella, *A Teaspoon of Treachery*, from her living room.

"I think it's the best thing you've written yet," James said when he was done reading.

"You read my others?" she asked.

"Right after the show."

She had created a protagonist for this book who was more vulnerable than in her previous works, who made mistakes. Her main character was a warm-hearted but cynical baker. *At least,* she thought, *the experience is useful research.*

"Maybe we should actually move in together," James suggested one evening, looking over to her as he scrubbed dishes in a sink full of soapy water.

Daksha watched him wash a plate with his hands in the water, noticed the way he checked to make sure he hadn't missed spots before rinsing. He placed it carefully on the dish rack beside him and then washed a wine glass. When he was done he used the still-wet glass to give a sprinkle of water to the jade plant that sprawled further along the shelf, looking almost too large for the pot, she noticed. The gesture reminded her of his kindness that day of the competition.

"I like it here," she said. "But you're welcome to stay."

It's a test, she thought, wondering if he was willing to fit into her life.

"I thought you'd never ask," he said.

Daksha published *A Teaspoon of Treachery* for real. The agent who agreed to represent her said that the bit of baking show fame she had achieved, especially in a scene so touching to the audience, made her personal brand more interesting to publishers.

The advance she got when the book sold wasn't enough to buy a mansion, or even a fancy marble countertop for her kitchen, she joked to Brenda, but it would be satisfying to see her own work on the shelves of bookstores at last. She kept working at the diner too. There, she got to hang out with Brenda. And the owner never asked her questions about her background. Sometimes, at work, she still leaned over the pastries, just to inhale the perfect balance of flour, butter and sugar.

★

One winter day, feeling uninspired to write, Daksha decided to bake. James was away, judging a pie competition at a farmers' market outside of the city. It had been ages since she'd been the one to turn their oven on. Since James moved in, he made most of their meals. He was a joyful chef, putting on music and singing along as he worked, sometimes using a wooden spoon as a makeshift microphone. Cooking was, for him, a party. Unlike for Daksha, who still preferred the quiet.

Her apron was on a metal hook attached to the kitchen wall. She slipped the neck loop over her head and tied the waist string behind her back. Daksha flipped through her cards of saved recipes until she found one for cinnamon buns, instructions she had jotted down when she was preparing to go on the show but had never made. When she was a child, the sticky treats were her favourites, though they always got the pre-made kind from the grocery store, the ones topped with generic cream cheese icing.

Daksha made the soft dough leisurely, kneading and punching it, then flattened it out into a pleasing rectangle. On top she drizzled spoonfuls of golden melted butter, sprinkled brown sugar and cinnamon, a generous handful of pecans. Then she rolled it into a cylinder that she sliced into even pieces. *Each bun, arranged in the pan, is such a perfectly satisfying swirl, all coming together like a bouquet,* she thought, imagining how she could describe the buns in fiction, later on. Daksha took a picture in case she decided to post it later too.

As the pastries baked they filled the apartment with the warm scent of spice. She pulled them out of the oven when they were evenly browned, then turned them out onto a clean tray so that the syrup of melted sugar and butter that had pooled at the bottom was now on top.

She got out a plate, instead of eating over the sink like she did in the past. Daksha ate the first one warm, uncurling it toward the centre — the sweetest, stickiest part. Taking her time, she licked the sugary goo off each finger before washing her hands in soapy water. Then she put a second one on the same plate, because the first one was so good. She thought of giving the rest to her neighbours, as she hadn't for a long time, but instead she put them into a sealed container for later. To keep. She brushed the flour off her apron and hung it back on its hook.

Daksha jotted a quick note on the recipe card before putting it away. *Next time add cardamom*, she wrote in her loose script on the side of the faintly lined card, thinking that she wouldn't mind playing with the recipe.

"Maybe," Daksha said thoughtfully to her jade then, alone in the otherwise-empty light-filled room, "maybe it turns out I actually do like baking after all."

My next main character could be someone creative but quiet, like me, she mused then. *An introverted painter, or a wildlife photographer. A graffiti artist,* she thought excitedly. *One who paints trees on buildings just before they get demolished.* She pictured such a woman, wearing black to blend into the night, painting in the shadows but making bold and colourful works visible to everyone in the light of morning. *Yes, she would be imaginative, but a private person too.* Daksha got her notebook from the shelf in the living room and sat down at the table. Facing the window in her own kitchen was by then her favourite place to write.

She didn't want to forget the specifics as they came to her. This new character was already so vivid: not only the black clothing she wore, but also what she liked to eat (a peanut butter and jam sandwich on white bread twice a day), the way she spoke (halting, thoughtfully, as if she were choosing her words from a carousel of possibilities). She pushed aside her recipe cards to bring her notebook closer. Before she forgot, before James came home and asked her how her day went, before she opened a bottle of wine and poured them each a glass, before she offered him a cinnamon bun, Daksha wanted to make sure she wrote all the important details down.

The Illness

ASHOK MET MIRA THE DAY SHE CAME TO HIS FAMILY home for tea. Mira was wearing a silk sari which she rearranged after settling into her spot between her parents on the long, formal sofa. The fabric was green and shimmered. Her heavy black hair and the gold chain around her neck shone too. Three gleaming gold bangles around her wrist clattered every time Mira lifted the delicate cup from its saucer. When she didn't have her tea gracefully in hand she would touch the bangles with her fingertips. Ashok presumed, by that familiar gesture, that she wore them often, and he wondered if she was superstitious, if she wore them for luck. Ashok stole quick looks at her across the rim his own cup. Later, he would decide that he had fallen in love with her right then.

He hardly heard the small talk around him but tuned in when his parents asked Mira if she liked to cook.

"I don't like to. I'd rather not." Her voice was quiet but sure.

"Well, our son seems to want to be the one to make the meals anyways," Ashok's father said in response.

Mira met Ashok's eyes then. She smiled at him and he felt the heat of the afternoon close in so that his palms and his temple were suddenly damp with sweat. After they had all finished their chai, Mira and Ashok were asked if they would like to see each other again. They both nodded, *yes*. From then on they were free to meet on their own as long as they were in public. Usually they went for walks, both wearing more casual Western clothes.

Ashok had a degree in hospitality and was working in a hotel restaurant as a sous-chef. "After my older brother became a doctor, I could do something different. You know, they had one top-marks kid with an ideal career. My brother's path gave me freedom."

One day, Ashok mentioned the idea of moving all the way to Canada. "I could open a restaurant there and it would be a success, I'm sure. My brother thinks so too. He's lived there for years now and said he could sponsor me."

Mira, who had an accounting degree, said boldly, "I could help you. I know all about running a business. All my life I've wanted to do something so exciting."

"Me too," Ashok said, imagining the two of them going together. He reached for her hand then.

Soon after, they were married.

The couple arrived on the prairies in the summer. At first they stayed with Ashok's brother, who had a large house in a suburb at the edge of the big city. The basement they slept in had a sitting area and a bedroom with grey-blue acrylic carpeting. Mira loved the plushness of it under her bare feet, the slight bounce of the underlay as she stepped across it.

Each morning Ashok walked eight blocks to the corner store to buy a newspaper and back again. Then, together, the couple looked through the classifieds, specifically the section with restaurants for sale. They spread the paper out on the plush basement floor then sprawled themselves down side by side to read it. The fine print of the newspaper was like an array of paths they could take, as if their own possible futures were laid out before them, crowded with promise.

When they finally found a restaurant they could afford it was three hours away, in a town that even Ashok's brother had never heard of before. *This,* Ashok thought, re-reading the ad circled with blue pen, *is how an adventure really begins.*

In the town, the streets were wide, with no pedestrians on the broad sidewalks and hardly any cars. Stopped at a traffic light on the main street there was only their vehicle and three others waiting for the light to change. "All this for only four of us," Mira noticed as the signal went from red to green.

When they pulled up to the restaurant, Mira was skeptical. "Why is the parking lot so much larger than the building?"

"That's good, it means our customers will find a good spot easily, even when it's colder out." He had heard a lot about the harshness of winter, the icy streets and snow-covered trees, from his brother. He found the building ugly but had gotten used to that. There seemed to be little thought to architectural aesthetics in most places he'd seen so far in Canada. Everything seemed to be created with only functionality in mind.

Mira ventured, "Maybe it would be nice to be closer to the city. To family."

"This is the adventure. Our adventure," Ashok said. "Isn't this what we wanted?" Mira could see that his heart was already set on this place, and so she decided, from that day, she would also make the best of it.

The restaurant was originally a breakfast café. It was owned by an older couple who wanted to sell and retire. Inside it was sturdy and clean with a well-laid-out kitchen and a bar with stool-seating, twelve tables for customers that they planned to leave behind for the new owners. There were large windows on all three sides of the dining room, all looking out to the over-sized parking lot. Mira and Ashok signed the lease that same day. They moved to the town with four suitcases of their belongings, the same ones that they had brought with them from home.

There were only a handful of other restaurants established already in the area: the fast food places along the highway, the Chinese eatery and one advertised as family dining, which Ashok and Mira learned was food that the white locals were more accustomed to. They were the first two South Asians to arrive there. It didn't seem like it should matter, even if Ashok's brother kept mentioning it.

Their lives became busy. Ashok and Mira soon had two children, a boy and a girl. They rarely had breaks from work and didn't take holidays. When the children were small, they sometimes wished they had their parents, or Ashok's brother's family, closer, so they could help the young family now and then. Instead, they learned to manage.

Mira dropped the children, Shivani and Dev, off in the mornings at preschool and kindergarten, then stopped at the bank or post office before going to the restaurant. Ashok went straight there to start preparing food for the day. He chopped vegetables and meat into tidy cubes to be marinated, prepared sauces ahead of time and stored everything in carefully marked plastic containers in the cooler. When Mira arrived she cleaned the bathrooms, vacuumed the restaurant, then together they wrapped sets of cutlery in white paper napkins, checked glasses and plates for hard water spots that they wiped away with soft cloths.

Ashok always felt a thrill when the first person came in for lunch. "Welcome my friends," he exuberantly greeted the diners. "My beautiful wife will take you to our best table."

Mira was more reserved. "Would you prefer to be beside the window or here in the middle, where it's warmer? How is your day going?"

Ashok liked to have conversations with people who came in, especially if they sat up at the bar, which he took as an indication the customer was looking to talk.

"I recommend the lassi today. The mangos are finally in season," he would say cheerfully, sometimes delivering the beverage to the customer for free. "Here, on the house this time!"

"I watched you drive up. Your truck looks like it's brand new. Business must be good!" he joked the first time he met Sam, a local contractor.

Sam laughed. "Never good enough. Let me know if you need work done around here. I'll give you a discount." He became a regular, coming in at least once a week to have an order of pakoras and a Kingfisher, and chatted with Ashok about the football he watched on television. Sam also told Ashok stories about the time he spent in India in his twenties.

"I think back to that year all the time. Everything about India totally blew my mind." Sam dropped his voice then. "Made me a better person. More tolerant than I was before, than my parents ever were, that's for sure."

After the lunch rush, Ashok washed dishes while Mira sat at the bar sipping a soda, or a cup of black coffee, entering numbers into their accounting ledger. As she worked, she wrapped a lock of her long hair around her index finger. Each time she lifted her hand the same three bangles, the ones she had been wearing the day they first met, and always wore still, clattered against each other. Ashok knew his wife didn't like to be interrupted while she was so focused, but when he watched her work it still seemed to him as if all the light in the room still radiated from her, like the first day they met. Like she was the centre of everything.

Feeling her husband's gaze, Mira giggled. "Later, Ashok. At home. Imagine if a customer walked in."

"You can read my mind, my love." Then he went back to work. Neither of the two could imagine a time they wouldn't be together. It felt like they would be healthy, young and over-whelmingly busy forever.

Ashok's brother came by regularly. He brought his family with him. They rarely stayed the night, but liked visiting in the restaurant, where Ashok always cooked them a special meal. After eating they would stay for hours, catching up over cups of tea, fountain pop for the kids, as other customers came and went.

"It's a nice place. You've made it very inviting," his brother encouraged, putting his arm around Ashok's shoulder. "Like I always said, you were destined for success."

The restaurant was their second home. When the children were young, Mira picked them up after school and brought them there to watch cartoons while she and Ashok kept working. In later years, the kids brought friends to do homework or watch TV on the screen mounted over the bar. Ashok or Mira brought them still-warm samosas, the recipe they'd perfected for the restaurant that was much less spicy than the ones they made for home. Once their son brought another teenaged boy who complained, "It stinks like curry in here." He didn't invite that friend back again.

By the time they were in their thirties, Ashok found he was occasionally disappointed by how ordinary their life was. Boring even, he thought.

"Remember how we wanted to be adventurous?" he asked his wife one day. "We could have gone on to California or a beautiful city in Europe. We could have opened five more restaurants, all over the world."

"This is a beautiful place, in its own way. We used to think it was exciting that we moved this far."

"A country so cold you can hardly stand outside in the winter? Working jobs where we can't take more than a single day off? I don't know what we were thinking."

"We should start cross-county skiing together. Or you could learn to ice skate. Take a couple hours off in the afternoon and go. The kids have so much fun playing hockey. They make the best of the weather." Mira continued, "We can have our fun when the children finish school."

Mira had always felt it was important to provide the kids with stable lives until they graduated from high school. But she dreamed of travelling too, Ashok knew. He would wait as she lingered outside the travel agency at the shopping mall, reading the lists of flights on sale in the window, taking brochures for vacation packages to Bali or France.

Mira told her husband that she would love to take a foodie trip to Italy. "The kind where you learn to cook their food by rolling out fresh pasta, plucking ripe figs from the tree, eating meals at outdoor tables, picking fruit in ancient olive groves." She sighed dreamily, "Imagine. It sounds so peaceful, so different from anywhere we've been. So romantic."

Mira opened a separate bank account for them that she slipped extra money into, whenever they had it. She called it their Adventure Fund. "One day we will retire and have the rest of our lives together to do all kinds of wonderful things," Mira promised.

Of the two of them, Mira was the strong one, physically. She took up jogging and rarely slept past six. Most mornings she went for a run first thing, leaving the house when it was still dark out, stars still dimly shining in the grey-black sky. As she ran, the sun rose, soft light giving way to full morning by the time she was home again. Her route was consistent: along neighbourhood streets, through the park, behind the hospital and funeral home and back again in time to have breakfast with her family.

Mira also volunteered at the school, organized fundraisers for Shivani and Dev's outdoor pursuits club and drove elderly residents of a care home to doctors' appointments, thinking of her own aging parents back home. When they could, they donated meals from the restaurant too. Mira filled aluminum pans and delivered them to the local shelter from the trunk of her car. Others in the town got to know them well. Respected them. Even loved them.

★

Then, in her mid-forties, Mira's health changed. She lost weight and became prone to colds, sometimes spending the day in bed with body aches that came hard and stayed, fatigue that she said came from so deep inside her. She stopped wearing her gold bangles and when Ashok asked about them she said that the bit of weight on her arm bothered her. Mira set them down on her dressing table in their bedroom and left them there, silenced. Sometimes Ashok would notice Mira touch her wrist, feeling the spot on her bare skin where the gold once was. Sometimes he would reach for her hand too and notice their absence, but mostly it was the sound he missed, the intermittent jangle that he had become so used to.

Ashok hired part-time staff, teenagers who worked half-heartedly, and he managed the restaurant on his own. He never heard directly that the quality of the food suffered, but there were signs. Unfinished plates, smaller tips and then, fewer customers. By then, he didn't care as much. Looking up from the flames of the gas stove, Ashok sometimes still expected to see his wife at the bar, doing her work with a lock of her hair wrapped around her finger, the ledger book in front of her. When she wasn't there for him to bring bites of this or that for her to try, or to pour her a fresh cup of coffee, the joy of making perfect meals for others seemed to fade too.

For a long time, local doctors didn't know why Mira's health declined. People in town wondered if she was unhappy, menopausal or, worse, seeking attention. Ashok felt concerned about her mental wellness too. "Why don't you try getting dressed? Come with me to work. I'll drive," he pushed his wife.

"Don't you think I want to? Don't you see how much I want that too?"

Ashok's brother stopped trying to keep his distance when he noticed their growing frustration. "Let's order tests. Get her to a specialist," he suggested. "We know our Mira. We know she would not exaggerate about any of this."

By the time Mira was diagnosed with cancer at almost fifty it had metastasized — into her bones, making them brittle and prone to breaks. If she laughed or cried, she could break a rib, causing her weeks of sharp pain. Ashok's brother came more often, just to see her, making the long drive to only stay for an hour, but he came at least once a month. "You must rest. Watch TV or read. Don't try to do too much," he advised.

"All I do is rest," Mira sighed.

People in town came together to help the family too. Neighbours made sure the lawn was mowed. A group of them hung Christmas lights on the house at the end of November, knowing that Mira liked to have them up for Diwali too. In early spring, the same group efficiently arrived with their ladders to take the lights down again.

One day the next door neighbour Janice pulled up in her car just as Ashok was taking in a stack of Tupperware containers filled with food that had been left on their doorstep by a well-meaning friend. He wished he felt more grateful for the delivery, but instead he felt overwhelmed by the steady stream of silent, ghost-like drop-offs. People seemed to only stop by when they knew no one was home. Perhaps by the way Ashok carried the containers in, Janice sensed that he was overwhelmed. She walked over and offered to help.

"Why don't I come in and get all this sorted?"

Ashok nodded, not trusting himself to speak. The inside of his eyelids tingled, threatening tears.

Janice stayed for two hours. She organized all the food — dividing a large lasagna into two containers and putting one in the freezer, chatting with Ashok as she did so. "This is far too much for one meal." She marked the dates on all the other containers, just as Ashok would do in the restaurant, and put the muffins on the middle shelf of the fridge.

"These muffins are a good easy breakfast, Ashok." Janice said his name the way most people in the town did. "Ash-ook." His wife was the only person left in his everyday life who said it the way it was meant to be said, he realized then. *Don't think like that,* Ashok told himself.

She loaded the dishwasher and got it started. "We'll get someone in to clean for you once a week or so. It won't cost too much and it'll help. You'll feel better. Now I'd love to say hi to Mira if she's up for it."

Janice sat in the bedroom with Mira for a while and told her a funny story about a group of teenagers down the street who went for a joyride in a parent's car. The kids got caught just as they pulled into the Just Chill drive-through. "You won't believe it, Mira, but one of the boys, that Carson fellow with the red hair, if you know him. Well, his own mother was inside having a coffee with a friend at exactly the same time!" Janice laughed. "Those children didn't even get their milkshakes! Boy, are they in trouble now." Ashok heard Mira's quieter giggle too.

"Thank you," Ashok said sincerely as Janice slipped her coat back on.

"All these years, you've been so generous with everyone. Every time we came into the restaurant you treated us like royalty. If you need anything, I'm right next door."

After Janice left, he went into their bedroom to be with his wife. Mira was sitting up. The television was back on. She muted it when Ashok came in. It was re-run of a sitcom they used to watch together he noticed, glancing at the screen. On the bedside table there was a woven silk shawl. He had purchased it in a store downtown after seeing it in the window and had given it to her for their anniversary. The emerald green, the richness of it, had reminded him of the sari Mira was wearing the first day they met.

"I feel bit better today," she said to her husband. "It was so nice of Janice to come. I miss knowing all the news."

"Soon enough we'll be through this and you'll hear all the gossip yourself again. Then you'll wish you didn't have to know. Who did what, who went where, all of that nonsense."

"I have a good feeling today, Ashok. Maybe I'll really be okay."

They heard the front door squeak open and close. It was Shivani. Her studio apartment was only a short drive away so she stopped by often.

"Wow, the kitchen looks great, Dad. You got it all cleaned up," she said, poking her head into the bedroom. Shivani was still wearing her puffy winter coat, he noticed.

"It wasn't me," Ashok replied. "Thank Janice. There's lots of food there too. It's all labelled. Help yourself, okay?"

"I can't stop. Dev called me from school to see how you were, so I thought I'd pop in. I'm heading out again in a minute."

After Shivani left, Ashok leaned in to kiss his wife, feeling cheered up again too. "We will get through this together," he said, as he had become used to saying.

He held her hand again then, touching the same spot on her wrist where her bangles used to be, feeling their absence. Mira's skin was colder than he remembered it being. Fear rose in his throat. *Could he live without her? No,* he thought. *There's no way.* It was a thought he pushed away each time it arrived, though more and more, it felt like the reality that was before them, especially when he really, really looked at her.

"Let me get you a blanket, you must be feeling chilly. I'll turn up the heat too." He left the room and felt momentarily relieved. Sometimes it was easier when he wasn't so close to her. When he was, the pain at times felt unbearable.

For three years, Mira's family wondered if every important occasion might be their last. Perhaps there would be no more Raksha Bandhan celebrations, and this would be the final time she would be there to tie colourful strings around her family's wrists for symbolic protection. Maybe this heart-shaped cake would be the last Ashok would bake for Mira on Valentine's Day. Or perhaps they would never again clink glasses of sparkling apple juice on New Year's Eve. When Ashok's brother's family visited, his wife regularly burst into tears so Mira ended up trying to comfort her.

"I'm okay," she told her sister-in-law. "I'll see you again soon. We'll come your way and stay the weekend."

People didn't know what sort of gifts to buy Mira for various occasions either. Gifts meant to last, like household objects or jewellery, or gifts for sick people, like slippers and bathrobes. Neither seemed right. When the four of them were together — Mira, Ashok and their grown-up children — they often ended up in tears.

"It's your birthday!" Mira once admonished Shivani. "You still need to be happy today. Please can we just celebrate you?" After that, the Ashok, Shivani and Dev spent the rest of the evening pretending they were fine until Mira went to bed and they could go back to being sad again. They sat together in the living room and talked about Mira's health, which was all they were really thinking about the whole time.

"She looks tired, but the doctors say her red blood cell count is slightly up, so that's a good sign," Ashok told them.

"I was thinking that she seems better than last week," Shivani said.

"Me too," agreed Ashok. "We have to stay hopeful." Saying such things to his children made him momentarily buoyant, as if there really was hope. In those moments he imagined they might get a call from the doctor saying the diagnosis was wrong, or there had been some kind of breakthrough and the cancer was suddenly curable. Maybe someone had made a mistake and there was a chance Mira would get better.

By the last winter, Mira hardly left the hospital and so Ashok went there every evening. In December, it was so cold that plumes of white billowed from the tailpipes of other cars on the street. As always, he drove slightly below the speed limit.

Ashok made the familiar left turn into the mostly empty parking lot that was hidden from the main road by snow drifts shovelled into peaks. He liked to park at the far end, even though it was away from the hospital door, because he found it easier to park with an empty space on either side, though he had to walk in the cold for longer.

When he slammed the car door too hard, the sound was startling in the quiet, making Ashok wince. That winter was so frigid that his heavy boots squeaked as he walked across the layer of snow and ice toward the salted walkway.

The doors slid open. Inside, the hospital was decorated for Christmas. Glittering garlands and gaudy ornaments hung from an artificial tree at the far end of the open atrium. The tree rose up higher than the second-floor walkway.

"Go on through, Mr. Lal," the woman behind the reception desk said, covering the receiver of the phone with the palm of her hand so the person on the line wouldn't hear her. Her desk was protected by a clear wall of Plexiglas, the edges decorated with snowflake stickers.

Dev and Shivani had gone to high school with her, and Ashok remembered that her older sister used to come into the restaurant, never alone and always with a date. Ashok had once heard the sister say, "The spices in this food are so sensual," in a way that he found funny. He wondered how his wife would have reacted if he had said such a thing, that the breakfast she made for them each morning was exotic or sexy. She would have raised her eyebrows, like he was ridiculous. Then the pang — he hadn't had breakfast at home with Mira for so long.

Ashok continued down the wide corridor on the first floor of the hospital. An unoccupied wheelchair was angled slightly as if left there in a hurry. He slipped off his coat before going in, feeling hot. It was always warm here. One time, he heard that they did that purposely, to keep patients sleepy.

Mira's room was about the best one could hope for in a medical facility. It was a private room, and there was a large window that faced the open area behind the hospital, a park that spread down along the river valley. Ashok's brother said they were lucky they weren't in the big city. Luxuries like rooms with only one bed and a view were much more rare there.

In the middle of the hospital room was the bed. It was an industrial and ugly thing made cozier with a homemade quilt in shades of blue that his wife's friends had made together for her. Mira was propped up with several pillows. Her eyes were closed, her mouth gaping as she slept and her head leaned to one side. The same green scarf that Ashok had given her was around her, sliding off one shoulder.

Shivani was sitting in a high-backed chair beside the large window. She was knitting, a puddle of burgundy gathered in her lap as the needles clicked steadily. Her black hair veiled her face as she looked down. Along the windowsill were bouquets of flowers, subdued pink roses and white carnations mostly, in generic glass vases. Some were fresh and others drooped, wilting.

Shivani looked up then. She gave Ashok a hug. "I'll get you a tea, Dad," as if he were the one who needed looking after.

Mira woke and pushed herself up, struggling to do so. "Oh, you're here. You must have shut down the restaurant early?" she asked, unsure of the time.

Ashok shrugged and walked over to the bed. He straightened the pillows, pulled the fabric back around both shoulders. He kissed Mira's papery forehead, smoothed her thinning hair. Her breath smelled slightly sweet and rancid, like old apples. When they were younger, Mira's skin was beautiful, the smooth brown-ness of it. Now, she was so pale, nearly translucent, so skinny that her jaw was sharp and her collarbones jutted. Through her clothes you could see the sharp outlines of her bones. When he helped her dress or bathe, he was shocked by the looseness of her skin on her skeletal frame.

She used to ask him, before she got sick, if he thought she was getting fat. He remembered her softness sometimes, her old roundness. He missed the space she used to take up in his arms. Now Ashok was afraid to touch her.

After Shivani left the room, Mira said weakly to Ashok, "I don't know if I can do this any longer."

When Dev was home from school, Shivani was visiting or other friends were around, Mira still talked about fighting the disease, still speaking the lines they expected to hear from her. But she often told Ashok that she was tired. He knew what she meant. Of course, he would never say it to her, but he was tired too.

Shivani returned with three paper cups on a tray, handed one to Ashok. "Black tea with one cream for you, Dad. Coffee for me, and a mint tea for you, Mom."

"Put it down, please. I'll have it later."

"She's hardly drinking," said Shivani to Ashok, picking up her knitting again.

"I am." Mira's voice was croaky. She tried to clear it. "I am drinking, just not right now."

"You need to keep your strength up," Ashok agreed with his daughter. They were all quiet again. A television down the hall played an old *Seinfeld* episode. The sound of the canned laughter irritated Ashok.

"Why don't you go home?" Ashok turned to Shivani. "I'm going to be here for a bit. You go relax, eat."

Shivani sighed. "Okay. I think I will. Thanks."

After Shivani was gone and it was the two of them, Ashok closed the door to block the sound of the sitcom and pulled the chair, still warm from his daughter, closer to Mira's bed. Out of habit he sat down softly. As if Mira were still asleep and he might wake her.

"So?"

"So, I'm sick of it," she continued saying as she had earlier when it was just the two of them. "I don't know why I'm supposed to keep going like this. The fun is all over, and I'm stuck here, always feeling so awful, surviving on painkillers, with nothing to look forward to." Ashok could see how hard it was for her to speak. He nodded, not wanting to belittle her by saying something artificially cheerful or meaningless. When it was just the two of them he didn't try anymore.

A nurse opened the door again. "Just checking in," she chirped, then left the door open. She and another orderly chatted in the hallway, discussing their weekends. The ventilation system clicked on and hummed slightly cooler air into the room. A food cart clattered by. The smell made Mira turn her head away, toward the window.

"I saw a fox. I saw the same one yesterday too, but I wasn't sure if I was imagining things until I noticed it again today," said Mira after a time, her voice so low and dry he could hardly hear her over the industrial sounds around them. "It walked right by the window. She's injured, with only three good legs — the fourth is useless, broken. It just dangles in the air. She must be hungry. I don't know how she'd find anything to eat if she's injured like that."

Ashok was quiet, not sure if Mira was hallucinating. It happened, most likely as a result of the meds she was on. Foxes and bobcats weren't uncommon, but they were stealthy. Rarely seen. He had never come upon one before.

The two sat together like that for a time, with long silences between few words, until Mira nodded off again. Ashok finished his coffee, threw away the dead flowers and tried to put the living ones back together into new arrangements. Then he walked over to the food kiosk where he bought a pre-wrapped cheese sandwich that he ate sitting beside sleeping Mira, using a napkin as a plate on his lap. He bought a can of orange pop from the machine in the hall and drank that too. Mira mumbled in her dream. Ashok looked out the window to the black night, put the remains of his meal in the trash and closed the blinds.

He texted Shivani, "I'm leaving. She's asleep."

Shivani wrote back a moment later, "Okay, I'll see you there tomorrow." And in a second message, "Thanks, Dad." He wanted to ask her what for.

There was no one at the front desk at this time, but Ashok said goodnight to the uniformed security guard by the exit door. It was dark outside. The parking lot was lit by overhanging streetlights, white bobbles in the black sky. There were still a few cars parked with wide gaps between them, but no other people around. Ashok sensed something move nearby. He looked over and saw low eyes shining yellow in the night, at the periphery of the lot.

It was a fox, just bigger than a house cat, watching him. The animal neared the closed garbage bin, sniffed the air, circled the container with its nose close to the ground, then turned around to leave, having found nothing. As it lumbered unevenly away, tangerine fur reflecting the moonlight, Ashok saw that one foot dangled from the animal's lifted rear leg, as Mira had described. The fox paused and looked back once more before carrying on, leaving tidy, uneven footprints in the snow.

Mira died as the winter faded and gave way to warmer weather. When the grass was turning green, but there was still a chill in the air, and the leaves on the trees were still buds.

The day after she passed, Ashok taped a note on the door of the restaurant. "Closed Indefinitely."

★

Later, Ashok wondered if the fox made it, surviving on garbage can scraps or learning to hunt on only three legs. Or if it didn't.

★

After the funeral, while the rest of the town and Ashok's brother's family lingered in the reception area, he and Shivani stepped outside, craving a break from the murmured condolences.

He asked her, "Did your mom tell you about the fox?"

"What fox?"

"The one that had been visiting her."

Shivani laughed. "I'm not a little kid, Dad."

"It's one hundred percent completely true. I saw it with my own eyes," Ashok said. "I'll tell you all about it."

He stood and held his hand out for his daughter to take and heard a familiar sound, the faint ting of metal jangling. Shivani was wearing Mira's three gold bangles. They shone in the afternoon sunlight.

"These look nice on you." He gestured toward them.

"I hope you don't mind. I just saw them on the dresser. It seemed right to wear them. They make me think of her. Every time I hear them. I just don't ever want to forget." She hiccupped the last words. "Now I'm crying again. Mom would have hated us crying like this all the time."

"She would have understood. And she would have wanted you to have them, I know." Ashok took a last look around, inhaled the quiet. "You should go through her things. Take what you like. I even think her old saris are in a box somewhere. Perhaps in one of the old suitcases downstairs. You'll want them to remember her."

"What about you, Dad? Don't you want them?"

As he looked away from Shivani he saw the shining green of early springtime all around them, a colour that would always remind him of Mira. A smattering of cloud in the sky floated by. The afternoon light flickered on the shining cars in the packed parking lot.

"Everything about your mother is inside me, in my heart," Ashok said to his daughter. "There's nothing I need. You take whatever you want. Pass on what you like. I want you to."

She nodded. "We don't need to decide now. There's no hurry. Let's go, Dad. People are getting ready to leave. We should say goodbye."

The two went back in and joined Dev, who was waiting near the door, chatting with some of his old friends, hearing stories of his mother's kindnesses, saying goodbye to almost everyone who lived in the town. They stayed until the staff had thrown away the leftover food and poured the remaining coffee down the drain, stacked the chairs and lined up the tables along the wall. Then there was nothing left for them to do but leave too.

"I'll make us dinner at home," Ashok offered Dev and Shivani, as well as his brother's family, who were lingering just outside, in the last warmth of the day. By then the sun was low in the clear wide sky, just beginning to set. "I'd like to. Mira would have liked that too. She would want us to be together. At least for today."

"You're tired though. We can order in. Pick up takeout, something easy," his brother argued.

"I'm not tired and I'm not quite ready to be alone. But I miss cooking. It was the thing I loved to do most for her. Let me."

"Okay then. We'll all help. You can put us to work. There's no hurry. We have all the time in the world." Ashok heard his brother pause uncomfortably after saying that. After all, who knew how much time they really had, both brothers seemed to be thinking as their eyes met. They both turned away as their eyes filled with tears.

At the house they spent two hours cooking together and the rest of the night eating the feast Ashok prepared: a spiced vegetable dish of potatoes, cauliflower and peas, khichdii made with mung beans and rice, which was Mira's favourite. He smiled as he stirred it, thinking of how, when Shivani was little, she called mung beans moon beams, and so for years, they all did too. Ashok made crispy puffed puris, which he knew Dev and Shivani loved most. It was the kind of meal he and his brother would also have eaten as children. Mira would have too. He brought a bottle of scotch out from the back of the cupboard after dinner, which he usually saved for only the most special occasions. He poured a glass for his brother and his wife, the children who were now adults too.

The next day Ashok was alone in the house again, as he had become accustomed to. He put on the TV to a morning talk show and was sorting through papers that had piled up on the console by the front door. The day felt mostly ordinary. If he didn't think about it for too long, he could imagine that Mira was still alive, that he might go to the hospital later to see her.

He came upon their most recent bank statement in the pile. It had been months since he'd opened their mail. Shivani had been doing it for them and even signed into his account to pay the phone and electricity bill for them sometimes. Ashok saw the statement for the adventure account Mira had set up for them so long before. There was more there than he knew. He finished going through the pile, throwing some papers away and filing others according to Mira's system. Then Ashok switched off the TV so that the house was silent again. He walked down the hall to their bedroom. There, he straightened the duvet on his side of the bed. Mira's remained untouched, as it had for months.

Ashok found a suitcase in the walk-in closet and filled it with a stack of shorts, two pairs of pants, underwear and socks from the dresser drawers. He thought of places he didn't want to go without his wife. He couldn't imagine Italy without her — it had been her dream trip after all. Not home to visit relatives — he couldn't bear answering all of their questions about her. Not yet. Ashok filled a wash bag with his toothbrush and toothpaste, a razor and shaving cream. He added those items to his suitcase then zipped it shut.

Outside the house, he waved to Janice, who was just leaving for work. She didn't stop to ask him where he was going. Ashok felt relieved. From the front seat he sent Shivani a text. "Check on the house, could you? I'm going on a road trip for a few days." He sent it.

Then sent another. "Maybe a week or two. I'll let you know."

Shivani responded instantly, sending him back a row of question marks.

Ashok sighed.

"I need to clear my head. I'm fine," he messaged.

He had waited long enough for another adventure. He and Mira had both waited too long. All he needed now was a direction. *East. Yes, toward Montreal,* he decided. He started the engine and gripped the steering wheel.

"It's time to go, Mira," he said. His eyes tingled. *No,* he decided. *I've cried enough for now.* He imagined his wife was beside him and could hear her saying, "Hurry up. Let's get out of here." Ashok turned on the radio and eased out of the driveway. Then, without a map or an agenda, he headed toward the highway.

Heads Are Going to Roll

WHEN THEY HAD FIRST OPENED THE BRANCH OF THE engineering company out west, Arnold considered asking one of his kids to go run it. Maybe his son. *It would be good for him*, Arnold thought. *A healthy challenge, a way to prove himself by working away from the head office, where everyone knows him as the boss's son.*

Arnold thought about his own dad, who had sure never tried to open any doors for him like that. His dad only ever told him that he should "work hard, become a real Someone, the kind of man who really matters."

Arnold mentioned the potential move to his wife. "What do you think?" he asked her. He was working on asking for her opinions, like his kids said he should.

Her eyes went glassy like she was going to cry, then she turned away from him. "You wouldn't send my grandbabies away from me like that, would you?"

I mean she can go see them, he thought. *For ski holidays or birthdays, Christmas even, whenever she wants.* But making his wife sad like that was too much for him.

So instead, the Calgary office was being run by strangers. And the group wasn't keeping up, profit-wise. They had plenty of work but weren't making the kind of money the Ontario offices did, the accountant said at the meeting of the board of directors. The executive team speculated that, looking at the numbers, the senior managers were soft, too soft. It looked like they were ordering in free lunches, paying overtime instead of hiring employees on salary. With all that coddling, the workers were spending too much time on the few big projects they were bringing in. Weren't making the profits they could be.

Should be! Arnold thought. *The game is to make money, right? Otherwise, what's the point of it all?*

"Heads are going to roll!" Arnold exclaimed to the board, slamming his hand on the table in a sudden jarring way, as if he had been startled awake from a pleasant dream.

When Arnold was young, he had a strong jawline, smooth and tanned skin. He was used to being respected, trusted, flirted with. Over time, the skin on Arnold's face had settled into softer folds, and his way of conducting business became less assertive too. He still liked to talk, made lengthy phone calls to long-time clients and mostly remembered their wives' names. But he liked to leave cold calls to the younger associates. Arnold had a big way of speaking. At company picnics and the Christmas party he took as much time at the microphone as he wanted to, sure that he was an inspiration to the others gathered there.

When he slammed his fist down on the table that day, it was like some dormant feeling, a slumbering passion, came awake within him again. Arnold said right there that he would take a trip out west. Insisted even. He would deliver the warning himself.

Yes, he was willing to fly all that way to give the sorry outliers one more chance to get it right. And in so doing he could prove to everyone else on the board what he was still capable of. This mission across the country was a task that would show he was still useful! *A job I can do for the betterment of the company,* he thought. My *company.*

Buckled into his seat on the plane, Arnold felt his heart racing with the thrill of having such an important task before him, then remembered what his doctor said about his blood pressure and took a deep breath, lifted one finger in the air until he was noticed and ordered a whisky from the flight attendant to settle himself.

I should fly more often, he considered as she handed him the drink. *Travel regularly, like I used to.*

Arnold's daughter had advised him not to actually say anything about heads rolling, but he had been repeating the words in his head for days. In a whispering, singsongy way under his breath. "Heads are going to roll roll roll." It was a strengthening mantra, he found.

Lately, Arnold had started wondering what he might do if he wasn't still working. He was aware that the current board of directors didn't have to keep him on if they didn't want to. It helped that his own kids sat around that table. They couldn't exactly ask him to leave, could they? Certainly his wife didn't want him hanging around the house all the time; she'd said so often enough. So he kept his corner office on the eleventh floor and stayed busy enough most days until lunchtime, when he could slip out for a hearty meal, the kind they hardly had at home anymore: a steak or a good burger with fries, and a drink or two.

On the flight to Calgary he tried to rest, leaning his head back and closing his eyes. But the longer he sat, the more outraged he felt. *Who are these weaklings pissing away my life's work?*

Arthur took a taxi straight from the airport, not stopping for lunch. He showed up at the bright, modern office on the south side of downtown and paused at the glass door. It seemed it was, well, bustling. People were talking on phones and gathering around computer screens together as though discussing important issues, problem solving. In fact, for a moment, he wondered if he was doing the right thing, coming here to talk about rolling heads and all. *Don't they appear to be busy enough?* Arnold felt the weight of his age then, tired and achy from the flight. He should have spent time in his hotel room first, he thought, maybe ordered room service or had a quick shower. Another drink maybe. A nap.

"Bah, onward, old man," he muttered sternly to himself. "Heads heads, roll roll roll."

Inside, Arnold was met by a young woman smiling up at him from the reception desk. He wondered if she was actually old enough to have a job in an office. And was she wearing that salmon-coloured headscarf for religion or fashion? He didn't know. *If it's religion, why has nobody told me?* Sure enough though, she knew who he was and stood up when she saw him like he was important. *I am important!* Arnold reminded himself.

The young woman smiled at him. "They're in the kitchen. Can I get you anything? Take your bag?" She gestured to the suitcase Arnold pulled behind him, which he had nearly forgotten about, despite the awkward height of it. It was made for a less-tall user. Arnold, of course, wouldn't let her take it. He felt foolish, as if she could imagine the contents of his suitcase. In the largest centre section was a pair of neatly folded clean underwear, a fresh shirt, his pyjamas and his toothbrush. Just the thought of the receptionist accidentally seeing these intimate objects made him feel weak. Or old. Arnold wondered if she, in general, found his wheely bag ridiculous (as he himself did — *Aren't I capable of carrying regular luggage?* he had thought as his wife packed it for him).

Then Arnold tried to think of what this young woman could get him. An Advil or an orange juice maybe. Anything to regain the upper hand.

"I'll go right in. And I'll have a coffee."

"There's a pot in the kitchen," she said, still smiling. "You can help yourself."

He walked down the hall in the direction she indicated. Through the window looking into the kitchen he could see the three managers spaced out around a long table. *Too relaxed!* Arnold thought. They were leaning back, chatting. Arnold twisted the cool metal handle. He paused before opening the door, which he did, of course, without knocking. *Hadn't the young woman with the scarf implied they were expecting me?*

Between each person were one or two empty chairs. Arnold didn't want to walk all the way around the table and risk looking unsure about where to sit, so he took a spot right by the door. The managers also stood up when he walked in, then, satisfyingly, sat back down when he did. Arnold appreciated the show of respect. He nodded approvingly, and then leaned over to shake each man's hand.

Then Arnold panicked. *What the fuck are their names again? Shouldn't they have told me when we were shaking hands?* He had met them all, of course. They had come to the Christmas party in Toronto but there had been so many people there. So many new people. Arnold hardly had time to hear their names let alone remember them. Arnold pulled a black notebook out of the side pocket of his bag and flipped it open. On page two, he had their names jotted in blue ink. "Steve. Allan. Vijay." Right.

Arnold remembered that he didn't mind Steve. Steve could talk golf. Allan was the strange one, a quiet guy who didn't say much. And Vijay, well, the boss man had never talked to him much before. He had no say when he was hired but heard that he was a good choice for Diversity, so how could Arnold argue with that.

"Let's get right to it, your profits are shit," Arnold said as he had planned. Arnold liked to start conversations with a swear or two, having learned over time that people really respect the guy who cuts to the chase. He wondered for a moment how he could get himself a coffee from the pot on the counter across from him. He should have done so before sitting down and starting his big talk. *A glass of water even.* "They weren't great to begin with and they've only dropped from there," he carried on. His tongue felt sticky in his mouth.

Nobody responded. Another employee came in, also without knocking, wearing jeans and a short-sleeved shirt, which Arnold noticed and didn't like. *Maybe,* he reminded himself, *there's some kind of cowboy culture in this city that makes people think it's fine to wear jeans to work.*

"Hey," the employee said, as if a meeting between the big bosses wasn't something he should worry about interrupting. The man took a white cup from a cupboard and poured himself a coffee, then took two creamers from the fridge. He smiled at them as he left.

Vijay cleared his throat. "Sir, with respect, we're in the middle of a recession. Our people are working hard to deliver on the projects we have, hoping for long term payoffs when things pick up again. But right now, well, we're bringing in all the work we can. Our sales guys are out there and our team is working hard to deliver quality work on time."

Is there a recession? Arnold wondered.

"There's no recession!" he said, as if making it so. "There's only a losing attitude." He wanted to call them all losers more directly. *A loser's attitude!* he wanted to say, but checked himself. *After all, I'm still a nice guy.*

Arnold paused, leaned back in his chair. "What do you drive?" It was a question he liked to keep in his back pocket to ask other men, as a way to establish power. The guy with the nicest car had the most power, obviously.

"I ride my bike in, or take transit in the winter," said Steve. "But my partner and I have a small SUV for driving to the mountains on the weekends. We like to ski."

Allan said, "We got a condo downtown so I could walk. We rent a car when we really need one."

"I have a VW station wagon. Hybrid. Fits the whole family but still great on gas," said Vijay.

Jesus, it was worse than he thought. *It's a fucking night-mare.* Arnold felt outraged. He couldn't believe their meagre lifestyles and how it reflected on him to have associates living such sorry lives.

"You should all be driving Porsches! Nice cars! Make it happen! You're supposed to make the profits, we give you bonuses and you all go buy yourselves a decent goddamn car! Christ! That's how it's supposed to work. Let me go talk to the people!"

Arnold stood up, pushing his chair aggressively back as he did. Vijay, Allan and Steve all stood up too and followed him out. Vijay shrugged at Steve, who shook his head. Allan coughed in a way that sounded like he was trying not to giggle, then cleared his throat and followed the others.

Arnold strode to the centre of the bright, open office, taking long steps down the aisle between the white work tables stacked with notebooks and folders, coffee cups and computer monitors. He clapped three times to get everyone's attention. People looked up and stopped what they were doing, but not as quickly as he would have liked. He heard a worker at the back say, "Seriously?" Arnold gave the youngster a look. *Clearly she doesn't know who signs her paycheque.*

"Attention everybody! This is my company and I have something to say." As Arnold stood in the centre of the room, he spoke with such vigour that his face trembled around the cleft in his chin. Now, the Calgary staff looked toward him, some with their mouths visibly wide open in astonishment. *Or in awe,* he thought — which made him feel hot, sweaty, wonderfully alive. And also, still thirsty.

Arnold paused then, looked around the office, nodding toward the three other men standing a distance away from him.

"I built this company from nothing. Nothing! And I'm telling you what a shame it is to see the profit margins like they are. Do better!" He paused again, ignoring the unpleasant way his tongue was still sticking in his mouth as he spoke. *If only someone would think to hand me a glass of water. Isn't that basic decency after all?* "Let's get these men some respectable wheels!"

He was surprised when no one applauded. In fact the room was remarkably quiet.

"If you were all doing your job right," he continued to the silent group now looking toward him, "your managers could all be driving Porsches by now! But no, they're driving station wagons! Riding bicycles! That's on you!"

"Let's get to work! Let's make some real money!" He lifted his fist into the air, pumped it up and down as though coaching football players.

After Arnold made the speech, he took long steps to retrieve his bag from the kitchen, and left the office rolling it behind him, the room still satisfyingly quiet. Arnold felt he had really gotten through to them. Again, he thought of pausing for a glass of water, but the timing was all wrong.

"I'm going to check into my hotel. I'll be back in the morning to talk strategy. Let's make some dough around here," he said to the managers before he left, in what he felt was a benevolent, helpful way.

As he pushed open the door with his free hand he considered that he should have found a way to say the part about the heads that were going to roll, should have trusted his own instincts. *If I had, this day might have ended even more perfectly.*

There was a buzz in the office after Arnold left that rose to a guffaw. "What kind of dinosaur would say such wildly hierarchical things?" one person asked. That they should all be working overtime so freaking Allan could drive a Porsche?! Two people resigned that day.

Feeling that he had handled the visit so deftly, Arnold cancelled his trip into the office the next day. Looking at his reflection in the mirror as he brushed his teeth that morning he thought, *Why shouldn't I leave the details to others to work out? Didn't I give the inspiring speech, as only a man with real experience like me could? Won't they look at how successful I am and see what there is to look forward to if they just get their profits up?*

In the end, head office still made the decision to shut down in Calgary a few months later. The company made Vijay an offer to move to Toronto, which he did. He was the last to lock the door of the empty office behind him, hand the key to the building manager, before he drove across the country with his family in his VW, pulling a U-Haul behind them. Vijay sold the car soon after, traded up. He also took up golfing. Allan and Steve both took the payout package and moved on, over to the competition across the river, just on the other side of downtown.

By then, Arnold had made the decision to finally retire. He realized that at home he could watch all the sports on TV. Not only golf but also soccer and Formula One. He had a pen and a spiral-bound scribbler he kept flipped open by his side, in case he wanted to make notes for himself: which player to watch, his projections about who might win and who might lose. *I've earned this kind of relaxation*, he thought, sipping one of the green smoothies his wife made for him, or if it was the afternoon, sneaking a beer or two. *Why shouldn't I?* After all he had proven to them, in the end, that he was Someone, a man who really mattered.

The Doctors' Lounge

L EKHA SHIVERED ON THE WOODEN BENCH OUTSIDE THE entrance of the clinic. She noticed the glass doors glide open and looked over, hoping it was her mom. Instead Dr. Khatri stepped out, squinting into the overcast afternoon light. She gestured Lekha toward her. The teenager obediently slid off her headphones, slung her backpack over one shoulder and walked toward the older woman, wondering if she was doing something wrong.

"There's no need for you to sit out here to wait, Lekha. You must be cold. Come in like the other kids do. I'll help you get settled."

Dr. Khatri led Lekha into the fluorescent-lit facility, across the atrium and down a wide hallway. She pulled open a heavy door that led into a large kitchen — three circular tables, a long countertop, with a coffee maker and a plug-in kettle on it, a microwave and a plain white fridge. The kitchen had the lingering aroma of instant noodles and tomato sauce. The soupy smell made Lekha feel queasy.

Dr. Khatri tapped the back of a plastic chair at one of the tables. "Here you go, Lekha. You can wait here."

Attached to the kitchen was a sitting room, casually called the doctors' lounge though, officially, anyone could use it. There were several other teenagers there, some that Lekha recognized from school. They sprawled across the oversized furniture in the open, more comfortable carpeted lounge area, their feet in brand-name sneakers were up on the square coffee table. On the TV was a talk show, a father and son arguing. The kids watching heckled.

"Tell him, old man!" one exclaimed.

"He's probably not even your real dad!" said another, making them all laugh.

"They're just actors, guys, cool down," advised Sai calmly, the only one of them that Lekha knew well.

When he noticed Dr. Khatri and Lekha, Sai dropped his feet to the carpet. He said to the doctor, "Can we go home now, Mom?" His black hair fell over his face and he pushed it off to look up at them; there was a smattering of scarlet acne across his cheeks and forehead.

Dr. Khatri, instead of responding right away, continued talking to Lekha. "Or wherever you're comfortable." She didn't move to introduce Lekha to the rest of the kids, the ones Lekha hadn't met before but pulled out the chair her hand was on. The feet scraped against the floor. "I'll tell your mom where to find you."

Then she turned back to her son. "Sai, I told you, I'll go as fast as I can."

Sai groaned and looked back to the TV screen. "How's it going, Lek?" He glanced over at her again. At school, Sai was popular but easygoing. While his friends were boisterous, Sai tended to be more in the background. Quieter than the rest of them. He always said hello to her, even in front of them. One semester they were in the same biology class and talked sometimes. When he came back from being away for a few days Sai asked her if he could copy out her notes.

"Do you even know her?" one of his friends asked as Lekha had popped open her binder and handed her tidy handwritten pages to him.

"We're old friends," he replied casually. "We've known each other for a long time."

Lekha had in fact first met Sai at the playground when they were both four years old. That day she was celebratorily throwing fistfuls of sand up the metal slide then watching them fall again. The sand glittered magically, as if flecked with tiny crystals that shone in the sunlight. Coming down it made a satisfying hissing sound that reminded her of running water. Sai watched for a few minutes and then joined in, swinging his arms through the air as he threw too. One time, Lekha remembered, after she had flung all hers, Sai shared the sand from his own overflowing fists.

"Here," he had said. She turned her hands and Sai dropped his sand onto her open palms. "Let's throw at the same time."

For a while their mothers only looked on from side-by-side benches at the perimeter of the playground. After a few minutes they said hello and started talking. Dr. Khatri asked Lekha's mom where she was from and the two discovered they were originally from nearby regions of the same place, only Dr. Khatri had immigrated when she was very young, and so considered herself mostly Canadian. When Lekha's mom mentioned she was hoping to find work now that her daughter was about to start kindergarten, Dr. Khatri said they were looking for another caretaker at the busy clinic she ran. Lekha's mother took the job.

After being invited to wait inside, Lekha dutifully waited for her mom at that very spot at the table in the doctors' lounge, as if it were assigned to her, reading or doing her homework. She never went past the kitchen, and so maintained a space between herself and the other kids. High school let out over an hour before her mom was done work, so even if she walked slowly to the clinic she ended up waiting awhile. Usually there were at least one or two other students when Lekha arrived. They were mostly doctors' kids, wearing T-shirts with luxury logos on them and brand-name jeans, including Sai, who seemed to feel at home there.

Those kids always preferred the more comfortable furniture, not the hard plastic chairs that Lekha sat in. At times, Lekha resented that they seemed to feel so comfortable while she didn't. *What would happen if I went and sat down with them, took up a spot in the lounge, right in the middle of the couch, in their space? Why shouldn't I?* Lekha wondered, annoyed at herself for not being bolder.

When there were no adults there, as there often wasn't in the late afternoon, the kids behaved like they were in a classroom with a briefly absent teacher. They opened the squat box that contained cubes of sugar, popped several of them at a time into their mouths like candy. The teens drank the little plastic creamers from the bowl in the fridge then left the dripping containers on the counter. They played makeshift games of basketball, ripping sheets of clean paper out of their school binders, crushing them into balls between their two hands and then chucking them toward the garbage cans, not even caring if they missed. Lekha never would have wasted new paper like that. Knowing the cost, she also made sure to write on both sides of each page.

The kids often wanted Sai's attention. "Watch this, Sai!" they said as they tossed their balls of paper into the trash bin across the room.

"Almost," he encouraged.

Through the overhead system, Lekha heard the janitorial staff paged to certain locations in the clinic and imagined the gore her mom might be called to wash away. Over the years, Lekha's mom never complained about the details of scrubbing smears of blood from linoleum floors, swapping out soiled bed sheets, mopping floors and wiping down medical equipment with bleach. She made friends with the other caretaking staff and the nurses and pushed her cart of supplies from room to room, adjusting her routine when more urgent cleaning was required.

"I don't know how you do it," Lekha once said to her mom on the way home. "Isn't it gross?"

"My job is as important as anyone's," her mom replied. "When I come in and clean up the worst things, that's when everyone is the most grateful. It's good to be needed, Beti," she said using the affectionate word for daughter. "Plus, it's a decent job, with good benefits for us."

Lekha understood. Her mom was making the best of it.

Now and then, Dr. Khatri liked to sit with Lekha while she was waiting, usually pulling the chair slightly away from her before taking a seat. The older woman told her one day that she had always wished for a daughter, and that if there was anything Lekha wanted to talk about, worries she couldn't talk about with her own mom who might not understand, she said conspiratorially, Lekha could always talk to her instead.

"If I think of anything I will." She blushed, feeling awkward. She didn't know why Dr. Khatri thought she would trust her more than her own mother. As if, because her mom wasn't brought up in Canada and didn't have a fancy education, she also didn't understand her own daughter.

Once, after Lekha's mom had been working at the clinic for years, Dr. Khatri invited the two of them over to her house. Mother and daughter pulled into the long, curved driveway in a wealthy suburb on the outskirts of the city. They sat in the light-filled dining room off the back of the house, and Dr. Khatri brought them tea and a bowl of spiced peanuts, then a plate of Oreos and a glass of milk that she put down in front of Lekha. Sai walked in and reached for a cookie but didn't sit with them. He and Lekha were both in junior high by then.

"Hey, Lek." She didn't mind the way he had always shortened her name so casually. In fact, she liked the way he said it.

"Hey," she said back.

The doctor then gave them a tour of the house. Most of the artwork and the furniture were made by certain people who were, apparently, noteworthy. As Lekha and her mom were leaving, Dr. Khatri said, "Now that you've seen the house you can understand why I need help. We have our regular service, but if you ever want to pick up extra hours, let me know."

Lekha noticed her mother straighten beside her. She had assumed the visit was social and not related to work. Lekha had too. Lifting her chin, Lekha's mom said, "Okay, thank you." Dr. Khatri watched them get into their small car again. Slightly frowning, as if disappointed, the doctor held up her hand in a rigid wave from the front door as they turned the car around and drove away. Lekha and her mother never went back to the house again.

At the end of her shift, her mom gestured to Lekha with a tip of her head from the doorway of the doctors' lounge. Lekha's mother was still youthful herself, strong from the physical work she did all day. Her hair was always neatly twisted back into a low knot. While her mom waited, Lekha packed up her books into her backpack and took her jacket from the back of her chair. Then they caught the bus home together. Their neighbourhood was mostly full of people who also came from other places, extended families living together in close quarters. The bus was full at that time of day so sometimes they would stand all the way home.

The two of them ate together — simple dinners of lentils, rice and vegetables, putting aside the leftovers in the fridge, carefully sealed in plastic containers. After, they liked to share a bar of milk chocolate or have a small square of store-bought cake together.

They rarely argued, and if they did, it was a quiet disagreement that didn't last. Lekha never heard her mother shout, and, when she thought about it, had also never seen her cry.

Lekha graduated from high school and went to university three hours away, where she shared a dorm room with another nursing student. At first, she found it hard to study and take care of herself. She often didn't have time in her day for meals, so she ate a bag of chips or fries and gravy from the cafeteria instead. She was usually still reading her textbooks past midnight, then woke up in time to get dressed and rush out the door before her morning classes. In nursing school, Lekha cleaned up blood all the time. She did it automatically mostly, but she thought of her mom too, spending all those years cleaning up after strangers on their worst days.

After university, Lekha found a cheap place to live and a job at a women's health collective. She met Dylan at a work fundraising luncheon. The staff were split up so there was one person from each team to represent their association at every table. Lekha ended up at the empty spot beside Dylan and had to introduce herself to their group.

In a lull between speeches he gestured toward the silent auction items lined up on narrow tables around the room. "Care to go look with me? I never know what to bid on."

"Sure," she said. He was so familiar with her, at ease, as if they hadn't just met.

"Do you golf?" he asked as they examined a pamphlet for a package at a nearby course.

"Never," she laughed.

"You know, I'd really love to take you out for dinner," he said then. As if there was something appealing about the fact that she had never golfed. She wondered if he was handsome or if he carried himself in a confident way that made him just seem to be. He was tall, with short hair, squarish glasses, and a few freckles across his nose. She thought they were cute.

★

Dylan made them a reservation at a place he told her he had been wanting to try for their first date, a trendy spot downtown. When Lekha arrived she had to go down a narrow set of stairs to enter the restaurant. It was cozy, with exposed brick walls and dim lighting. He was already waiting for her.

"You look beautiful," he said, standing up to pull out her chair.

She was wearing her favourite dress. It was black, sleeveless and fitted without clinging uncomfortably. It was one of two outfits she wore to dress up, and she'd already worn the other to the fundraiser. Lekha had also put on her favourite beaded earrings and brushed on a bit of mascara. She put up her hair in a way she'd never tried before, in a high bun with loose curls framing her face. Her carefully applied lipstick was new. It was called Deep Ruby. In the store, she had tried it on and thought she looked glamorous. "Definitely yes, that's the colour for you," the salesperson had agreed.

The lipstick made Lekha feel bolder that night too.

"Wine?" Dylan asked.

"Sounds great."

"Red or white?"

"Either is fine."

"No preference?"

"I don't really know much about it so it's fine if you order what you like."

Her ordered a whole bottle of the chianti. It seemed extravagant. Lekha had never ordered more than a glass at a time. By the time the bottle was empty, their meals were done and they'd shared the tiramisu, and they ended up leaning in much closer to each other. Dylan pushed aside the dessert plate and linked his pinky through hers. He pulled, so that it felt to Lekha as if he was drawing her whole body towards him. "I really want to kiss you," he said.

They were both startled when the server approached to clear away their dessert dishes. The wave she was being drawn in by receded again. "Another bottle?" the server asked.

"Just the bill," said Dylan. "Let me get this," he said to Lekha before it arrived.

She thought of arguing but wasn't sure she could afford it anyways. "Thanks. Next one's on me."

On the way out of the restaurant Dylan put his hand on the small of her back for a moment. When he pulled it away Lekha felt the absence of it, like another wave pulling away again, so that outside the restaurant, when he did kiss her, she took his hand and placed it there again.

"We could go to my place?" he said.

"Good idea," she replied.

"You're sure?"

"Totally."

In her whole life so far, Lekha felt like she had never done anything spontaneous. She thought back to the doctors' lounge, where she never did leave her assigned spot away from the other kids, the way she was always responsible, studious, good. Lekha wanted Dylan. And she almost never did anything only because she wanted to.

After that first date, they spent as much time as possible together. For months. Instead of waves of longing, she felt immersed. Obsessed, maybe even in love, so that everything outside of the two of them, for that time, fell away.

Lekha also became a person who preferred a certain kind of wine. They frequented a bar where they got to know her name as well as his. She stopped working so much unpaid overtime, and discovered what it was like to really live at the centre of a big city, to know where the good places to eat were. They planned meals to make too, not by looking at websites but instead by flipping through the pages of the cookbooks in Dylan's extensive collection, hardcovers with colour photos and recipes that used elaborate ingredients. Truffles. Anchovies. Olive oil that was hand-pressed in Italy. They bought groceries together at the outdoor market on the weekends. As Dylan's girlfriend she felt like she not only belonged but was given entrance to an interesting world of parties, animated conversations over cocktails, elegant meals that lasted for hours.

In the beginning she loved the way he wanted her all the time. She couldn't get enough of him either. He had his hands on her even when they were with others. Dylan often gripped onto part of Lekha when they were alone too — her ankle, if they were watching a movie on his couch, her hand while she was speaking with an acquaintance at a bar. Walking down the street, he would put his arm across her shoulders and pull her closer to him, leaning down toward her. At the start of their relationship she thought he was generous, loving, so openly affectionate; he made Lekha feel important, like he really needed her.

While she was dating Dylan, Lekha hardly called her mother at all, instead she sent quick texts. "Busy day! I'll call you this weekend. Love you." When she did call, she told her mom about work but didn't talk about her new life. She had started spending her saved money on things her mother would never buy — linen tops, luxury jeans, Italian coffee and fifteen-dollar cocktails. *She doesn't need to know about any of it,* Lekha thought. *She won't understand.*

She couldn't actually picture introducing Dylan to her mom, couldn't envision him visiting their townhouse, sitting in their plain kitchen, eating a meal with them off their CorningWare dishes. She tried to imagine what it would be like to introduce them. *What would he say to her? What could they possibly talk about?* She couldn't picture two more different people.

Lekha also felt like her relationship with Dylan was an indulgence that she wanted to keep to herself. Like she was living a secret, exciting life. She wasn't sure her relationship would survive her mother's more practical appraisal. Her mom might tell Lekha that she wasn't being true to herself, that he wasn't the right guy for her, he was far too clingy. She knew her mother had always hoped she would marry a man with the same background as them, or at least someone they could easily welcome into the family, someone who didn't need to have every dish, every quick expression explained. *I don't want to hear it. Not yet. I'm having fun,* Lekha told herself. For once, she wasn't thinking about the future at all. And, for a time, it felt excitingly indulgent.

Dylan's condo was in a trendy building, a historical sandstone in a hip neighbourhood. Inside, the apartment was renovated but oddly divided. The living room was bright and modern, with two large windows that looked out to the busy street, the original flooring was freshly sanded and finished. But the bedroom was small and windowless. The wardrobe and dresser Dylan had purchased with his ex-wife were for a much larger home, and so loomed, taking up all the spare space. There wasn't even enough of a gap between the mattress and the furniture for the doors or drawers to open all the way. At night, Lekha felt closed in by the looming antiques. She often borrowed his bathrobe from the hook on the back of the door, tiptoed out of the bedroom and sat alone in the armchair by the window, looking out to where the stars might shimmer if they weren't hidden by the glow of the city.

Still, she spent most nights at his place and avoided inviting him to her basement apartment, telling him honestly that she found it embarrassing. One time they had to stop there so Lekha could pick up some clean clothes for the weekend. She could see that he was antsy to leave too.

"This can't be where you live," he said, looking around.

Lekha shrugged. "It's a place to keep my stuff."

When she had signed the lease for her apartment, her priority was to work as much as she could, save money and move up in her career so her place was the cheapest she could find. Her clothes were mostly there, mostly still in boxes jammed into the closet, but there were no pictures on the walls or books unpacked onto the built-in shelving. Her fridge was empty but for a bottle of ketchup and a half-full plastic bottle of ginger ale.

Dylan opened her fridge as he waited for her to pack a bag. "I'm pretty sure this is flat," he joked, picking up the soda.

"I know," she replied, irritated.

For months she told herself that it was almost like she and Dylan were living together but she could never bring herself to take more than a couple of changes of clothes and her tooth-brush to his place. Often, especially when she hardly saw or spoke to her mom, Lekha began to feel as though she was living nowhere at all.

★

One evening, she went with Dylan to his friends' housewarming party. She didn't know the couple well. They had recently moved into an open-plan luxury condo in a new development. Everything in the home was visibly expensive, from the clean lines of the furniture to the handmade ceramic dishes they served appetizers on. When the women offered to show people around, Lekha and Dylan went along. The tour consisted mostly of them showing their guests their art collection.

"Isn't this place incredible? They both had such great taste even before they met," Dylan murmured to Lekha.

"Is this a Grant Smith chair?" asked Dylan's friend Cam.

"I have always wanted a Levi Kaitze painting," a woman said, turning toward Lekha.

The woman on the other side of her responded before Lekha could think of what to say. "Well, now I do too! It's just gorgeous." Lekha nodded to be polite.

She remembered the time she and her mom went to Dr. Khatri's house and was reminded of how unimpressed her mom was with the doctor's references to the items in her home. Similarly, Lekha now found herself pretending to be more interested than she was. Dylan was talking to another old friend about an abstract sculpture perched on a pedestal.

She watched how Dylan asked people all the right questions. He inquired what they liked about a particular piece, what drew the hosts to a certain artwork. In the same way he talked to her when they first met, with intense interest. He glanced over to see where Lekha was and winked at her.

The next morning, as they sipped their lattes, he said, "Wouldn't it be great to own a chair like that one day." He pulled out his phone and started scrolling through images of them. "You have no idea how much these things cost."

It was true. She didn't. *And,* she realized, *I don't really want to either.*

One time, near the end of their relationship, Lekha and Dylan went to an Ethiopian restaurant with friends. Dylan said, "Lekha grew up eating spicy food. Like, even as a baby. You should tell them about it, Lekha. And they basically never ate in restaurants."

"Restaurants are pricey," she reminded the group, feeling as though she was admonishing them. They were, after all, sitting in one. She avoided telling them about the level of spice in their food when she was growing up too, finding Dylan's disbelief ridiculous.

Dylan had always liked it when Lekha talked about her background, her childhood visits back to the country her parents were born in, and more than once he told her that he thought she was exciting. Her heritage made her so different from other women he had been with, he commented.

Later that night Lekha told him, "I feel really embarrassed when you talk about my life like that."

"But it's so interesting. It makes the rest of us look so ordinary. White bread. You know."

It annoyed Lekha when he used his skin colour as a way to laugh off important conversations. It was an easy way for him to not have to feel any discomfort, she thought. He reached for her and intertwined his fingers with her smaller ones. She pulled her hand away.

"Anyway, I make enough. If you stick with me we can eat at all the restaurants we want." He leaned over and kissed the top of her head, not noticing her annoyance.

"We had everything we needed when I was growing up. I don't feel like I missed out." She didn't like the way Dylan seemed to think her childhood was pitiable, in a way that reminded her of Dr. Khatri's suppositions when she was younger. Lekha shifted away from him, not wanting him to touch her then at all.

One day Lekha was helping Dylan change the linens on his bed. As he lifted the fitted sheet off, she noticed an old blood stain about the size of her palm, rust coloured with jagged edges, near the centre of the satiny blue quilted pillow top, on the side Dylan never slept on. Dylan shrugged and tossed her an edge of the new sheet to pull across. "I've had this bed a while. Got your side there?"

She thought at first about how important appearances were to Dylan. He wanted things to look a certain way on the outside. And yet, underneath his expensive sheets was a stain of menstrual blood from one of his exes. She thought of her mom, all the stains she'd washed away over decades. If Lekha's mother had encountered such a spot she would have scrubbed it clean, bleached it away. Either at work or at home. She wouldn't have shrugged it off. In fact, she couldn't have without fear of being judged or, at work, even fired. She saw Dylan as her mother would in that moment, looking past Dylan's careful exterior to the person he really was. *An ordinary man with intense ambition. A guy who wants to be seen as being perfect and successful. Someone like him never really has to worry that he won't be, even if he never thinks twice about old stains. He so clearly has everything going for him. Everyone likes him, respects him.* She felt then as though he'd never really had to earn anything.

She looked up Dylan's ex-wife online later that day, something she had done when she first learned about her and felt insecure, but hadn't since. The ex had straight blonde hair, perfect teeth. In every photo she was smiling and confident. In several pictures she was unselfconsciously wearing a bikini, often holding a glass of white wine or a paper-umbrellaed cocktail up to the camera. Her fingernails, in these close-up photos, were always professionally manicured, Lekha saw as she zoomed in. Lekha kept her fingernails as short as possible, a habit from nursing school.

In one vacation photo Dylan's ex was taking a surfing lesson, in another she was actually skydiving. Lekha felt deflated, thinking how different she was from this woman. She looked back at Dylan's older pictures too and saw a succession of people with their arms around him, friends and lovers. They all looked nothing like her. No wonder he found her exotic.

She then flipped to her own account and scrolled through her photos. Most of them were posted by others — family and co-workers who arranged themselves into semi-circles. There was one of her and her mom at her nursing school graduation. They both looked happy, even though the photo was blurry.

Lekha noticed that Dylan had tagged her in pictures that she hadn't approved so they hadn't been posted yet. They were selfies, part of Dylan's outstretched arm visible in several. Because he took the photos in each one he was larger than her, distortedly oversized. Lekha had never learned how to camera smile and so she looked unprepared, as if halfway through an expression, in all of them. So unlike Dylan's ex who exuded wide-open, care-free joy in pretty much every snap.

Lekha told herself she didn't ghost Dylan. She closed her internet browser and texted him. "I need time. Some things came up. I'll call you." But she didn't phone.

In the time they were together, they had always talked every day, slept together almost every night, so he knew right away that something was wrong. Dylan texted her back and tried calling but she silenced her ringer, deleted his repeated text messages after only glancing at them.

She told her co-workers not to put through his calls anymore. "It's a long story," she said when they looked at her curiously. They all thought he was such a catch and had told her so often.

Over weeks the messages became sadder: "I love you." "I'm sorry." "I don't know what I did wrong." They didn't make her feel any regret. Lekha was surprised by how quickly she moved on. By then, she only felt sorry for Dylan.

Dr. Khatri phoned one day when Lekha was at work. She stepped outside to the hallway to take the call.

"I have an offer for you," the doctor said. "We're looking for a supervisor, a staff member to lead our outreach programs. I think you'd be perfect for it."

"I can be there tomorrow," Lekha replied right away.

She called in sick to work the next day, rented a car, packed an overnight bag and made the long drive home. She passed her old high school on the way through town, then called Dr. Khatri from the clinic parking lot. The doctor met Lekha at the sliding front doors.

"Let's have a coffee," said Dr. Khatri, walking briskly, as she always had. "Your mom's working today, so you might see her. I didn't say you were coming. I wasn't sure if you would want me to."

Lekha moved slightly away from the doctor, to shun the implied closeness between them, though it was true that she hadn't told her mom she would be there. The two stepped into the doctors' lounge where the furniture was new since she was last there, sparser and more modern, though the room still smelled like leftovers. There was no one else there and the coffee pot was empty so Dr. Khatri started a new one, sitting down across from Lekha while the bean grinder whirled. They didn't start talking until the coffee began to ping as it fell to the bottom of the glass carafe.

"Basically, if you want the job it's yours," said Dr. Khatri. "There's no one we'd rather hire. So why don't you tell me more about how things are going with you. Seeing anyone?"

Lekha had a cup of coffee with Dr. Khatri, who handed her a printout of the posting for her to look through on her own. Before she left Dr. Khatri said, "I had always hoped when you were younger you would call me Aunty, but you were always so formal. I hope if you take the job you'll at least start calling me by my first name."

After, as Lekha waited outside on the bench for her mom to finish her shift, at the same spot by the door where she used to sit when she first started coming to the clinic on her own after high school, she thought back to the doctor's comment. It was strange, when she thought about it, that she always called

Dr. Khatri by her professional name, though she had known the older woman for almost her whole life.

That day the sky was clear, the summer air warm. Lekha thought she saw Sai walk by. Dr. Khatri had said he still lived nearby and worked at a law firm close to the clinic. But he didn't notice her sitting there so she didn't call out to him either. Lekha considered that she might get in touch with him if she moved back, see if he wanted to catch up. *Maybe over a glass of wine.*

Lekha's mom stepped out of the clinic. She looked smaller, though she still walked tall, spine straight, her hair pulled back like it always was. When she saw her daughter, she looked concerned, held out her arms as though Lekha was a child. Lekha hugged her.

"Everything's fine. I have a car here, Mom. I can drive."

Lekha opened the passenger door for her mother then closed it again before walking around the car to get back in the driver's seat. She held the steering wheel loosely, shifted the beige rental into gear, pressed the button to open her window before moving. They eased through the parking lot, then she accelerated to full speed as they reached the wide main street that ran through the city. The cool wind rushed in, forcing out the stagnant air from the car in a gust.

"Why don't we stop somewhere, Beti? Have a bite maybe? It feels like we should treat ourselves. Celebrate this surprise visit. I'm so happy to see you." Her mom spoke louder than usual, to be heard over the sound of the wind rushing in through Lekha's still-open window. Lekha closed it again.

Her mother continued, "I've heard there's a good Thai place not far, people at work have been talking about. Over on Thirty-Ninth."

"I'd like that, Mom. It's been so long since I've seen you. So much has happened since then."

"I've been wondering what you've been up to. And why this surprise visit. Take the next turn then," her mother advised. "It will take us right where we want to be."

After dinner, back at her childhood home, Lekha closed the door of the bedroom that used to be hers but had become the sewing room and dialled Dylan's number. He answered just as she was about to hang up. Dylan sounded out of breath, as if he had run to pick up the phone.

"What the hell, Lekha?" he said instead of hello.

She paused, trying to breathe away the embarrassment, the shame, that clutched her vocal cords. Actually hearing his voice made Dylan seem more real to her again. "I'm calling to say sorry. I handled things badly. I'm out of town now. It was a last-minute thing. I'm moving." She used the job offer as an excuse. "One day I'll try to explain."

"Lekha, I was worried sick. There has to be more to your complete disappearance than a job offer."

"I needed space. It wasn't working for me anymore. *We* weren't working."

"You could have just told me that. I would have understood. We could have at least talked about it, figured it out together."

Lekha didn't disagree with him. There was no point by then, but she knew that he wouldn't have actually understood. Dylan wasn't used to people not wanting him in their lives anymore. Even with his ex, he had been the one to leave. A small part of her felt a rush of triumph that she had ended the relationship, not him.

The conversation turned out to be shorter than she imagined it would be. Less messy.

She said, "I'm sorry." And she mostly meant it.

Dylan responded briskly, "Good luck. I hope you find what you're looking for."

Lekha heard her mom downstairs, the familiar squeak of the floor in the kitchen as she put away dishes, the murmur of voices from the television. She decided she would stay a night, maybe two before going to pack up her things from her apartment again. After that she would have to decide where she wanted to live. Maybe she'd rent a place walking distance from her new job, an apartment she liked. The written offer from Dr. Khatri included a generous bonus, one that gave her more options. Enough to take a vacation even. Maybe with her mom.

She remembered Dylan was still on the line. "Me too," Lekha said to him. "I hope I find what I'm looking for too."

Part Three

Braids

NIRAJ'S FAMILY WENT BACK TO THE ALL-INCLUSIVE RESORT after it was fine to travel again. He did his best to make everything feel like it did before, like their vacations used to be.

Each morning Niraj tried to be the first to arrive at the hotel's designated beach area. He left when their hotel room still dark, with only a line of early morning light shining in where the curtain didn't quite meet the bottom edge of the sliding glass doors. The only sound then was the hum of the air conditioner. The kids, not yet awake, were each covered by only a twisted sheet, duvets kicked aside, limbs outstretched. Often Emily was still asleep too, her book splayed open on the nightstand beside her, her chin-length hair fanned across her pale cheek.

Niraj wore the swim shorts and flip-flops he had pulled from the back of the closet at home, slung two towels over his shoulder and carried a tote bag in one hand. He turned the handle and creaked the heavy door open and shut as quietly as possible. There was usually no one else in the hallway at that hour, and hardly anyone on the curved outdoor pathways. Groomed trees arched pleasantly overhead, lush green against blue sky, perfectly curated. Leafy cover gave way to the modern, open swimming area — three pools connected by streams with jets along the walls to keep the water circulating between them. There was a bar on the far side and one at the centre of the largest pool. Beyond that was a set of stairs that led to the narrow strip of sand, the wide ocean, the straight line of the horizon.

Niraj's family mostly spent their time there, at the beach, instead of the swimming pools.

"After all, isn't that the point of going so far?" Emily reminded them, as if their trip was more than a common journey, like it was an adventure, or even some kind of achievement. "We can go to the swimming pool at home."

At the shoreline the employees sang, "Good morning, sir," then continued their work, pulling apart the recliners stored in neat stacks overnight, placing them in even rows that faced the ocean. They clicked the backrests into position at forty-five-degree angles, popped open striped umbrellas, then set out low tables for afternoon cocktails. Niraj nodded hello then looked away. It was awkward, he felt, witnessing the workers arranging the same set up every day, but he still liked getting there early. In the same way that he liked to arrive at his office before everyone else, back home.

When everything was laid out an employee would say, "Okay, ready!" and call him "sir" again, as if they had created the whole scene just for him. Then Niraj laid his towels neatly across two recliners, pulled the rough fabric taut so there were no wrinkles. He saved one for himself and one for his wife, more in the shade because she sunburned so easily. It felt greedy to save more than two spots, so he let the kids make do.

The beach towels were, satisfyingly, nearly the exact width as the chairs. Once they were arranged, Niraj put one of the cheap objects from his tote bag on top: a paperback novel from the shelves in the hotel lobby, the blue plastic shovel or the smooth red crab sand mould that came in the package of beach toys they had purchased from the gift shop and would leave behind when they left.

The towels, plus these dispensable items, told the other guests that the seats were taken. No matter what time Niraj came back to the spot with his family, no one else would have moved them or sat there. It was a system to mark temporary ownership that, to his continuous surprise, always worked. Niraj returned to their room with the canvas bag deflated in his hand, usually before his family was even dressed for breakfast. By mid-morning, all of the beach chairs and the ones around the swimming pools were similarly reserved for the day.

Usually, he felt pleased with this quiet accomplishment. But that day Niraj was uneasy. He had woken up too early, before his alarm sounded, before the staff had started arranging the chairs, so he ended up passing by several workers in white protective suits. Cinched hoods and industrial gas masks covered their heads, their faces were shielded. The labourers were spraying the entire grounds — the sidewalks, furniture and even the playground — with a mist of pesticides, getting the job done before the tourists were meant to be awake.

Niraj was aware he was seeing something he wasn't supposed to. He held his breath and circled wide around them, kept walking toward the beach, where he sat down on the sand, close to the water, so it almost reached his toes. He inhaled morning air, cool and salty through his nose and into his chest, then exhaled evenly, trying to calm himself. Niraj focussed on the easy rise and fall of the waves in front of him as he breathed, until he could carry out his routine, willing his mind away from the apocalyptic image of the white-clad sprayers covering everything with an invisible layer of poison. *Why didn't I notice before?* he wondered. *How else could there be no bugs in a place this tropical?*

Every time he relaxed that morning, the picture came back to him, and he felt his breath shorten. Sprawled on his lounger, Niraj tried napping as he usually did through the morning, but found he couldn't rest. When he tried, the image of the pesticide sprayers troubled him again. Niraj opened his eyes and looked over to his teenage daughter, Charlotte. She was sitting on a wrinkled towel laid out on the ground, facing away from him. Charlotte was digging her fingertips into dry sand, pulling up handfuls and then letting the grains fall through the gaps in her fingers.

"Hungry?" Niraj asked, bothered by not knowing what his daughter was thinking about with such intensity.

She pushed her fingers back in for another handful before answering but didn't turn toward him. "No."

"Maybe thirsty? Get one of those lemonades you like?"

"I'm fine."

Niraj tried to think of something else he could ask her, but Charlotte kept her gaze fixed toward the horizon, as if she didn't want to talk to him.

A couple of years earlier, Charlotte would still play with her brother, Luke. Now Luke played alone, or with other kids he met, ones closer to his own age. Even with no other children around, Niraj saw that Luke was happy enough. He spent an hour building a sandcastle that he then gleefully destroyed. Like Emily, Luke seemed to be enjoying the vacation in the same way he always did, with complete enthusiasm. Niraj felt himself outside of this carefree joy this time. Charlotte seemed to feel outside of it too, but in her own bubble, also separated from him.

Niraj watched Luke wading in the ocean. He ran full speed into the waves before racing back out again as if being chased. Thin and shirtless, always impatient. Each time a wave reached to the waistband of his loose shorts he held on to them, finding this less of an annoyance than it would be to stop his solo game long enough to re-tie the drawstring.

Charlotte leaned back on her elbows, her emptied fists clenched. Still looking outward.

Emily checked her watch then put down her book. She gave the sunscreen tube a shake, then squeezed the cream into her palm. There was a sputtering, farty sound as it emerged, loud enough to make Charlotte glance back at her mom. Emily rubbed the cream into her pale shoulders in a series of quick, practised ovals, down her arms and then her legs, leaving streaks that disappeared in moments. She did this every two hours, as prescribed on the label.

On Niraj, the white sunscreen stayed visible so he avoided putting on any more than he needed to. He was born in Canada, but he looked much more like his Indian mother than his British father. Luke inherited Emily's fair complexion and so they covered him with waterproof sunscreen every morning, even before they headed to the beach. Charlotte had darker skin and Niraj's black hair too. Niraj thought that she looked even more like his mother than he did, especially after a few days in the sun.

Down the beach a local woman was braiding another tourist's hair. The blonde customer sat on a folding lawn chair while the hair stylist stood over her, wearing a broad-brimmed hat, a long loose dress and rubber-soled sandals. The tourist wasn't wearing a face mask, though the local woman was. It was plain blue, generic, the kind that used to be freely available all over the place. While the pandemic was mostly declared over since better vaccines were developed, many of the locals still hadn't been able to access them. And so the residents kept their face coverings on.

Charlotte opened her clenched hands and brushed the sand off her palms, then stood up.

"Dad, can I get that done?"

She must be arguing with Emily again, Niraj realized then, otherwise she wouldn't have asked him. He saw the opportunity though, a chance to connect. He paused and took a sip of his drink before answering, noticing that the ice cubes had already melted in the heat. Niraj took his time, looked down the beach in the same direction as Charlotte.

Niraj thought of telling her about the time when he was backpacking through Europe and let his then-girlfriend dreadlock his shoulder-length hair. He had a few pictures of himself from back in those days, and thought how his daughter might not even recognize him. When he came back to Canada and started university, he made friends with a group of visiting students from Ghana, who shook their heads and laughed at his dreads. "Man, that hairstyle just doesn't suit you," one said. Niraj ended up at the barber off-campus the next day for a buzz cut. Niraj had thought that the dreads made him look good but back at home, he felt silly, sheepish. He thought it might be the right time to tell Charlotte that story but he didn't want her to feel embarrassed, like he did then. He wanted her to enjoy the vacation. Be happy.

"Sure," he said more confidently than he felt. "If that's what you'd like to do, then why not."

"Not here," Emily cut in. She squinted to look up at her daughter and sighed. "We can ask at the salon later, Char. It'll be cleaner."

Charlotte glanced back at the braider, then, accepting the compromise, acknowledged her mother. "Fine."

She turned toward the water where her brother still played, lifted her arms high above her in the air as she walked away from her parents, stretching upwards. Niraj was struck again, as he often was, by the feeling he was losing her. Had lost her even.

"Race you!" Niraj called, as if she were no different than she used to be. He jumped out of his chair and ran past her, toward where Luke was still leaping through waves, wondering if Charlotte would follow.

Slowing at the crooked edge where the shoreline slithered toward the beach, Niraj's feet hit the cool water. It reached to his ankles then retreated outward again, sucking at his heels. He lifted his feet out of the slurping sand, left imprints that disappeared with the next rush. Niraj took another step deeper and noticed Charlotte wading in behind him. As the waves were pulling him into the ocean, now from around his calves, she darted past him and lowered her whole body into the cool water. "I win."

"This time."

Niraj considered how Emily and Charlotte were bickering more often, even when he didn't see anything to disagree about. And then, just as quickly, they were close again. He found the bumpy relationship between them unsettling. And he felt excluded too, not really knowing what was going on, so that the next afternoon when Charlotte said, "Dad, now Mom said I can't get my hair done," Niraj found himself taking his daughter's side.

"Come on, let's just go and see what they can do."

Inside the hotel salon it was quiet and calm, the air fresh, scented with something bright and herby: peppermint or rosemary. The pale walls were lined with dark wooden shelves. Delicate bottles of luxurious products perched along them like cylindrical birds. Music — a flute and an earthy drum beat — played from a ceiling-mounted speaker, the volume low. Behind the sleek reception desk was a picture window that looked out to a smaller, semi-private pool. The ceiling sparkled with crooked lines of sunlight.

"How can I help you today?" asked the dark-skinned woman behind the counter. She was wearing the short-sleeved button-up shirt assigned by the hotel and silver hoop earrings. Her nose was almost invisibly pierced with a pin-prick gem that shone blue. The woman's black hair was in narrow braids that were pulled to the side so they fell elegantly over one shoulder.

"Your hair's so pretty," Charlotte said in a burst. "Can you do mine like that?"

The woman walked around the counter so that they were facing and gently lifted Charlotte's chin. Niraj was touched by the serious attention she gave his daughter, as if really seeing her.

"I think we can do something good for sure." Then looking at Niraj said, "I have time if you're free now."

"Okay. I'll leave you here then," he said to his daughter. "Charge our room, Char, you can sign for it." The woman slipped on a disposable face mask then and gestured for Charlotte to follow her.

He wondered about the cost, but decided not to ask. He didn't want to interrupt the moment for his daughter.

Emily was relieved when he got back to the room and told her where Charlotte was.

"You should make more decisions," his wife said to his surprise. "It's hard for me to always be the one in charge."

"Huh. I thought you wanted me to stay out of these disagreements."

"She's your daughter too. And she needs both of us." Niraj considered that she was also saying he was still important in Charlotte's life. It made him feel hopeful. Until then, he had only been thinking about how he was losing her. He hadn't considered that there were ways Charlotte still needed him. New ways, maybe, now that she was getting older.

As the stylist leaned over her, Charlotte noticed how her eyeliner swooped up a bit at the edges, and wondered how she made the line so even. She must use a liquid liner, not a pencil, Charlotte considered. It also didn't seem like she was wearing any other makeup. One of Charlotte's friends at home had started wearing heavy foundation, making her skin look dry, powdery. Charlotte had gone to the makeup counter at the mall to look for some once, thinking she should try it out too. A salesperson sponged a liquid on her face for her, but she couldn't find the right tone for Charlotte's skin. Despite her attempt to blend the pinkish beige cream, Charlotte still ended up with a line at her jaw where the makeup ended.

Charlotte liked the way the salon employee's face glowed, and decided that, even when she got older, she wouldn't cover up her skin either.

The woman asked Charlotte a few questions as she braided. The usual things adults asked, like "how old are you?" and "what subject do you like in school?" She paused now and then to answer the phone or get a glass of lemon water for Charlotte, leaving heavy black plastic clips in Charlotte's hair to hold certain sections apart from others. The braids took much longer than Charlotte thought they would, much longer than the woman on the beach spent, and she tried not to be obviously impatient or bored. *Don't act like a kid*, she reminded herself.

Charlotte wondered if she should ask the braider questions too, if she should try to make conversation, so she asked the woman if she lived nearby, thinking it was a neutral question. The stylist laughed and said that her home was several bus rides away. Of course, Charlotte realized then, she had never seen any houses or apartments nearby for locals.

There were a lot of things that Charlotte wished she could really ask about. For example, she wanted to openly ask the woman about her makeup, instead of trying to guess. She wanted to ask her for real what her home was like, if the commute to the resort was hard for her. Charlotte imagined that it must be by the way she had answered. But it seemed like things worked according to a system Charlotte didn't quite get, and adults didn't like to be asked too many questions.

By the time her hair was all braided, Charlotte's legs were tingling from sitting still for so long. The woman handed her a mirror to see herself up close. *I look like someone else*, Charlotte thought, seeing her hair all pulled back away from her face. *Older maybe*. The braids fell evenly, just below her shoulders so that her hair was shorter, and felt heavier too. Charlotte raised her eyebrows at herself, unable to tell if the hairstyle looked good or not, but she liked the newness.

The woman said, "It suits you. You look like you could be from here."

She said it in a semi-serious voice, so that it sounded a little like she was joking, but not really. Charlotte had also noticed that she looked like the locals, some of the staff. When she was younger, she never really thought about her own background, but lately had been wishing she could talk to someone about that too. She mostly wondered about her dad's mother.

The woman told Charlotte that if she took care the braids should last for weeks, possibly more than a month. Charlotte signed the bill by writing her name in the neatest, most grown-up looking way she could. She'd never been to a hair stylist without her mom and wasn't sure about adding a tip, so didn't. Her head felt heavy and tight, not quite painful, but aching. When she left the salon, the ropes of her hair swung unfamiliarly.

When Niraj, Emily and Luke came back to the hotel room before dinner, the curtains were pulled closed and the air felt chilly after the heat outside. Charlotte was back from the salon and asleep on top of one of the beds. Her hair in narrow braids, barely wider than a pencil, stretched across the white pillow-case. She was on her side, her hands tucked under her cheek. Niraj saw that her bright pink toenail polish, so carefully applied before they left home, was now mostly chipped off so that only uneven flecks remained. He felt a sharp sorrow, nostalgia, as if other veneers were falling away too. But Charlotte still breathed through her gaping mouth in her sleep, like she did when she was little.

Emily whispered, quietly enough to not wake Charlotte, "Well, let's go eat. She can catch up with us later."

She left Charlotte a note on the hotel stationary, using the pen decorated with the same crest of gold swirls as the paper.

Hair looks cute! Going for dinner! Get something to eat and come find us!

Emily's writing was bubbly, each exclamation point quickly added, so it was clear to Niraj that whatever disagreement that happened earlier between Charlotte and Emily was now over. She signed the note with a bloated heart whose ends didn't quite connect. Niraj glanced at the note and considered how differently he would have written a message to his daughter in his own cramped script.

Charlotte woke up and saw the note her mother had written, then changed into her favourite azure sundress. She walked over to the pizza counter attached to the main restaurant. With a resort wristband on, hotel guests could walk into any eatery and have whatever they wanted, not finish one plate before starting another. She had been thrilled at this when she was younger, when she first discovered that she could refill a drink as many times as she felt like, use a new glass every time. But since then she had learned not to order more than she could eat. On this trip Charlotte found herself sometimes not ordering more food even if she was still hungry, feeling almost embarrassed by the luxury of it.

The kiosk was decorated in red, white and green like an Italian flag. From where Charlotte stood waiting for her slice she had a narrow view into the kitchen, where she saw a row of cooks busy preparing food for the main restaurant. There was a massive oven, steam rising from tall aluminum pots. A person was bent over a pair of industrial sinks scrubbing dishes. An insufficiently small fan whirled in the corner. There was nothing else to keep the workers cool. No air conditioning, like in the guest rooms. When the server at the counter handed her pizza to her on a paper plate, Charlotte looked away from the back room quickly, knowing she had seen something she wasn't meant to, the hectic machinery behind the peaceful utopia tourists like her family came for.

She ate her pizza sitting alone on a patio overlooking the ocean then bent the grease-stained paper plate in half before dropping it in a nearby bin. Near twilight, the darkening water swelled and receded, the night air smelled of brine and seaweed. Charlotte shivered then turned away. Following the sound of drums down the wide curving path between the palms, Charlotte crossed over a bridge under which orange and white fish swam in an artificial pond. She saw her parents and brother sitting at a round table watching the evening's entertainment. Dancers in long skirts swirled onstage, accompanied by drumming that made the glasses on the table vibrate. Seeing them from a distance, Charlotte felt like her family were strangers and she was all alone.

Charlotte sat on the empty chair beside her dad, then touched her head, as if checking to see if the braids were still there.

Niraj looked at her. "Well. You look different." As much as she had looked young when she was sleeping, now she looked older. Her face, no longer hidden by her thick hair, was narrower than he remembered, childish roundness not quite gone, but nearly.

"Sick, I can see your scalp," said Luke.

Emily smiled and said, "Beautiful, honey! You look really beautiful," in the same voice she used to exclaim over a kid's drawing or a good mark on a test. She reached over to touch a braid. "How does it feel?"

"It still pulls, but the lady told me that shouldn't last too long," said Charlotte, ignoring her brother's comment of disgust. She also tried not to respond with irritation to the way her mother always talked to her like she was just a child. *If I do we'll be mad at each other for hours again, or her feelings will be hurt, which is even worse. It's not worth it,* she decided.

The next day, their second-last day before flying home, Emily suggested the family should leave the compound and explore, not only laze around on the beach all day. Niraj felt relieved to skip the hustle for a shoreline spot, still haunted by seeing the pesticide sprayers. He remembered again the way they looked in their white hazmats and gas masks, as if in an ominous movie.

"Great idea, let's do something new."

They made it to the market, a twenty-minute stroll away, by late morning. The area around their resort catered to foreigners, and so the market was full of things tourists buy — multicoloured woven blankets; carved wooden statues that the sellers told them promised love, luck or wealth; dresses embroidered with floral designs hanging from crowded racks. Niraj found a shady place near the stalls Charlotte and Emily were looking at and kept

Luke with him. He noticed how Charlotte always stayed in front or behind her mom, never quite beside her, though Emily paused and waited for Charlotte to catch up if she was lagging, or hastened if Charlotte was too far ahead.

A group of local boys gathered nearby. One of them said, in Charlotte's direction, "Hey, where are you from?"

Charlotte looked over but didn't respond. She looked as if she was evaluating, deciding if she should tell him or not, working out if the situation was exciting or unsafe. Emily was distracted by a table display of linens, so seemed not to notice the interaction.

Another teen speculated, "American?"

"Hey," said the first boy again, "are you American?" He slowed the last word, speaking in an exaggerated drawl, like he was from the States too. Niraj didn't like hearing his daughter evaluated this way by a group of boys so called out her name and gave the teenagers a look. They glanced toward him, then sauntered away, taking their time. One looked back at Charlotte again as he left, as if challenging her to follow. Charlotte paused, then turned and walked toward her dad and brother.

So many of the locals here, in this place with a long history of colonization, were of mixed origins, like him. Like her. *By appearance, Charlotte could fit in easily with those kids,* Niraj realized.

He wondered if he should tell her more about their background then too. He could tell her about his mother, and the kind of strong person she was. Niraj's mother had been born in a small town, a village really. She was uncommonly smart and went as far as she could in the school close to her home, then went on to Canada on her own to study and become an engineer, winning a full scholarship for her degree. She had made the move against her family's wishes. They thought there was no need for a girl to get so much education, she had once told Niraj.

Emily was the one who had embraced his heritage back when they were dating. She took yoga classes and remembered the Sanskrit names for all the poses she learned. She bought cookbooks with Indian recipes, even went to temple with his mother. When they got married, she wore a cream-coloured dress for the ceremony then a red and gold sari for the reception, one his mom helped her choose. On their wedding day she helped Emily put it on.

Emily knew more of Niraj's mother's stories about her upbringing, heard all about her childhood on the walks the two women took together. But then, he noticed that she didn't talk to Charlotte about being biracial either, as if that part of his history had stopped being as important to her after his mother passed away. Maybe she got too busy, so that understanding things like cultural identity wasn't as pressing to her as it once was. Or perhaps it didn't seem like it mattered to the kids when they were younger, so Emily stopped thinking about it too. Possibly, she expected that he would one day show more interest too. *When I didn't*, Niraj thought, *Emily gave up.*

Niraj used to talk to his daughter about all the kid things that mattered to her: the important plot points of *The Little Mermaid* movie, if she should dress up like a tiger or an alien for Halloween, if it was worth saving up for roller skates. He read bedtime stories to her whenever he made it home from work in time and took her and Luke to the playground on the weekends, stopping for milkshakes on the way.

Now that Charlotte didn't just have the simple worries of a little kid, he wasn't sure how to talk to her sometimes. *In the same way that I never had important conversations with my mother, because they seemed too hard*, Niraj thought wistfully. *What if I lose Charlotte too?*

"Let's go for a walk down the beach when we get back?" he proposed to his daughter as she sat down beside him. "Might be our last chance to look for seashells before we head home."

Charlotte shrugged. "Sure, why not. There's probably nothing better to do." He put his arm around her.

It's a start, Niraj decided. "You're right. There probably isn't."

That night Niraj stayed up late, scrolling through social media on his phone, and found himself reading articles about the chemical pesticides used at resorts and their many side effects, in the same way he used to read all the news and statistics about the pandemic case counts every evening. Emily put down her book and turned off the lamp on her side of the bed while he was still scrolling.

When Niraj looked over Emily said in a quiet voice, as if she had been waiting for him to notice her, "Charlotte's confused about a lot of things. I think you should tell her more about your side of the family. It might help her, give her something real to hold on to. I think she needs that. I keep waiting for you to notice."

Then Emily whispered, "And how long do you think she's going to keep those braids in?"

Niraj put down his phone and clicked off the lamp on his side too. "Maybe next year we should try going somewhere new for a change for our vacation. Go camping in the summer instead, or take a ski trip in the winter, somewhere closer to home. It feels different here this year."

"Maybe it's us. Maybe we've changed," Emily replied into the dark.

The family packed their things the next morning, planning to get to the lobby in time to catch the first shuttle to the airport. Niraj took a last look around the room while the rest of his family waited in the hallway, as he always did, to make sure they hadn't left anything behind.

Emily had donated the books that she had brought from home, left them in the lending library in the lobby. The beach toys were still in the room, with a note in Emily's bubbly writing for the cleaners that they were to be given away if possible. They left their plastic card keys on the desk too, where the staff would find them.

"Okay, ready. I think we have everything," Niraj said to his family. Out of habit, he turned the handle and closed the door quietly, like he did in the mornings, as if not to disturb anyone inside.

Charlotte wore the outfit she had on when they left home two weeks earlier, jeans and a tank top. Her zip-up hoodie was tied around her waist, so that she was ready for the chill of the airplane. Luke still wore shorts and flip-flops because he was hardly ever cold, even at home. The kids went ahead, while he and Emily stayed a step behind. They walked down the hallway in their pairs, each pulling their rolling suitcase behind them.

★

When the flight attendant gave them their seat numbers, she first offered three together and one apart from the others. Charlotte quickly volunteered to take the single spot. Niraj saw the look on Emily's face, that she didn't like the idea.

"Is there anything else?" he asked.

"Oh wait. Yes, I have two together: A16 and A17. And another two side by side: A27 and 28. At least that way no one has to sit by themselves?"

"Perfect, we'll take those," Niraj decided.

"You can sit with me," he told Charlotte, before she could object.

At the gate, Charlotte found a single-stall washroom, locked the door behind her, took off her disposable mask, which her mom thought they should wear in the busy parts of the airport, and looked at herself in the mirror. She smoothed her hair, then gathered the braids into a high ponytail, checking the look from each side. She puckered her lips and wished she had taken her phone out of the backpack she had left with her parents so she could take a picture of herself. Charlotte pulled a fat hair elastic from the pocket of her jeans and slipped it around the bundle of braids. With her hair up she felt older. She looked at herself again, pleased that she looked different, *not like all the other kids at school.* Then she slipped on the mask again before leaving the bathroom so that her own breath was warm on her face.

On the plane, Charlotte held on to the curved end of the armrest and leaned away from her dad to watch out the window as the island fell away. Moments later there was only ocean under them, until the aircraft rose so high that she couldn't see anything but the cotton ball tops of clouds. Charlotte opened the fold-down table on the seat in front of her and saw a stain — circular and dark. She was annoyed that it hadn't been wiped away, so that she was reminded that someone else had been in the exact same seat right before her, looking out the same window.

Charlotte touched one of her braids, liking the now-familiar feel of it between her fingers, and thought again about how she looked like the locals, she could pass for one of them. *I could even work at a resort like that, at the front desk or maybe even the salon, and wouldn't stand out.*

Her dad was flipping through the free magazine provided by the airplane. When he was done he slipped it back into the vinyl pocket in front of him. He took off his mask then, so Charlotte did too.

"You would have liked my mom, you know. Your grandmother. She would have liked you too." Niraj started the conversation he had been wanting to have with Charlotte for days, ever since she got the braids.

"Really?"

"She was a lot like you. Smart. Determined. Imagine, she just moved across the world all on her own when she wasn't much older than you. She knew what she wanted to do, and she knew she had to work hard. Unlike you though, she didn't have her parents to turn to. They never forgave her from moving so far away, so I never got to know my grandparents either."

For most of the rest of the flight home, Niraj remembered stories from his mother's life and shared them with Charlotte. The stranger beside him kept his headphones on for the whole trip so didn't seem to mind. Niraj told Charlotte where her grandmother had stayed when she first arrived (a dorm room she shared with a Scottish student), what she ate (Western food — pasta and boiled eggs — things that she had never eaten before), how his parents met and what their wedding was like. They had eloped on the beach in Tofino, because both of their families disapproved of the marriage.

224 *An Astonishment of Stars*

Niraj didn't tell Charlotte how he had treated his mother badly as a teenager, and how he regretted it later, especially now that both of his parents were gone. How embarrassed he was by her back then. *Not yet.* He wanted tell Charlotte the good parts first. *The rest can wait for another day.*

By the time the plane began to descend, Charlotte was asleep. At first with her head leaning back onto her own seat, then her body fell so she was resting on Niraj's shoulder. He kept still. Niraj didn't want to wake her, feeling, at last, needed again.

He leaned over and watched through the window, across Charlotte's sleeping body, as the plane began to descend. It broke down through the clouds, back toward land. Grey mountain peaks came into view below. Then they glided further toward the adjacent patchwork of prairie and farmland. The wheels thunked as they emerged from the aircraft's body then hit the asphalt runway with a slam. There was a high-pitched squeal as they slowed, and Charlotte was startled awake. She sat up straight.

"Don't worry," Niraj told her. "We just landed. We arrived right on time."

The Gossip

PEOPLE IN THE NEIGHBOURHOOD WERE BOUND TO ASK where the baby came from. I'm sure I saw Grace, walking her dog, looking the same as always only the day before. And I can't have been the only person who was more than a little surprised.

I was coming home from the bus stop that afternoon when I first saw them, on the porch of their house just down the street, that nice-looking bungalow. I was still wearing long pants and a jacket from the chill of the morning so I remember I was feeling too warm, maybe having something of a hot flash too, so it really took me a double-take to see clearly.

And like that, there it was — a brand new baby, dark-skinned like Grace, being held in her arms! Awkwardly, I'll say. The little one was wearing nothing but a plain white onesie. Draped over Grace's other shoulder was a gauze blanket, but it wasn't doing much good there, was it? That blanket was so new it still had fold lines from being in the package. I could see the creases from the sidewalk! Personally, I would have washed it first and hung it out to dry before using it, but I suppose people have different opinions about that kind of thing.

Grace's husband was there too, of course, hovering nearby, watching as if that baby might somehow fall unexpectedly. As if Grace might just drop the baby. And doesn't he have those arms to catch the tiny thing! Olivia from the fourplex on the corner says he works out all the time. She sees him leaving for the gym early in the mornings and then again later at night. Twice each day, if you can imagine!

Their poor dog was curled up on a corner of the porch that afternoon, attached to a post by a long rope, eyes completely set on Grace, wondering what might happen next if he looked away, I'm sure. And of course, wondering how this new creature fit in too. That pooch never needed a leash when he was with Grace before, never even looked side to side when he was on the front deck or they were out walking. Long-haired brown dog, retriever type, maybe you've seen him. A rescue I heard. But a good-looking one, I always thought. Well-behaved at least.

Well, let me tell you, I did a double-take. No baby, then — snap — suddenly one appearing like that. At first I considered how some people never show and you hardly know they're pregnant. Me, I was gigantic from four months with all three kids. Everyone knew that we had ours coming, believe me! But you've heard those stories too I'm sure about people going into labour without even knowing ahead of time. I thought maybe it was like that. Or, giving her the benefit of the doubt, as I like to, I considered that maybe she carried her baby small. After all Grace is so slight herself.

Either way I meant it kindly when I said that day, "Wow, Grace, you never even looked pregnant!"

And then she replied to me, straight, without even smiling, "Oh, I didn't have her from my own body." Just like that, she said to me, "We hired a surrogate." She wasn't embarrassed or anything when she said it, by the way, so I don't think she'd mind me telling you either.

I heard later from Terry, you know, the older fellow just down from us, that Grace and her husband spent pretty much all of their savings to have that child, that's how much they wanted one. Had I known I might have given her one of mine! Of course, I'm only kidding. But I imagine it's not cheap to get someone to have one for you.

Yes, this was just after they did all that work on their house too. Ali who lives two houses down from me on the north side speculated that they might have to sell the house now to make ends meet. We only wondered about that for a minute though. (I mean, really, how could we even know their full situation?) Then we both went into our own houses to get on with the evening. For me that meant cooking dinner and calling my mother, like I always do.

Mrs. Gunderson, the elderly lady who lives across the street, waved me over one day later that week as I was stepping out to get my mail from the boxes. Her apartment is right on the main floor so she pops out for quick conversations. She sees me coming and sometimes even waits there for me, I'm sure of it. Ready for me with all her questions! Stores them in her cheeks like a squirrel until she can let them all out! It sure feels like it anyways! There's always something with her.

Anyway, she asked if I knew why Grace didn't adopt like other people do. "Aren't there are so many babies out there already?"

I admit — I wondered then if she assumed I should have that kind of information because Grace and I have the same skin colour. But when I think things like that I remind myself that I shouldn't imagine such smallness of people. Of course, everyone is curious and mostly have good intentions too! That's what I try to focus on.

I told my mom on the phone that day what Mrs. Gunderson asked, about why Grace and her husband didn't adopt. Just as something to talk about when there was a lull in our conversation. But what a mistake! I heard her get completely quiet from her side of the phone line. My mother didn't say anything for a bit, which is always bad news. Usually it means I've said something she doesn't like. Uh oh! Watch out! I sat down on the kitchen stool and got ready.

"Sometimes an adopted baby grows up and leaves you," my mom began. "That happened to your Auntie Oishi. Remember how she adopted that sweet baby girl all the way from India. Did the paperwork and the interviews with the social worker. Put all that effort in. Always treated her like she was no different from her other kids. After all, the little girl looked like them even!" She went on. "That ungrateful child grew up into a wild young woman and no one ever heard from her after that, did they? I bet she never even calls you. When you were little you two were close as anything," my mother reminded me, like I'd forget! "I'm not sure my sister has been the same since. I'm surprised you don't remember all that pain we went through before you say things like that about adoption, like it's an easy thing to do."

I could see what my mom meant in a way so I apologized because that's always best when she starts feeling hurt like that. She can get so upset about events that happened a long time ago, then she really goes on and on.

Yes, I phone my mother nearly every day while I'm cooking. Though sometimes I'm not sure she even wants to talk to me. But then, if I don't call, my sister tells me how our mom thinks I don't care because I don't bother to reach out. So I call even though she talks to me like I'm nothing interesting, to tell you the truth. That's how it feels sometimes. Or like I'm a child still. Most of the time I'm just trying to think of what to say, any neutral subject we won't disagree over. It's not easy, believe me!

Personally, I think that if you get to look that good like Grace, well, I'd have gotten a surrogate too. And if we could afford it, of course. I mean, really, who wouldn't! My girlfriend Clara agreed too. I go visit her every week or two even though it's an extra bus ride to get there and takes time out of my day. Last time we got together, I was saying to Clara how I was a mess after all that baby-having. And let's face it, I've never looked the same.

(Of course, I wouldn't tell my mother that because she loves her grandchildren more than her own children, so she wouldn't like me implying that I resented how having them ruined my body. She would say how her grandbabies were worth it and then of course she would tell someone else, one of her friends or my sister, something like how she always thought I was vain, if you can believe it. Me! Vain! No one who really knows me would say that! If she talked to my sister, word would get back to me within minutes, and then I'd be stewing over it for hours. No, when it comes to her, better not to say anything.)

Clara said that she thought it would be worth it to let someone else go through it all on one's behalf too. "Mostly because of the hormones" was her opinion. "Think how steady you'd feel. I just couldn't shake the blues after having both of mine. It's sure not easy. Jim would agree, wouldn't he?" she asked loud enough for her husband to hear.

He must have been listening the whole time, because he bellowed from the next room, "Damn straight! Boy, did I suffer with her mood swings after she had the kids!" We had a laugh about that. Sometimes men forget that we have to tolerate all their feelings too! And sometimes they sure don't know what our bodies go through.

Of course, I dropped off a card from the dollar store for Grace, signed all of our names on it and I thought of making her a meal, but who knows what they like to eat. And it's not as if she's all worn out from childbirth. Maybe I was feeling a little jealous, I don't mind admitting. Things seem easier for Grace than they are for most people, in general. You can't think like that though, right? I have to remind myself now and then. I'm human though, just like everyone else, and I can't help but notice that some people seem to have it easier than others. That's just how life is. It can't always be fair, I always say.

Anyway, I thought I could take over a bouquet of daisies or black-eyed Susans from the garden, later in the summer when there's more of them because everyone likes flowers to brighten the house up. Or I could ask her to stop by for a glass of wine or two, since, well as far as I knew, she wasn't even breastfeeding. Can she even breastfeed? Maybe I'll ask her one day if we get to talking.

★

For months after the little one showed up, Grace would walk over to the Mini Mart. That's what the corner store was called then, there used to be a sign up and everything. Grace would saunter over with the little one strapped onto her in a cloth carrier, roly legs hanging, toes no bigger than jelly beans. She'd walk so slowly, you know. Like she had all the time in the world. "It's the right distance," she said to me one day in passing, "so that I don't have to take a diaper bag or anything. I can go straight home if I need to."

Grace didn't ever have the dog with her then, poor thing was probably shut inside most of the time, I'm sure. I wasn't sure how he was and didn't want to intrude by asking. We still stuck to small talk, Grace and me. No, I still didn't get to know her much better after she had the baby. Even though sometimes it works out that way, that acquaintances become friends once they have something in common.

Alice, the woman who owned the Mini Mart, knew almost everything that was happening in the neighbourhood. She tended the shop morning to night and generally liked to chat when we'd come in to pick up a carton of milk or a bag of hamburger buns.

If you were standing near the cake mixes you could see into the back room where Alice's private space was. I'll admit, I found that a little unprofessional. There was an old leather couch and a TV that was on most of the time. She liked talk shows mostly, as far as I could tell. There was a kettle and a toaster back there too, so she had her comforts. As far as jobs go, it seemed like a pretty good situation for her there.

I could tell when the store had been quiet for a while because she wasn't behind the counter but instead came out from the back when the front door opened, the little bell at the top of it jangling to let her know, and I always felt bad, like I was interrupting.

If she was halfway through a good TV show, *Oprah* or one of those big ones, you could see she was still trying to listen, and maybe rushing good paying customers like me out, not showing interest in the way we'd come to expect. A bit unprofessional, see? Inconsistent, I'll say, to be kinder about it.

Alice's husband kept to himself in the apartment upstairs, where they both officially lived. I hardly ever saw him around the store itself though. Left things to his wife to run. As you walked past and the second-floor window was open though you could hear the shows he watched that were the opposite of what Alice liked, mostly sports for him, it seemed.

Who am I to say how anyone should make their marriage work? If they like their space away from each other, so be it.

Alice was the kind of person who knew just the thing though. I'll give her that. Like it was a skill she had. If you went in with a headache to buy Advil she'd say things like, "Why not buy a banana too? Eat it on your way home, then have a big glass of water when you get there." And sure enough if you did, your headache disappeared, before you even took the painkiller.

Once I stopped there early in the morning to get a coffee to go. She suggested I go sit in the park on the wooden bench by the pond to drink it. "You might feel better all day," she mentioned in a pleasant way that wasn't too pushy. (You see, when she wasn't rushing people out for her shows she could really be quite thoughtful.)

"The kids," she suggested, "will be just fine taking care of themselves for a little while at home." I thought it was fine advice so I went to the park and even took off my sandals for a bit. Imagine, me in the park barefoot like that! It was nice, I won't lie, sitting outdoors on my own for a few minutes. Not rushing around looking after things like I usually am.

Another time, I stopped in for a can of beans and was feeling a bit blue thinking about one of those disheartening phone conversations with my mom. Alice must've seen it, so she said to me, "Buy a watermelon, one of the small round ones, they're the sweetest. Have the first piece to yourself before you call the kids in. You'll feel better after."

And didn't I do just that, I bit into that juicy slice, standing there by myself right over my kitchen sink. I won't say if I cried. Oh no, that's a secret between me and that melon. After, of course, I cut up the rest into nice triangles and shared it around like always.

I never told her that her advice worked, but I always did what she suggested. What could be the harm in it? And I always try to stay open-minded. She had some good ideas, I'll admit that too.

But you know, after the time with the watermelon, well, I felt a little embarrassed when I saw Alice, like I'd let my feelings show more than I was comfortable with. Like she knew I'd get all weepy like that!

For a while I sent the kids instead if we needed something, gave them extra for a slushy as incentive. That always worked with them. They always picked the blue so their lips and tongue were that same colour for hours, that's one of the things they like about it. It makes me laugh too. They look just ridiculous.

When Grace took her new baby to the Mini Mart, Alice would hold her for a long time, bouncing outside right in front of the doorway if there was no one in the store, or ringing a customer's things through the cash register with that baby still held in one arm, like an old pro. The little one happy as anything with her! Smiling away! I still don't know if Alice ever had kids. She wasn't the kind of person to go on about herself, but she obviously knew what she was doing. Some people have that kind of instinct, I think, whether or not they actually have a family of their own.

One day I remember seeing Grace use the time while Alice held the baby to stretch. The empty cloth carrier still attached at the waist flopped down to Grace's knees so it looked like she was wearing an apron, her arms up in the air as if she might lift off. I thought of how good it would feel to reach upward like that, to be that unselfconscious, right there in front of the world. Personally I'd feel so foolish. Stretching away for everyone to see! But it looked like it felt good, I won't lie.

Grace sometimes sat on the bench outside the corner store drinking an iced tea or lemonade from a bottle. One day I passed by, she had an ice cream, one of those chocolate and nut covered ones on a stick. I admit that I wondered some about a grown woman who would buy such an indulgent treat in the middle of the day like that just for herself. Of course, I didn't say all that. I checked my instinct. *Why shouldn't she take a nice break?* I thought instead. So I said, "Good for you, treating yourself!" Grace looked at me but didn't say thank you like I thought she might.

"I always worry about a parent who is too self-sacrificing," I told my husband, Rian, later that day. "One can't maintain such selflessness for too long." Maybe hoping he'd get the hint. I thought he might wonder if I was talking about myself in a way. He didn't wonder a bit. He shrugged then went back to eating his dinner the way he does.

"Rian didn't know what I was trying to say." I made the mistake of complaining to my sister later, who didn't really understand either it seemed. Maybe I wish I was the kind of person who might buy myself an ice cream in the middle of the day, I wanted to tell them both. But I didn't bother. There doesn't seem to be any point in it.

At least Clara made a joke of it. "Who would sit around eating ice cream when you could go home and pour yourself a glass of wine instead? That's what I'd like to do!" We had a laugh about that.

We all took Alice for granted, I see now. One morning the shop just didn't open, and a week later it was still closed up tight. All those posters on the outside advertising cell phone plans faded so quickly in the weather. They still look terrible, all worn and forgotten. After a while the whole building was boarded up and it just stayed like that. Even the upstairs apartment stayed vacant.

People who were in the know said that it turned out that the store was losing money that whole time. It was busy enough. Steady at least, I always thought. And Alice sure never seemed worried. But the bank took it all, Mrs. Gunderson said she heard. Just like that.

Some people moved away not long after. Not directly because of the Mini Mart but maybe because the neighbourhood didn't feel the same. As if Alice were the keeper of people's spirits too. Not that I believe in that funny woo-woo stuff, but maybe sometimes there's truth in it.

I felt a bit blue about the shop closing myself. I'd gotten used to it being part of things. And I worried about Grace some too. Wondered how it might change her days, and also if she might have known this was coming. Maybe Alice talked to her about it those afternoons, when they visited, when it was just the two of them chatting. Maybe they talked about their troubles, like money problems or family worries. Maybe they became more than acquaintances and by then were real friends. It made me feel as though I'd been left out, when I thought of it like that.

★

When I told my mom the Mini Mart closed she also said, "Isn't it a shame?" But then right away said, "Now couldn't you maybe move to a bigger house too?" Which is a thing she likes to say regularly enough. She wishes I lived in one of those same-same suburban houses she could show pictures of to her friends and feel proud of instead of our little fixer-upper. One she'd feel more comfortable visiting, she likes to say.

Oh, I know, there's a lot of work to be done on this old house. Rian is always promising, "I'm going to get to that," whenever we talk about the work that needs to be done around here. But he likes living here for his own reasons and I don't mind.

But my mother took the opportunity that day to tell me again that we should move close to a regular supermarket instead too. "And close to where your sister lives," she said. Like those are the most important things in life — supermarkets and my angel of a sister. I could hear her coming up with the whole plan right there.

"Someone's at the door I have to go," I said to my mom then, even though there was no one at all. Even though I knew she'd find that rude. *So be it*, I thought. I wasn't in the mood to talk anymore.

And so of course right then Grace and her husband went walking past, on the opposite side of the street, but it was the first time I'd seen them all together in a while. They looked so happy it almost brought tears to my eyes.

He was pushing the little girl in one of those jogging strollers, the expensive kind with three big wheels, and Grace had the dog on a leash, the type that attaches around the waist. Grace had one hand on her husband's back so they were all walking together and I could see how close they were. As if they really liked each other. I really felt that, watching them that day. It was a nice thing to see but somehow affected me in a sad way too.

Well, I can tell you that dog was still not looking around like regular ones do, only giving that stroller a bit of a side eye now and then. I bet Grace could even take it off the leash again if she wanted, but I'm glad she doesn't do that anymore. Just in case. Anyway, that dog is wise, I think. The way he isn't too involved in what's going on around him, just does his own thing.

I really should have taken a real gift over or invited Grace to stop by with the little one in those early days. I feel sheepish about it still. After all I like to be friendly.

As I watched them pass by that day it occurred to me that I could offer to walk the dog for them instead, or bring him over to keep me company sometimes. It might be nice to have a quiet mutt like that around while the kids are at school. Some company.

But then, imagine if anything went wrong! What if he found the spirit to go running after a stray cat? No, best to keep my distance, I decided. Let them be. After all, they seem to be getting along well enough. Grace seems to be managing just fine without me fussing over her. And isn't my plate full enough already? It sure feels like it, most of the time.

In a Name

KAVISHA TRIPATHI LOOKED PAST THE WHITE GRID LINES of the windowpanes above the kitchen sink to the broad elm outside. It was the end of autumn. Brittle leaves were scattered across the yard. The ones still on the tree trembled, barely holding on.

"So where do you want to go for your dinner tonight, birthday girl?" Kavisha looked away from the changing weather outside, toward her own cheerful kitchen. She leaned her lower back against the hard lip of the stone counter. Her daughter, Meena, was sitting on the linoleum floor putting on her striped socks. There were dark patches on her green T-shirt where her hair, still wet from the shower, touched her shoulders. Kavisha thought Meena might ask to go to their usual family restaurant, but as she had been getting older she had become less predictable, keener to try new things.

"There's a vegan place on Sixth Street called Plant that Charlene went to with her parents for her birthday. She said you have to make a reservation, because it's so busy. It's really cool, she says."

"I love that you want to try something different, sweetheart. I'll go down there in person while I'm out. See if they have a last-minute spot. I'll tell them it's a very important day." Kavisha smiled.

Meena stood up and kissed her mom's cheek. The two were nearly the same height.

"Wear your winter coat. It's supposed to snow," Kavisha said. "And why don't you ever dry your hair?"

"I hate wearing my winter coat, Mom. I'll be fine." Meena took her jean jacket from the hook by the door and ignored the comment about her hair. Kavisha raised her eyebrows but didn't push the matter. Meena turned back before leaving. "Don't worry, okay? I have a hoodie in my bag too. I'll put it on if I need to."

"Okay, sure. I guess you're old enough to decide these things for yourself."

Alone in the house, Kavisha finished loading breakfast bowls and juice glasses into the dishwasher then sat down at the dining room table to make a list of errands on a yellow sticky note. She took her time writing things down, sipped her coffee and scrolled through her work emails on her phone, responding to some and deleting others. She kept adding to her to-do list as tasks came to her. Finally, she pressed the paper to the back of her phone so she wouldn't forget to take it with her, then got dressed for the day, already feeling weary.

The restaurant, Plant, was in an old brick warehouse on a street that bustled with foot traffic. Kavisha squeezed her car into a spot on a nearby street and walked the short distance, wrapping her coat around her as she faced into the wind. She glanced up to the shifting clouds above.

The wooden door swung open easily. Inside it was bright, with large windows. The room was still empty of people but for a woman setting tables, and the staff working in the open kitchen. True to its name, there was greenery everywhere: creeping up the walls and hanging from planters suspended by ceiling hooks that were installed in between elegant bamboo light fixtures. Lush vines wound overhead too. Tall palms in basket-weave pots curved toward the brightness from shaded corners.

The woman setting tables put down a stack of cloth napkins and came to greet Kavisha.

"Well, hi there," the host said, as if surprised to see her. Her long blonde hair was pulled up into a top knot but her bangs were short. She wore a sleeveless black dress and an assortment of jewelry — a heavy silver necklace with a turquoise pendant at her throat, earrings so long they swayed. She had a tiny silver hoop in her nose, and Kavisha noticed that she was wearing a bindi, a small sparkling gem that shone like a diamond at the centre of her forehead. Kavisha wore them herself sometimes, for weddings and celebrations, and felt a twinge to see the woman wearing one so casually.

"What can I do for you this morning?"

"I'm hoping I can make a reservation for three for tonight. It's my daughter's birthday."

"Beautiful," she said, in a way that Kavisha felt immediately irritated by. "Let's see what we've got." She reached for a tablet, tapped the screen with an electronic pen to turn it on so that it lit up. Blue light from the screen reflected into the glimmering gem above her brow. "Well, look at that, I have one spot left at seven."

"Great, I'll take it," said Kavisha.

"I'll need your name then."

Kavisha felt a rush of frigid air as the door swung open behind her. She followed the employee's eyes. A couple in office clothes entered the restaurant. *It must be close to lunchtime after all*, she thought, feeling the pressure of time. She still had so many things left to do.

"I'll be right with you, as soon as I'm done here," said the hostess pleasantly to the duo. "Sorry, your name?" she looked back to Kavisha with an expectant smile. Her whitened teeth shone.

Kavisha paused. It was a familiar feeling. The pressure of the waiting customers, the host expecting a swift response. The young woman's pen hovered over the screen without touching it. Kavisha noticed her fingers were long and bony, her nails polished black.

"Just put it in my husband's name, he'll probably get here before us," Kavisha said quickly. "And it's much easier." It was. Simple. British in origin, easy to spell, common. The hostess's pen moved easily on the screen as she wrote in the reservation details with a flourish, dotted the "i" with a confident tap.

Kavisha wished that in this recurring situation the person would respond by saying that they didn't mind, they could take the extra seconds to write her name, even if it was harder. Now and then she made a point of taking the time to spell it out, helped the person get the pronunciation right, though she was very aware that it wasn't her job. But Kavisha found the process exhausting. That's when her husband's name came in handy.

"Okay great, see you tonight at seven!" The woman smiled and then waved the next two customers toward her.

Kavisha left feeling, as she often did, embarrassed. She was intelligent, independent, called herself a feminist, and yet used her husband's name more and more often. It made her feel as though she had developed a bad habit, like secretly smoking. Kavisha used his name for all sorts of interactions with increasing regularity: making complaints to the city about overflowing garbage in the alley, registering Meena for after-school activities, writing simple queries from their shared email — the most impersonal communications, both with and without telling him. It was a relief. And it was astonishing how different these daily experiences were with such a simple name to toss to strangers.

After her daughter was born, exactly twelve years ago, Kavisha held her newborn's full weight in the crook of her arm, trying to see the person this new baby would become. They were told that they had to decide on a name right away, that there were forms that needed to be filled out before they took her home. Kavisha had felt overwhelmed, as though they were being asked to define their baby for the rest of her life. Her husband didn't think it was such a big deal.

"You decide," he had said, looking down at their baby. "It matters more to you than it does to me."

Kavisha's husband was complex in his own ways. Yet his name was jotted on the side of paper coffee cups with astounding ease. She was used to telling baristas, "I'll wait by the counter." Friends encouraged her to make up a fake name, anything she liked, to use in such situations. But she couldn't bring herself to, as though adopting a false name was a kind of deeper betrayal. Instead, she quit shopping at clothing stores where they insisted on identifying her on the whiteboard attached to the change-room door. It wasn't worth the trouble. And then, at some point, she started using her husband's name instead of her own.

The icy wind pushed at her back as she walked to the car, this time pressing her onward. A swirl of litter lifted off the sidewalk in front of her. When she got into the vehicle, she turned up the heat, then referred to the sticky note that she had pressed onto the dashboard. The square paper fluttered in the suddenly warm air.

★

She called the shoe repair shop to see if it was open next, remembering that the owner often worked odd hours. Kavisha thought she might give the shopkeeper her husband's name right away. After all, they were his brown leather loafers in the crinkled plastic bag on the passenger seat.

"Drop them off and I'll get to them," said the man's gruff voice on the phone line. He hung up without asking for a name or saying goodbye.

The repair shop was a short drive away, on the corner of a busy intersection. It was in a stout building with a handmade sign advertising both leather repair and motorcycle attire. Kavisha pulled up in front and flipped the visor to check her face in the mirror. She pinched her cheeks before flipping it closed again, an old habit.

Outside the shop Kavisha paused to read a note taped to the inside of the glass door. Printed on plain paper was a grainy photo of a white dog. The dog was medium sized; its mouth was open in a way that almost looked like it was smiling. It was friendly looking. Endearing. Underneath the photo was a message:

"Dear Customers, you may remember our shop dog, Maeve, who recently passed away. We are still grieving and appreciate your understanding. Maeve would have wanted us to keep the store open. This was her favourite place to be."

She found the sign so unexpected, a bit absurd. *Imagine putting such a feeling in writing for everyone to read,* Kavisha thought as she entered the shop.

The hinges of the old glass door creaked. Brisk air rushed in with her. It was warm inside. There were long rows of black leather jackets, chaps hung on racks, an orderly line of helmets, shiny and round. *This would be a pleasant place to spend your days if you were a dog,* Kavisha considered. Quiet, with an earthy, animal-like smell, a predictable undertone of glue and solvents. She remembered seeing the old dog there in the past, when she had come in to look for a wallet for her husband's birthday after he hinted that he had seen one he liked in the store. The dog had been a lazy presence, unbothered as she reached over it for the wallet she wanted.

Kavisha nodded hello to the man who looked up from behind the counter at the back of the store. His hair was shorter at the sides and longer at the back. He had a neatly combed handlebar moustache. She guessed he was in his fifties, maybe older. His black T-shirt was tight across his belly, under which hung a canvas tool belt. The man was heavy, solid in his unapologetic presence. She could imagine him splayed on the leather seat of his motorbike, arms and legs open wide to the world racing toward him. He looked like a guy who rode the big reclining kind of bike and had for a long time.

Kavisha liked the man despite his unpolished manners. The way he took pride in his work, dedicated himself to a certain lifestyle. She even admired the way he shared his loss and his own grief. So unexpectedly, so openly.

"Hi there," she said not too loudly, trying to be respectful. Kavisha pulled the shoes out of the bag and set them down on the long, narrow counter at the back of the store, where the shopkeeper was looking down at a boot held loosely in his hand. The counter separated the retail section from the brightly lit workshop behind him. There were many kinds of footwear behind the counter too, lined up on the floor and arranged on metal shelves, dozens of pairs of them, each with a yellow paper tag attached. Sets of slim heels stood like thin soldiers between narrow-toed dress shoes and freshly shined workboots.

"I just talked to you on the phone," she explained.

The repair man put the boot down on the shelf, beside its twin, without saying anything. He scooped both of her husband's shoes up by the heels with two fingers of one hand. His hands were darkened by leather dyes and polish. The deep colours burrowed into the grooves, making the fine lines in his skin seem like they were drawn on, doodled. He looked at the shoes from all angles, turned them over to see them from below. The bottoms of both were pulling away from their leather bases. The man set one shoe down and tugged at the rubber base of the other, causing it to gape even more. He peered between it and the leather like a dentist inspecting an open mouth, then looked at Kavisha and said, "This shouldn't have happened."

"I know," she agreed. "They're not that old."

"This will take me a week. Maybe more. I'm pretty busy."

"That's fine," she said, still holding the emptied bag in her hands. "Just call when they're done. He's not in a hurry."

"Okay, what's the name?" He flipped open a receipt book, scribbled on it with a ballpoint pen, then looked up at Kavisha. Waiting. His moustache, streaked with grey, covered his top lip.

Kavisha thought of saying her husband's name. But the man was so unhurried. She imagined telling him that she too had pets who had died. A family cat and then a dog when she was a child. The aged terrier they had to put down the year before Meena was born. When she hears their names, she still misses them, the warmth of their bodies tucked in beside her on a sofa, curled up at her feet as she slept at night, the happy presence waiting to greet her when she arrived home each day. It had never occurred to her to announce her loss to anyone, to give it space like that, but she feels now like she should have.

The repair man tapped his blue ballpoint twice on the blank page of his notebook. The phone rang and he looked over at it. Kavisha said, "Go ahead and get that, I'll write it down."

"Sure." The man held the pen out to her. The plastic was cool and light in her hand. He turned the book so it was facing her. Kavisha pressed the pen to the paper, wrote her own name and her phone number. Her loose script was bold and easy to read, the blue ink sharp on the white page.

"Here you go," she said

He took the pen back. "Huh." He drew a circle around her name and read it out loud like a question. "Kavisha?"

"Yes, that's right." She was relieved that she didn't have to correct him. But of course it wasn't actually that hard to pronounce, when people just took a minute. He jotted a tag number beside it and handed her a square slip of paper with a matching number. Kavisha slipped her portion into her coat pocket.

"I'm sorry about your dog," she said before leaving. "Maeve."

The man nodded.

After the shoe repair shop, Kavisha stopped at the drugstore, the grocery store and the gas station to fill up her tank, places that didn't ask for her name at all. Driving home, taking the narrow roads, the snow began to fall. Fat flakes left circles on her windshield that she swept away with the squeaking squeegees of the car wiper blades. She thought that they'd have to leave in good time for dinner, in case the roads got icy. She didn't want Meena to miss out on her celebration.

Kavisha thought of the meaning of her daughter's name: precious stone. Beautiful and, also, resilient. She'd never asked her daughter if she liked her name or not. Maybe she would, over dinner, Kavisha thought. She could also tell Meena the reasons why she chose it for her, why she still thought it suited her all these years later.

Stopped at a red light, Kavisha pulled the sticky note from the dashboard. She crumpled it in one hand and dropped it into the empty plastic cup holder beside her. She looked up to the overcast sky to where a vee of geese travelled southward through the snow. The birds flew in neat formation. When the light changed to green, Kavisha pressed her foot down on the gas pedal to carry on home.

As she let herself into the house, she noticed Meena's sneakers, damp from the wet snow accumulating outside, left haphazardly by the door. "I'm home," she called.

Kavisha hung her coat in the closet, pushing others out of the way to make space, then rubbed her hands together to warm them up from the cold outside. She took off her boots too, put them neatly side by side on the rug, then lined up Meena's sneakers beside hers. A damp autumn leaf clung to the side of Meena's sole. Kavisha pulled it off and opened the front door briefly again to drop it outside, then locked the door with a practised flip of the deadbolt.

Meena's neon school backpack was on the floor too, gaping open from when she pulled her lunch bag out, it looked like.

Kavisha picked the bag up to close it and noticed a thin, pale-coloured notebook inside. There was a pen-drawn doodle on the front. She took it out to look more closely. "Property of Meena!" the drawing announced in fat bubble letters, decorated with stars and what she assumed was meant to be a guard dog for the note-book's contents, but was in fact a fat puppy with hearts for eyes, reminding Kavisha again of the sign put up by the shoe repair man. Lines of ink radiated out from Meena's name like rays of light. Kavisha smiled and wedged the notebook back into its narrow spot, then zipped the canvas bag closed.

Upstairs, she knocked on Meena's bedroom door before opening it. "We have a reservation for seven at that restaurant you wanted to go to. It seems like a great place. Let me know if you need help deciding on an outfit."

The radio was on and the sound of a boy-band pop song bounced in the background. Meena was in front of the mirror, putting her hair up. She dropped it as her mom opened the door.

"Oh, I totally know what I'm going to wear!" Meena came to the door excitedly and kissed her cheek. "Thanks, Mom!"

Kavisha had a long shower in the bathroom connected to her bedroom, the water warming her from the chill outside. Still wearing her white bathrobe, a crooked towel wrapped around her wet hair, she took her wooden jewellery box off the long dresser and sat down on her bed with it in front of her. She flipped open the time-worn clasp at the front. The hinges made a familiar creak as she carefully lifted the hand-carved lid of the amber box. She had always opened it in the same way, as if discovering lost treasure.

Most of the items near the top were cheap costume jewel-lery: sterling silver hoops of various sizes, a pair of fake diamond studs, pendant necklaces she'd bought on vacation. There was a red beaded choker she had picked up from an artisans' market years earlier and never worn. Kavisha lifted that section out and put it down beside her. Concealed in the bottom section was her precious orange-gold collection.

When she was a teenager, her mother had handed a few of her possessions down to Kavisha, including a set of bangles; a short, simple necklace; a pair of narrow, drop-shaped earrings. She was given more over the years, and just before her wedding her parents gave her a pair of larger earrings that had a small ruby at the centre of them, another necklace that was uncomfortably heavy to wear, and a thick bracelet with a clunky clasp. Giving a daughter jewellery was an old custom, a discreet way to pass on some wealth to her alone. Kavisha thought of her parents every time she touched the sun-hued metal.

Kavisha picked up a pair of earrings that she thought Meena would like. They connected at the top like ordinary hoops, but the bottom part widened into semicircles, like the shape of the moon as it waxed or waned. There were slender lines on those crescents that reminded Kavisha of the rays of light on Meena's drawing of her name.

These are perfect, Kavisha decided, putting the earrings down on the bedside table. Then she put the costume jewellery back at the top of the box and closed it gently. Kavisha stood up, cinched and re-knotted the belt of her robe before picking up the earrings again, feeling their cool weight in her closed hand. The slight sharpness of the metal edges pressed into her palm as she walked downstairs to find a case and the right tissue paper from the crowded drawer in the kitchen, so she could wrap them up right away.

Kavisha put the earrings into a miniature box, one that a silver necklace had come in, a gift from her husband. She wrapped the box in green tissue paper with white flowers on it, tied a darker green ribbon around it, made a bow at the top. Then she slipped the package into the oversized pocket of her robe.

From her other pocket she pulled out her phone. Kavisha found the number for the restaurant and dialled it. Looking through the kitchen window she noticed the old elm was nearly bare, having lost the last of its foliage over the course of the day. The brown and yellow leaves, now all on the ground, were fixed beneath a skiff of wet snow.

The phone rang only once. "Plant!" said a cheery voice on the phone, startling her.

Kavisha took a quick breath before speaking. She pressed her free hand down on the counter. "Hi there, I made a reservation today for seven o'clock and I just wanted to change the name it's under."

"Right, seven o'clock. I think I remember you. For the birthday right? No need to worry about the name, it doesn't really matter. Just check in under the one we've got when you get here."

Kavisha's throat tightened. The kitchen floor was cool under her bare feet; her hand still on the counter steadied her. She imagined her daughter beside her when they got there, hearing her mother say a name that was not her own. *Meena probably won't even notice*, Kavisha told herself. *And probably won't think it's a big deal if she does.*

"I'll change it anyway, please," she responded, more loudly than she meant to. "It does matter. It's actually important to me."

The woman paused. "Okay, sure. No problem."

Kavisha cleared her throat, straightened her spine and said her name, then spelled it into the receiver.

"Okay, got it. Change made. We'll see you soon!"

Kavisha hung up the phone and fixed the loosened belt of her robe again. She felt lighter as she walked back up the stairs to finish getting dressed. There was no need to hurry; they had plenty of time before they needed to leave to make it to the restaurant on time.

The Worrier

A MRIT HADN'T ALWAYS BEEN SO WORRIED. WHEN HE WAS younger he was a real troublemaker. A joyful shit disturber. He liked to replace the contents of the sugar bowl with salt, hide the TV remote control just for the fun of seeing his dad get flustered. He came up with elaborate plans to miss school, swiped chocolate bars from the corner store even when he had his weekly allowance jangling in his pocket. Amrit snuck out through his bedroom window in the middle of the night for the thrill of it, not minding that there was nothing to do but wander. Or he smoked a pilfered cigarette on the deck at the top of the playground slide at the elementary school nearby. Lying on his back facing the night sky, Amrit dreamed about living an exciting life, which was what he wanted more than anything.

His dad told him that it was okay for boys to get into a bit of trouble now and then. "When I was your age I got into some harmless mischief too." Then he told Amrit how he used to play pranks on his brothers and had even skipped school now and then. "As long as you don't get caught, it's okay. Just don't make a habit of it." Followed by, "And don't tell your mother I said so."

When Amrit was fourteen he decided to take the family car out for a drive. He backed straight into the fence across the alley, at full speed. The neighbour shouted that Amrit could have killed them, which shook his parents enough that they started taking the problem of their son's audacious behaviour more seriously.

"We will pay to get the fence fixed but you owe us," his dad said, unusually sternly. "We want the full amount. No shortcuts."

Amrit thought this might mean he'd have to get a job at Arby's or stock shelves at Safeway like some of his friends did, but instead Amrit spent that summer doing chores around the house for his parents. The work wasn't too hard: sanding and painting the deck, cleaning out the garage, watering the rose bushes, mowing the lawn every third day.

His mother and father compensated him by the hour, minimum wage. It was money he never saw as they used it to pay off his debt directly. The ledger, a piece of lined paper pinned to the bulletin board in the kitchen, showed the tally: the date, the initial debt, the number of hours he had worked, the remaining amount owed, all in neat columns that were pencil-drawn by his dad using a ruler. His parents trusted him to jot down his hours each day on the paper himself. Amrit rounded up.

Amrit was also the kind of worker who rested a lot, going inside the house for gulps of orange juice from the carton. He took snack breaks, standing in the kitchen with the fridge door open for a long time, its interior light illuminating its unvarying contents. Amrit rummaged through the neatly organized containers of leftovers, then peered into the paper bag his mom left his lunch in before deciding if he wanted it or not. *As if she thinks I can't even make myself a simple meal,* he thought sulkily. But then, he never had. If it was something he didn't feel like having, he wouldn't even eat it. His mother didn't like to waste food so she would end up taking that very same lunch, the limp day-old sandwich, to work with her the next day, as her own.

On his work breaks, Amrit lingered inside for a long time, and even if he wasn't eating, he flipped on the TV for a while before getting half-heartedly back to the job.

"It's too hot out," he complained to his mom when she called to see how he was, muting the TV before she could hear it. He hoped she would feel sorry for him, feel bad for making him work so hard.

Back then Amrit was strong and tall, naturally athletic, good-looking with his flop of thick black hair and sharp jawline. Amrit spoke Canadian English with such a natural, confident accent. "How could we be so lucky?" His parents said. They also reminded him, "We came here for you. We wanted you to have every option open, so that you can succeed."

He bristled. "Quit putting so much pressure on me. This is my life. I have to be my own person." And then he walked away. It never occurred to him to look back, to wonder if they were hurt and that pain might show on their faces. And so he didn't.

Amrit barely graduated. He had lots of friends and was good at sports, but when it came to the actual work part of high school, he just wasn't interested. Though of course he was smart enough. His parents knew he was highly intelligent. By the time he was four years old he was already reading full books on his own — zipping through one and tossing it aside, then reaching for the next one. Amrit was a thoughtful child who grew into a young man with a prematurely serious expression. By ten he was often bent over a scattering of parts, unscrewing anything mechanical to find out how it worked: an electric keyboard, a radio, a toaster. In those days, he might even try to put the item back together again.

He still liked to take things apart as a teenager. In those years he grew bored more easily, so that a desiccated alarm clock would collect dust on the desk in the basement, unrecognizable as a sprawled collection of buttons, an emptied shell of hard plastic and a twist of multicoloured wires. Weeks later, his mother brushed the tangled mess of parts into an empty shoebox in case Amrit wanted it again. A month or so after that, she put the lid on the whole package and left it on a shelf in the storage room, not knowing what else she could do with all the pieces.

"He is too smart to worry about cleanup," he heard her tell his dad. "He is like a genius."

Amrit wasn't surprised when he didn't get into college. He knew he had filled out the applications half-heartedly, hoping he wouldn't be admitted. "The last thing I want to do is sit at a desk for another four years," he told his parents when the rejection letters arrived.

"Okay," they eventually agreed. "You take a break for a year, and then apply again."

"Sure," he said. "I'll still make you proud, you'll see."

His parents believed him.

Amrit went to work up north in the mines, near Yellowknife. While he was there he wrote poetry. How could you not with that kind of light, still lazily candescent at two in the morning? Amrit once described this radiance on a postcard to his long-distance girlfriend. The word "luminescence" stuck with him, so he bought a notebook and used a company pen to fill the blank pages with his own longing. He imagined the girl back home, plain and lonely, reading his words. Amrit thought he might even read the poems aloud to her when he saw her again, and considered how that might really turn her on.

The relationship didn't last. Neither did his interest in verse. He felt restricted by words after a time, disliked the effort of writing them down. There never seemed to be quite the right ones to say what he was really feeling. *There are people who live, and people who write about living,* Amrit decided then.

All that time he had spent taking things apart when he was younger made him useful at his job though. He understood how things worked. When a piece of equipment made a high-pitched grinding sound or came to a slamming stop, he could reliably work out the problem and rig up a quick repair. People got to know that he was handy. Amrit was given a raise and made good money for a time and spent hardly any of it — then again, there wasn't really anything he could buy there. He felt confident then that his parents would be proud if they could see him being promoted, respected, even though he was one of the youngest workers there.

Amrit imagined one day sending them on a vacation, all paid for, or telling them, "I told you I'd succeed, in my own way," as he handed them the keys to a new luxury car. His parents would see that he hadn't needed to go to college at all. Things were going just as he had hoped they would.

★

After a while, Amrit remembered his longing for adventure, so he left his job and used his savings to travel. First he went to Costa Rica with friends from work. From there he went further south on his own: Brazil, Chile, Argentina.

There was a place in Buenos Aires he stayed for a while. A hostel and party spot where Amrit spent over three months in a blur of cheap wine, coke and pot. One morning, sobering up, splashing cold water on his face, he noticed a drain pipe was dripping under the sink. Amrit went down to talk to the only staff person working there and offered to fix it. "All I need is a wrench," he said in English, making the motion with his hands.

Amrit used the tool to tighten the connection so that the leak, satisfyingly, stopped almost immediately. That night he partied with his friends as always, but at dawn, as he lay in his bottom bunk bed trying to get to sleep with his foot on the ground to stop the drunk feeling of spinning, he thought about how it had felt to use his hands again.

It seemed he was at a point where he should leave or else he might stay forever. Staying, Amrit might disappear into a life of booze and all-night clubs, which was fine, until it wasn't. There were other foreigners who had been there for more than a year, rarely seeing daylight at all. *It's time to move on,* he decided as he fell into a thick, drunken sleep. Amrit left the city later that same afternoon and never drank again.

He changed directions in his travels too. Though Amrit still had some money then, he travelled as frugally as he could, to make his savings last. Along the way he sent his parents quickly written postcards. One from a tiger sanctuary in Thailand, another from the Taj Mahal. "Cool place! Wish you were here! Love, Amrit." The places he sent them from were, for him, tacky touch points on the road of real adventure. He let his parents know he was alive at least, and still having fun. But he didn't tell them much more.

The experiences he loved were unexpected: happening upon a talented drummer busking in the train station in Marrakech, who he went back to listen to four afternoons in a row, or watching the sun rise pink and orange on the beach after an all-night rave in Canggu.

In Calcutta, he saw groups of children — street kids, cheeky and brave. They were young, not yet teenagers. They wore poorly fitting chappals, the soles of their feet were hardened and cracked. During the day some of them had things to sell to tourists: pencils, plastic flowers. The youngsters asked him for things in English. A pack of gum, American dollars. He handed them money, gave them exuberant high fives, bought whatever trinkets they were selling. Those kids, mostly boys with wide smiles, confidently shouted for attention, "Hey, Mister! Mister!" They reminded him of himself when he was younger. He too had been that bold.

Some seemed more troubled, so Amrit would offer to buy them a meal by gesturing toward a street vendor. After eating quickly, those kids asked for cash too, holding their hands open toward him. In those moments he dropped what he could, sometimes more than that, into their waiting palms. Amrit tried not to worry about how quickly his own savings were dwindling.

Back at home, Amrit's parents still felt hopeful. They were certain one day he would come back and go to school for engineering or a business degree. Tell them all the stories of his travels. He could upgrade, they reminded each other, he wasn't even twenty-five yet.

"Amrit was never one to be pushed," his mom and dad told their friends over tea. "Didn't we also want a big adventure when we were so young? We moved across the world ourselves before making a good, stable life in Canada."

In South Korea, Amrit started teaching English as a way to earn more money. Once, out of the blue, he phoned his mother and said, "I'm thinking of getting married. I met someone. She's from here. You'll like her."

Amrit's mother had always wanted a daughter-in-law. Grandchildren even. *Maybe just what he needs is a life partner to help him get on the right track,* she thought. She waited impatiently for the next call. But Amrit didn't contact them again from Seoul and then never mentioned the fiancée again. When he did finally get in touch again, his mother didn't ask about the woman either. After all, she still hated to push him.

"What if he's broken-hearted over it?" Amrit's mother asked his father as he was brushing his teeth one evening. She was standing beside him, speaking to his reflection in the bathroom mirror as she rubbed lotion into her hands in a practised, anxious way. "Better we don't say anything. It might only be painful."

By then Amrit's father was starting to worry about the kind of person his son really was. As the familiar vanilla-scented cream disappeared into his wife's skin, he thought about how his son might actually spend his whole life detached, wandering. *At this age, shouldn't Amrit have settled down? He is old enough to be a father himself, isn't he?* And then he wondered if Amrit already was. *After all, we know so little about his life.*

★

Amrit's run of good fortune ended abruptly. One night, closer to home in Mexico City, he went out with a woman he had just met. She was staying in the same hostel as him, an upgrade from the kind of place Amrit usually stayed in but he liked the location and was, in his mind, making the slow journey toward home, where he thought that he could easily find work again. He had gotten to know the American and her group of friends over most of a week.

"Let's go dancing! It's still early," he overheard her plead to her crowd. It seemed that her friends wanted to stay in for the night, but she was keen to party.

The others responded that they weren't in the mood, "I'm done," another woman said.

"I think I'm still hung over from last night," complained another. A different friend nodded sympathetically.

Amrit found the woman who wanted to go out attractive, pretty in an all-American cheerleader way. She had fair features and an outgoing personality. When they talked it seemed like she was flirting with him too.

"I'll go," Amrit offered from where he sat flipping through a book on bike repair he happened to find on the shelf in the lobby.

"Seriously?"

"No problem, it'll be fun."

"Great! Give me fifteen to get changed and we can get the front desk to order us a cab." Then she joked to her friends, "Have fun being lame."

"Come down whenever you're ready and we can just catch one outside. There's no need to bother the receptionist," Amrit suggested instead.

When the woman came back down, she was wearing a fitted purple tube dress and sandals with a thick wedge heel, the kind sold in the nearby market, Amrit noticed. She looked more apprehensive then. "You know, I read in the tourist books that cabs can be sketchy. I think we should get the desk to call us a taxi. A company they know. I don't mind waiting awhile longer if it's safer," she said.

"Trust me," Amrit was confident. "I've hailed rides all over the world and nothing bad has ever happened."

"Well, if you're sure." She was still hesitant.

Amrit promised, "It'll be fine."

It was dark out by then. The city air smelled of car exhaust and gardenias. He waved down a navy Civic with a lit-up *For Hire* sign in the window. She paused again before getting into the cramped back seat after him.

Amrit said, "Let's go."

They both heard the door lock click as the driver peeled off, before they even had their seatbelts on. *Why would he lock them in?* The woman looked at Amrit with wide eyes, shocked. Amrit felt the thud in his gut too. It quickly became obvious that the man was taking them in the opposite direction of the club.

"Hey, I think we should go the other way," Amrit leaned forward to talk to the driver, trying to sound calm. A drip of sweat slid down his back.

"Just a quick stop on the way," he replied in easy English. "No worries, okay?" which made Amrit sweat more.

Amrit tried the handle as they slowed in traffic. "Holy shit, man. At least unlock the doors. Hey maybe you could just let us out here?" They were still in a busy neighbourhood. *We can find a different ride.*

The driver said, "Sure, I'll stop as soon as I can, okay?"

As they slowed at an intersection. Amrit tried the door handle again. He slammed his shoulder against the door trying to push it open.

"Buddy! Don't wreck my car."

The woman beside him was whispering, like a mantra, "Oh my god, oh my god, holy fuck, what the fuck."

"I'll pull over for you here," the driver said, still friendly-sounding, upbeat. It seemed like an ordinary night for him.

The car eased into a narrow alleyway, unlit and sheltered from the glow of the city by buildings. Even the car headlights seemed dim. Three men were sitting on a low step in the narrow lane. Because they were wearing dark clothes they blended into the night. They approached the car like mirages, or ghosts. The driver at last clicked the button beside him to unlock the car doors.

"Just hand over your money," the driver advised. "There will be no trouble that way. We're all friends here. We can stay friends, right?"

Amrit refused at first. "No way. Fuck off. You're not getting anything."

"Let's go," he said to the woman. Amrit pulled on the metal handle and she slid across to exit through his side too. She was shaking but had stopped speaking. "It's going to be okay," he bluffed as he opened the door.

"I fucking told you," she hissed.

He heard the men talking to the driver. "Okay, no money. Let's take the girl then. We could have a good time with her, hey?"

No matter what, Amrit decided then, *I'll make sure she gets away*. He whispered for her to leave. "Just go, okay. You run. Don't stop. Just get as far from here as you can. I'll handle this."

He turned to the men. "I have cash. In my wallet. Try me." Then he stood in a tough-guy-movie stance, fists raised. As if he was ready for them. Amrit wondered momentarily where his acquaintance would escape to, but then a calmer feeling came over him. She would be okay, he decided, as long as she could get out of the pitch-dark of the alley back to the main street.

"Foreign asshole," one man said to him in English, forgetting about the girl then. "Let's fuck him up. It'll be fun."

Amrit glanced back at the woman one last time. He noticed the blur of her bare legs, her pale silhouette in the night as she ran away from them. The purple of her dress disappeared into the dark. As the men descended on him Amrit cried out. At the first punch he was winded, his breath forced from his body in a groan as he fell to the ground.

For the first time in his life Amrit realized, *I'm in really big fucking trouble.* He didn't remember anything from the night after that.

Amrit woke up in the same alley. They had left him like an old towel, a lifeless, boneless heap on the ground. He didn't know how long he was unconscious, but when he came to he felt his pockets immediately. His money was gone, along with his whole wallet, the leather one his father had given him for his sixteenth birthday. Even his hidden waist pouch with his passport in it had been taken. Touching his face, Amrit felt the swelling around his eye sockets. There was blood on his fingertips; it seemed to be coming from somewhere near his hairline. It was late morning, he tried to guess, looking around then, maybe early afternoon, judging by the light. The narrow valley between buildings was still shaded, but when he looked up the flash of sun hurt his eyes.

It took some time for Amrit to stand up and limp, dizzy and disoriented, toward a parked van to check his face in the side mirror. He didn't recognize himself. His face was so puffy and red-bruised. A cut above his eyebrow bled dark blood, a slow trickle, some smeared on his cheeks. Dirt clung there too. His vision wobbled, blurred and his body throbbed — deep, hot pain. Though he couldn't say just where it was coming from. *Everywhere.*

He found the strength to stumble out of the laneway, terrified that the men would come back for him. *Even though they already took everything.* For the rest of that morning Amrit hunched on a nearby street. When a local police officer tapped his shoulder, Amrit was so thirsty, so weak he could only say, in English, "Help me." The officer lifted Amrit to standing by roughly pulling on his arm.

"Man, you look like hell. Not from here, I guess. I'll give you a lift to the hospital." The cop unceremoniously pushed him into the back seat of his cruiser and, at the hospital entrance, opened the car door for Amrit to fall out of. The officer didn't help him into the building or wait to see if Amrit made it to the entrance.

After that night Amrit never saw that American woman again. Janet? Jessica? What was her name? He couldn't even remember. When he thought of her through the rest of his life he felt a piercing stab of regret. *How could I be so stupid?*

Amrit had always been treated like he was special, at least by his parents. Now he understood that he wasn't. When he was young, his parents were so proud of everything he did. They cheered him on at school basketball games, boasted to their friends about how smart he was. He was treated as if he were protected by a higher power, like he was smarter and more capable than most people. All his life, he wore his parents' pride comfortably.

That night, though, Amrit had endangered not just his own life, but someone else's. The shame of that realization was a weighted black cloak thrown over him. He felt the suffocating pressure of it all the time, so that he couldn't breathe. Amrit became afraid of everything, as entirely as he was once afraid of nothing.

After leaving the clinic, Amrit went to the police station, where they only said that they couldn't help him without any papers. He tried going to the bank to withdraw the last of his money but they also said, "Come back when you have some ID." From the hostel he retrieved his backpack, but there was nothing of value in there either: two changes of clothes and a pair of canvas runners, his toothbrush, shaving gear and deodorant. That was all. A lump, a sob so heavy it felt like stone, lodged in his chest as he held his useless bag in his arms. He didn't know how to ask for help, or from whom. The last thing he wanted to do was call his parents. Amrit had never imagined he would actually end up as a disappointment to them.

When Amrit went to the Canadian embassy they said there was a series of formal steps he could take to get his identification back, but when he thought of it he only felt weary, immobilized. He left and went back to the police station, which at least seemed a familiar place by then. Amrit slept in the shelter of a jacaranda tree there until they made him leave, but then they also directed him to a public square where he could find resources offered by NGOs. "At least they can give you a meal," one officer said. At the square, he found others like him lined up for help. Young people and old. Families with kids. So many others, each with their own tragic stories, their own feelings of failure.

★

Not wanting to call his parents and admit that things had gone so badly for him, Amrit let time pass in a blur. At night, he slept in a park sometimes or in a cot at a shelter if there was one available, and survived on free food offered by generous do-gooders. Amrit often had to duck into alleys much like the one he'd been assaulted in to relieve himself, hurriedly. His body pulsed with panic every time he was in a closed space.

He developed a loose social life, mostly lingering with other English-speakers. Amrit didn't want to have conversations; he didn't really want to get to know anyone. It seemed better to chat lightly with strangers and then move on. His adventures had come to a terrible, disappointing conclusion. He preferred not to talk about himself at all.

"So what's your story?" a new acquaintance asked as they finished up their free meal of corn tortillas, rice and beans. "How did you end up here?"

"Who knows, right?" Amrit regularly shrugged off such questions, not wanting to talk about it. "Well, I'd better move on. Nice meeting you. Good luck."

By himself, Amrit scanned streets during the day for hardly smoked cigarettes, a mission that passed the time and consumed him. As he focused only on the ground before him, he could forget about the other inhabitants of the bustling city — others who had places to be, people to meet up with, plans. Witnessing people living ordinary lives made Amrit despondent. There was no clear path in front of him, no destination, and that lack of a plan no longer felt like an exciting adventure. He especially didn't want to think about his parents. *Imagine how they would feel if they saw me now?* He shook his head as if in conversation with himself.

In this idle existence, he lost track of days, then weeks and months. Time didn't matter to him then. He was drained of hope and energy, most of the time he didn't feel anything at all. If Amrit started to, he learned to stop himself, or, within moments, grief and shame would circle his throat, throttling him. When that happened, Amrit would bend over as if he was suddenly winded and couldn't breathe. Like that night.

"A person on the streets in Mexico City can expect to live until they are in their mid-twenties," he was told one day by a well-meaning volunteer who handed him a paper-bag lunch. His age. Amrit wasn't sure if he cared if he lived or not then, and sometimes it seemed as if it would be easier not to. Not long after that Amrit met a different volunteer who took pity on him, which happened to be at a moment he was open to listening.

"Let's go to the Canadian embassy, let's get you sorted out so you can go home," the kind stranger offered. "I have some time today. I'll come with you."

As the stranger spoke, Amrit had the feeling that this might be his last chance to leave. A life preserver was being thrown to him and he felt, in that sliver of a moment, ready to catch it. The volunteer made it sound so uncomplicated. Amrit was reminded of the day he left Buenos Aires, when he could see that if he didn't make a change quickly, he might never change again. *I want to live*, Amrit decided. *Home. Yes. I want to go home.*

"Thank you," he said to the helper, who nodded and put a hand on his shoulder.

★

It was early in the morning when he dialled the number to his parents' house.

"Hello?" His mother's voice sounded as though he'd woken her up. He checked the time on the wall of the bus station where he'd spent the night. The handle of the payphone was heavy. Three people sat on the floor nearby watching him. The morning air smelled like cigarette smoke and old socks. *I should have waited an hour*, Amrit thought. *It's too early.*

He considered hanging up. Trying again later. Instead, he ventured, "Mom, it's me. It's Amrit."

She was quiet. *She's forgotten me.* Then his mom repeated his name back three times. "Amrit? Amrit. Amrit!" And then she shouted away from the receiver to tell his father "It's him!"

His dad took the phone then and said, "It is really you?"

"It's me, Dad. I'm back in Canada. I just got off a plane. I'm taking the Greyhound from Vancouver tonight and I'll arrive in the morning. Will you come get me from the station?"

When he stepped off the bus at the station he knew that he looked like a different person. He wore an ill-fitting pair of jeans and a golf shirt made for a much larger man. His clothes had been freshly washed when he was handed them at the embassy, but after two days of travel he felt sticky again, self-conscious about his own body odour. The waist of the jeans was rolled to keep his pants up, making a strange lump around his middle. He didn't own a belt. Amrit kept his head down, his shoulders hunched.

His mother reached out to hug him but he came toward her stiffly, his arms held close to his body. He felt the pain he had put her through and found it unbearable. "I'm so sorry, Mom. I should have called. I couldn't. I'm sorry. I should have," he rambled. He wondered for a moment if he had ever apologized to his mother before, at any point in his life. He didn't think so.

"You're here now," she said. "You're home."

His dad lingered a step behind. "My son. We are so happy to see you." Amrit was the one to draw toward his dad. He fell against his chest. His father held him close, as if he were an injured child, a boy who fell off a bicycle.

"Dad. I'm sorry. I made a mess of everything." He again pictured the girl running into the dark, the men moving toward him. Amrit wished then that he hadn't come home again. As his dad held him awkwardly, he closed his eyes and held in the sob that heaved in his chest as much as he could, and wished for the protective numbness he had felt only weeks before.

Over time, Amrit mentioned places he'd been to his parents but only briefly: The sprawl of Jakarta. The camels he rode in the Moroccan desert. The vibrancy of the Barranco district in Lima, which he thought was a place his mother would love to see. The quiet of the Hōnen-in temple in Kyoto, which, he said, his dad would prefer.

His mother gave up on him becoming a great success, a source of real pride for them and instead just hoped he'd find a stable job. A friend or two. At night, crouched in front of her god Shiva, she prayed for her son. That he might recover some of his old confidence again. But Amrit's shoulders still slouched inward, as if protecting his heart.

Amrit's mother died of cancer within only a few years and his father passed soon after. They left Amrit the house. Enough money to live too, frugally. Over time, he expanded into the space bit by bit, moving tentatively from his childhood bedroom into what was once a guest room because it faced the yard instead of the street, which he liked better. He eventually took down some of the framed prints of mountain scenes his mother had up, the ones he had never liked, but kept them in storage as though he might one day put them back. Though he lived in the same house he grew up in, it was becoming his own, with a mostly empty fridge and a phone that never rang.

Amrit rarely went past the store on the corner where he bought his groceries — premade sandwiches and fruit salad. Most days he left the TV on for the comfort of the noise, but he hardly watched it. Summer evenings, Amrit liked to sit on the front porch, thinking about things.

The street his house was on ran straight east to west so that at certain times of the year, the sun seemed to rise at one end of it and set at the other. There were hardly any trees, and those planted at the centre of the flat lawns looked parched, especially in summertime. From his front deck in warm weather, he caught glimpses of the lives of others: the clusters of boisterous children walking home from school together, the cars that arrived home from work at near the same time, disappearing into garage doors that gaped open just long enough for the vehicles to enter before closing again. Later, families emerged, sauntering out for evening walks together. Amrit watched them go by and if they waved he would say, "Beautiful evening!"

As he aged, his body bent inward even more. In his fifties, Amrit grew a layer of fat around his belly while the rest of him seemed to get thinner. Amrit was the first one out in the morning to shovel in the winter, so that the mail carrier, who came early, wouldn't slip, and he often shovelled a narrow pathway down the entire block, running the blade of the shovel across the new snow to reveal the concrete below, liking the achy feeling of remembered muscles. Now and then, Amrit took apart old computers, a useless VCR, out of that same curiosity that consumed him as a child. But now he also challenged himself to put it all back together again, in working order. He flipped through stacks of magazines he borrowed from the library and took his time washing his dishes after dinner, sweeping his own crumbs off the counter with the side of his hand rather than bothering with a cloth. He monitored the weather and made sure the drains of his house were pointed well away from the foundation, lengthening them with plastic extensions when it rained too hard.

He often observed a young couple across the street, watched as they moved in, painted the walls, planted flowers in pots on the front deck. He could feel the excitement of this life they were building, this confidence that the coming years would be just as happy. When a new baby arrived, well, some nights he could hardly sleep wondering if they'd be okay, sure they must be exhausted or overwhelmed by the sudden change in their lives. The mother, Grace, looked like his own mom when she was young, with her brown skin and long black hair, which made Amrit feel strangely paternal. If he'd had a sister, or even a daughter, Amrit thought, she might look like Grace.

When no family came by to help them out, he worried that maybe they had no one to step in when they wanted a break, or if they needed to borrow money. He heard in passing that the baby was a surrogate and didn't know much about how that worked but he guessed the whole thing was probably expensive. He remembered his own parents and how they had longed for grandkids, the way his mother used to reach out her arms when she saw a baby, always offering to hold it.

Amrit considered ways he could help them out but none seemed to quite fit. Neighbours gave him ideas when he asked, as they stopped to chat when they passed on their evening walks. Amrit was aware of the fissure inside him and didn't want others to see it, so he tried to sound carefree, lighthearted even, when he asked people what they thought the couple might need.

"I wonder what I could do for that family?" he said to the woman two houses down when she stopped by one afternoon with a bill that had accidentally been delivered to her house.

"Oh, there's no end to things a baby needs," she said as she handed him the white envelope. "Diapers or a little outfit, one of those bouncy chairs. Or how about one of those monitors so you can watch them sleep?"

"What's that?"

"You know, a camera that you put above the crib, and a monitor the parents can take downstairs while they have dinner or watch TV. So they know the baby's okay."

Amrit liked that idea and figured he could rig one up. He connected a camera module to a microcomputer, which would easily sync to any laptop. The tiny computer part took a full week to arrive, via mail order. It was, he realized, the first time he'd purchased a gift for another person for many years, maybe his whole life. The awareness gave him a new feeling of purpose.

He secured the cables and checked each connection. In the basement storage closet, Amrit found an old box with a broken clock inside and a bundle of wires he needed. He was grateful that his mother had kept a few things from his past projects. Working at the kitchen table, Amrit lost track of time. He started in the morning and stopped only for quick breaks until after dark.

When he took the contraption over to the neighbours and handed them the box with the monitor inside, they seemed surprised, speechless for a moment.

"It's a baby monitor," Amrit told them. "I hear they're handy."

"Oh wow," said Grace as she handed the box to her husband.

"I don't know what to say," said her husband. "Thanks." He set the box down on the floor and bent down to look into it. He picked up the monitor and turned it around in his hands as though he had never seen one before.

"No problem. I wanted to do something." Amrit still stood at the doorway. "Let me know if you have any trouble with it. I can help. Anytime."

"We will. And really, thank you." Grace kept the door open as he walked away, then waved one more time before shutting the door.

Amrit felt more confident to help out in other ways after that. He found an old wagon in the alley that he cleaned up and painted so it looked almost new again before delivering it to the family. He saw them pulling the growing baby across their yard in it one day, and the little one looked happy. When he was outside mowing his lawn he always pushed the machine across the street and mowed theirs too.

One day, on the internet, an ad came up for a package of stick-on stars, the kind that go on the ceiling and glow in the dark. Amrit thought of the night skies he had seen through his life. The past-midnight glow up north and then, in the winter, the darkness that lasted well past noon. The evening sky above the playground he used to stare at when he snuck out as a teen.

The stars over the Chilean desert where he had once camped with a friend he'd made playing roadside soccer in Uruguay.

He bought the stars for the child and, when the package arrived, he took them over, still in the plastic wrapping they came in.

★

The television was on in the living room, which Amrit remembered had been fully renovated, so that despite the house's age, it looked all new inside, like the after shots of a home reno show. The dad was watching car racing with the volume on low, the little one was asleep, curled up beside him. Their dog was there too, stretched out on the floor near the unlit gas fireplace.

"Why don't you come in? We could put these up in her room right now," offered Grace. "Maybe you could give me a hand while Sam's got Sadie. I think she'll just love them."

Amrit wondered if she only asked because she felt sorry for him but said yes.

The bedroom was painted pale yellow, the hue of a block of butter. There was a black and white family picture of the three of them hung on one wall, a life-sized tree decal, brown bark with green leaves, sprawled across another. A collection of stuffed animals — an elephant, a lion, a bunny — were lined up on a shelf. Amrit noticed that they hadn't installed the home-made monitor he'd given them but instead had a factory one, sleek and modern. He was embarrassed but then laughed at himself. "Well, that looks much safer than the one I rigged up."

"We still think it was very kind of you."

"I don't know anything about kids," Amrit admitted.

Together he and Grace put the stars up on the ceiling. By the time they were done, the child was awake again, so then the four of them — the family of three and Amrit — stood in the room together.

They switched off the light. Faded daylight came in through the pale curtains. But it was dark enough that the stars shone white in a way that felt real, almost as if they were standing beneath a real night sky, the stickers in random constellations of Grace and Amrit's own inventions.

Sadie, who was, by then in fact, nearly a toddler, chubby and rosy-cheeked, pointed up at the stars, wanting to make sure her father noticed. "Dada."

"That's right, sweetheart," he responded. "Just for you."

The greyish carpet was soft and plush beneath Amrit's sock feet. He thought that maybe he should install new carpet, a nice one like this, in his house too. It might be a job he could do himself. He could ask the couple for tips, how they did the rest of their renovation. Make a few updates himself. Modernize.

"Thank you," said the mother. "That's really something," said the dad.

"One day, when she's older, I'll tell her about the places I've been. All the adventures I had when I was young. Well, maybe not all, but a few of them." Amrit smiled. "Everywhere I went, even as the constellations changed, the stars in the night sky always made me feel like there was hope. Purpose, if you know what I mean."

By the time Amrit went home the sun was setting, tinging the sky pale pink. He took his time crossing the familiar street, whistling as he cut across his lawn to his own blue house, think-ing of what he might watch that night, that he might order a pizza for dinner. Thinking that it felt good to have been useful, to have given something. Maybe it still wasn't too late for him to be the kind of person his parents had wanted him to be, Amrit considered. There was, after all, still time.

He checked the mail and noticed that the scrubby rose bush beside the deck that his mother had planted long ago was thirsty, the leaves browning at the edges. Now and then a few hardy flowers blossomed, but the plant was overgrown and struggling along, as it had since his parents had passed away. Amrit had managed to keep it alive by running the hose at its base for a few minutes when he was watering the lawn but he did nothing more. He would soak the bush well that night, he decided. And then learn how to prune it properly. There had to be some way he could get it to produce more of the yellow roses his mother had loved.

He wondered how hard it would be to plant a garden too, replace some of the ordinary turf. At one time there were notices on the bulletin outside the community association advertising free workshops. He could meet people in a class, he thought. Gardeners, he thought, would be good people to know, imagining them to be quiet and optimistic. Amrit envisioned even replacing the whole lawn over time as he'd seen that some people were doing, and he could learn how to really care for it all too. *Yes, that would be meaningful,* Amrit thought as he pulled a vagrant weed from a crack between the sidewalk and front step and twirled it between his thumb and index finger. *Look, I'm starting to make things better already.*

An Astonishment of Stars

THERE WERE LOUD BANGS WHEN THE ENGINES DIED, followed by quiet, the rush of air over the wings while the jet's path bent toward the jagged peaks of the mountain range below. As the plane descended the hundreds of passengers closed their eyes, held their breath, gripped their armrests. The captain stayed calm, pointed to an alpine meadow well above the treeline, signalling to his co-pilot that he would land the plane there, and, incredibly, did.

The impact of the plane hitting the ground whipped passengers' heads forward then back again, bodies held into their seats at their hips by straining nylon belts. The plane hammered across the uneven earth, pounded up and down. It took time after the aircraft eventually stopped for the travellers to look around and realize they were still alive. Rescue helicopters arrived and ferried the survivors from the edge of the long alpine meadow to the nearest hospital to be checked over. The official reports said there were injuries but no deaths in the near-catastrophe.

The eerily undamaged jet was investigated by teams of officials, emptied of fuel and passengers' belongings. It was secured, and then left where it landed.

Years later, hearing of the abandoned airplane, a rich man leased the area from the government on a whim and hired an exclusive architectural firm to convert the structure into a home. It was an unusual place to live, but the idea wasn't unique. During and after the pandemic, the wealthy were looking for places away from civilization — buying up swathes of land, purchasing cruise ships for private use, controversially even building man-made private islands created just for them.

Workers used metal pillars to balance the aircraft, taut steel cables to anchor the body and wings to pins that extended through the shallow surface soil into the rock below. The architect put the narrow primary bedroom near the rear of the plane, another smaller bedroom closer to the middle, next to a full bathroom. The ceilings at the front of the structure were higher, so they put the kitchen and living room there, adding dormers to bring more natural light into those rooms, to open them to the scenery. Most of the original windows were preserved down the length of the structure, bringing in oval patches of light throughout the day. The cylindrical curve of the walls remained too, along with most of the overhead bins, still useful for storage. Around the front of the plane they built a wide patio with a long, sturdy staircase to the ground. The cost to install a septic system and running water was enormous, as were the solar panels for electricity, satellite for internet.

When it was finished, the rich man moved in but lasted only weeks before leaving again. He was quoted as saying that he wasn't prepared for what it was really like to live that far away from other people, and that he preferred to live somewhere more civilized. He donated the whole thing back to the government, who eventually established it as an environmental research station, a high-altitude location to monitor the climate as it changed over time. From that height, it was easy to study the altering patterns of weather.

Tonight, the wind comes from the north, urging the tethered airplane forward. Past midnight, Priya lies awake listening to the creak and heave of the metal structure around her. Four-year-old Aadi is asleep, wedged between his parents. His hair is wet with sweat — he is always hot when indoors, so used to his outdoor mountain life. Every night he stays in his own narrow bed only for a short time, then slips to their room, into the crevice between them, whispering, "Mama, move over."

Priya's husband, Tarak, snores in an even, not-unpleasant way that drowns out the industrial noises of their tin can home. Still, Priya can't sleep. She slides an arm out from under her son's body. There is little room on either side of the bed in the narrow space, so she eases to the end, puts one foot down then the other before standing. Like water, Tarak and Aadi move easily into the available space. Aadi shifts into the dent in the sheet she leaves, Tarak stretches to fill out the extra room in the middle. Priya steps over the dog, Charlie, sleeping in a circle, nose tucked under his tail. She takes her favourite knit cardigan — the only thing of her mother's she brought here — from the hook on the wall, puts it on over her flannel pyjamas. Charlie thumps his tail on the floor. When she hushes at him to be quiet, he loyally stands up and follows her. Feet bare, she walks silently down the low hallway. With her fingertips she touches the overhead bins, camouflaged by shining faux wood. Charlie's nails click on the hard floor a step behind her.

When Priya and Tarak first heard the story of the converted plane they were sitting outside, at a café near their downtown apartment, in the same city where they had met, in the environmental science undergraduate classes they ended up in together.

That day they were each scrolling through social media on their phones. It was a Saturday in mid-autumn. There was a chill in the air, but it was still warm enough to be outdoors wearing jeans and light jackets. Priya read parts of the story about the plane made into a dwelling aloud from her screen, turning it to show Tarak the picture. "Isn't that wild," she said.

Tarak glanced at the image. "Imagine the view," he agreed, then seemed to not think any more of it.

Priya kept reading, staying up late that night, searching for articles and enlarging photos on her screen to see the airplane's details better. The story was compelling to her — a near-disaster reimagined into something useful again, something beautiful. As if, Priya thought, the plane showed how resilient people were. How resourceful humans could be.

Over the next year, Aadi was born. Then, soon after, Priya's mother passed away unexpectedly. The time was so quick between the two momentous events, as if the souls of her mother and son switched places, so that Priya's joy was weighted by grief. She could never have imagined becoming a parent without her own mother nearby. The two had been close all her life. Even as an adult, so much about her daily life reminded Priya of her loss. Most days she had called her mom on the way home from work and had imagined one day passing the phone to her children too, so that they could talk to their grandmother. Most Sundays they had still made and eaten dinner together. Priya had always imagined that weekly tradition would carry on after she and Tarak had a family.

When Aadi was crying she didn't know how to make him stop, couldn't figure out what he wanted. She tried nursing him, changing his diaper, bouncing him up and down as she paced the bedroom.

"I don't know what's wrong either, but why don't I take him?" Tarak would say.

"My mother would know," she accused. Priya was afraid her baby could feel her incompetence, or worse, her sorrow, and was responding in kind. Arguing with Tarak made her feel mean. A moment later, ashamed.

"I wish we had the help too. Let me try, Priya. I'll take him so you can rest at least."

When she was exhausted enough she finally agreed, feeling defeated. "Just give him a bottle if he's hungry. I don't think he wants me."

Over time, Priya realized that, for her family, she needed to stop looking for her mother in the places she used to be. She started taking a different route home from work, listened to the radio on the drive now that there was no one she wanted to call to discuss her day with. Priya hired a babysitter and made plans to go to the movies with Tarak on Sundays. Or they went out for lunch so that she might forget the family dinners at home they once shared. Then she began looking at different employment opportunities and scrolling real estate listings in her spare time, thinking it was time to move too.

Searching through job postings on her lunch break one day, Priya stopped at an ad seeking a weather scientist to staff the renovated airplane they had read about all that time ago, and, without even talking to Tarak, put in her application right away. Four months later, she was hired.

They put their extra things in storage, sublet their apartment, said goodbye to their friends. They got Charlie from a rescue shelter, thinking he could be a good companion for Aadi in an otherwise peerless place. There would be no preschool or afternoon playdates for him so far away from their home, from the city, so distanced from everyone they knew.

Priya's job is simple enough. With her background in atmospheric science, she easily fills out a series of spreadsheets charting weather patterns, wind speeds, and then notes corresponding wildlife sightings and migration patterns. She submits information electronically every day. Tarak, working on his next degree, studies the changing climate's impact on mountain ecosystems. Every two weeks, a government helicopter brings groceries, packages, other necessities. It is a long walk back to civilization but not impossible to do in a day. Mostly, they are alone. Now and then hikers make their way from the backcountry campsite down the mountain, usually to see the plane.

Priya still imagines conversations with her deceased mother, thinks about how she would describe the spectacular landscape to her. When Aadi draws, she is aware that his crayoned pictures will never decorate her mother's fridge or walls, and then the sharp sorrow engulfs her, as if it were new again.

Nights in their airplane home are the hardest. Despite all the effort to make the airplane feel like a real home, its bones are metal. There is nothing organic in the structure of it, no wood or brick, nothing warm or soft embedded in its original construction. At night Priya considers how long a machine made for motion can be held still, against its nature. The plane's original purpose was to move, and she feels the tension in the way it is held, like a suspended breath in the heavy darkness outside, so different from the city nights she knew before. When Tarak and Aadi are so soundly asleep, Priya feels called to nightwatch.

She pulls her sweater closer around her, pours a glass of water and sits down at the table, looking out at the blue-black night sky pierced by an astonishment of stars, the outline of the wings faintly glowing. Charlie goes back to sleep on the rug in the kitchen, stretched out on his side, restlessly dreaming. When a line of light appears along the horizon, and the wind quiets, signalling morning, she walks to Aadi's room, where she falls asleep in his narrow bed, under the duvet they brought from their apartment, the colourful cover printed with alligators.

Hours later, Priya is back at the table eating breakfast, a bowl of the same kind of cereal she eats most mornings. When she was younger, it was the only kind of cereal her parents ever bought. The sameness that used to bother her is a comfort now.

She looks out through the window to where Tarak and Aadi are lounging like black bears on the wide rocks that jut from the surface. His work equipment in a waterproof toolbox beside him, Tarak reclines face up, sun shining down on him. Aadi has his yellow plastic bulldozer and is lying on his belly, driving it across the rock. His coat is unzipped as he prefers that it billows up in the wind, and he is wearing his rubber boots. He kicks idly at the rock with his toe. *I wish my mother could see him, how thoughtful and serious he is, more like me than Tarak,* she thinks. Priya lifts her hand to the window as if about to rap on it with her knuckles to get their attention. Instead, she lays her palm flat on the glass. From this distance, they would not hear her.

Days later Priya is looking out the same window. On the stove she is simmering a pot of chai. Growing up, her family often had a pot of strong black tea with spices simmering on the stove. Priya makes a milder blend — adding whole cinnamon sticks, ginger, cardamom, peppercorns and cloves to their list of supplies. The smell of the warm spices fills the plane. Tarak and Aadi have cheerfully gone for a walk with a packed lunch and snacks, planning to be gone for most of the day.

A stranger walks across the meadow and Priya watches to see if the rest of his hiking group follows him, but the middle-aged man appears to be alone. He stops and sits down on a boulder, looks up at the airplane, pulls a water bottle from his backpack and takes a long drink. From the same bag he takes a square cardboard box and sets it down on the rock beside him. He removes his canvas hat and runs his hands through his grey hair, wipes his forehead on the sleeve of his fleece jacket.

Priya switches off the stove. Putting on her cardigan, she steps outside onto the deck. The aroma of chai drifts outside from the kitchen. The man raises his hand in the air as an acknowledgement, and Priya waves back. Charlie races past her to greet him, barking happily, and he reaches down to pat his head. Priya walks down the stairs across the green toward them, and the man stands up, picking up the box so it is held in the crook of his arm, cradled.

"I saw your husband a ways back," he says as a greeting. "He said you wouldn't mind the intrusion. I hired a guide to get me to camp yesterday but he pointed me in the right direction this morning."

Priya notices him still looking at the plane. "Of course. People like to come and see. It's really extraordinary." Speaking to strangers is uncommon for her now, she realizes, feeling awkward.

"Yes, well," he replies. For a time they are both quiet, looking up toward the plane. Then, "I've been wanting to come but it took me a while. I couldn't decide."

"Why don't you come up? We can sit on the deck, you can see even more from there," offers Priya, gesturing to the plane. "I just made tea." Usually she wouldn't invite a stranger up, not when she's by herself, but to her own surprise she doesn't hesitate.

"Well, sure. If it's no trouble."

The two walk across the meadow, Charlie running ahead and then falling behind. Priya stays in front up the stairs to the deck, the wind pushing at them gently.

"Have a seat anywhere you like." She gestures toward the heavy chairs surrounding the wooden table that is permanently affixed to the outdoor space. The colourful cushions around it are faded by the sun.

Priya strains the spiced tea from the stove into a ceramic pot then brings it out with two cups, sets everything down and pours. The box is between them. She notices that the cardboard is soft, rounded at the edges from being handled.

They both sip their tea, making small talk for a few minutes, then the man says, "You see, my brother died on that plane."

"But they said everyone lived." Priya puts down her cup and crosses her arms, feeling cold.

"He was flying on his own. I managed to track down the woman who was sitting beside him, she said he seemed fine the whole flight. He chatted with her kids a bit but kept mostly to himself. He ate, had a drink, slept a while. After the plane landed, they looked over and he was just gone, slumped over. Heart attack, they said. The shock of it all, I think. But not technically because of the crash." He pauses.

"It must have been terrible. I think about it often," Priya empathizes.

"Almost seems fitting that he'd die on an airplane though. He was always a traveller. Did all kinds of odd jobs all over the place. Never had a family of his own, that I knew of at least." He smiles. "I always wanted him to meet mine, get to know them."

Priya thinks of her mother then too, the familiar ache of knowing her son will never know his grandmother either.

"I've had his ashes with me all these years. Never sure where he'd want to be in the end. But I was looking at the pictures a while ago" — he gestures with his chin toward the plane — "and thought maybe the right thing was to bring him back here."

Priya takes a sip of her tea and then says, "I know just the place."

She goes in and comes back with a windbreaker and her boots on, leaving Charlie behind so he won't be a distraction, hearing him whine as she closes the door. The two walk back down the stairs and across the meadow, down a hill that leads to a steep drop, looking over another rolling meadow of brushy green.

"This is the best view," she says. "You can watch the sun both rise and set from here."

The man wipes at his eyes roughly. "Perfect."

"I can leave you here if you like," she offers.

"No, it's fine with me if you stay." He pauses. "Maybe if you know where he is, you could watch over him for me."

Priya stays back as the man walks closer toward the drop. She looks up to the wide sky to give him privacy but she stays standing, touches a low bush beside her to steady herself. The man sets the box down on the ground to pull it open and takes a clear plastic bag full of ash from inside it.

He holds the bag in one hand and reaches in with the other to take a handful. The heavier bits fall like stones between his fingers while the lighter ash rises in clouds like dust, swirling into the clear air, hazing the view before them. After each handful, the man pauses in silence.

Priya thinks how different this is from the formal ceremony that was organized by older relatives for her mother. She envies the man this quiet space in which to say goodbye, this final intimacy. She imagines herself invisible so that she doesn't intrude on this farewell between the two siblings. This, she understands watching the man, is what she has wanted too.

There is little ash left, so he turns the bag to shake the remaining dust out into the air before putting it away in his jacket pocket. Priya hands the box back to him too. He wipes his hands on his pants before taking it, flattens it down to a thin rectangle that he tucks under his arm. The man looks outward for a time, then turns toward her and says, "Well, I guess that's done now."

She nods.

"Thank you." He meets her eyes for a moment.

"I'll look out for him."

He doesn't stay for long after that. Priya climbs back up to the deck to let the dog out, while the man waits at the boulder where she first saw him. Tarak and Aadi return; Charlie barks joyfully when he sees them. Aadi holds a fist-sized rock in one hand and a collection of short sticks in the other. He sets his treasures down on the bottom step before they all walk with the man back toward his camp, staying in a single line on the narrowness of the trail. Below the treeline, the family says goodbye to him. On the way home Tarak and Priya take turns carrying Aadi on their backs. Charlie stays close enough to keep track of them all.

They tuck Aadi into his own bed early, seeing that he's tired from the long day. Priya lies awake, facing away from sleeping Tarak, waiting for Aadi to wake and patter into their room. She thinks of her mother and wishes she could tell her about the day, talk to her about the man, the way the ashes lifted in the after-noon light before drifting downward. She hears Charlie shift on the floor as Aadi makes his way around the dog. Priya moves over to make room as Aadi wiggles into the space in the mid-dle, pressing his knees into her back as he curls against her. That night, for the first time, Priya is lulled to sleep by the creaking of the plane, still pulling, as if wanting to rise again.

Acknowledgements

SOME OF THESE STORIES HAVE BEEN INCLUDED IN LITERARY magazines. "Daksha Takes the Cake" was first published in *The Fiddlehead*, and "An Astonishment of Stars" was published by *Prairie Fire*, under the title "The Landing." *Thin Air Magazine* was the first publisher of "Invasion." Thank you to these magazines and the many others that make space for new writers.

Thank you so much to Jen Sookfong Lee for editing this book with such care and insight. You're a beacon of Canadian literature and it was a dream come true to work with you. I am forever grateful to you and ECW Press for believing in this book.

I was fortunate to also work on this collection with author and mentor Barb Howard as part of a four-month program through the Alexandra Writers' Centre. We used this time to talk through many of these stories, both over email and Zoom chats that always ran long. Barb, I am truly grateful for the time and effort you put into this project.

Thank you to the Calgary Public Library, and to all public libraries, for making the works of other authors abundantly available. To this day, nothing makes me feel richer than coming home with a fresh stack of books to read.

To each of my dear friends, the people who share my community and who know all about this writing adventure: thank you for (often literally) walking with me.

Lucie Chan, thank you for always reminding me how much art really matters. Sonal Champsee, ViNa Nguyễn, Samantha Jones, Precious de Leon and Monda Mahmoud: our conversations about craft stay with me. I'm grateful for your wisdom and encouragement.

To my mum and dad: your open door and generosity have made your house a second home for so many. My love of stories began with those I heard told around our table.

Mark, Nikhil, Ravi: you are my everything. You've encouraged me, believed in me, inspired me — and tiptoed around me so I could keep working (sometimes obsessively). Mark, your willingness to talk through my every win and frustration has been incredible. I'm so lucky to journey through this life with you.

KIRTI BHADRESA lives in inner city Calgary, on Treaty 7 territory, with her family. She is an avid reader, a non-linear gardener, an enthusiastic baker and a frequently outraged optimist with a soft spot for odd dogs.

Entertainment. Writing. Culture. ─────────

ECW is a proudly independent, Canadian-owned book publisher. We know great writing can improve people's lives, and we're passionate about sharing original, exciting, and insightful writing across genres.

───────────────────── **Thanks for reading along!**

We want our books not just to sustain our imaginations, but to help construct a healthier, more just world, and so we've become a certified B Corporation, meaning we meet a high standard of social and environmental responsibility — and we're going to keep aiming higher. We believe books can drive change, but the way we make them can too.

Being a B Corp means that the act of publishing this book should be a force for good – for the planet, for our communities, and for the people that worked to make this book. For example, everyone who worked on this book was paid at least a living wage. You can learn more at the Ontario Living Wage Network.

This book is also available as a Global Certified Accessible™ (GCA) ebook. ECW Press's ebooks are screen reader friendly and are built to meet the needs of those who are unable to read standard print due to blindness, low vision, dyslexia, or a physical disability.

The interior of this book is printed on Sustana EnviroBook™, which is made from 100% recycled fibres and processed chlorine-free.

FSC
www.fsc.org
MIX
Paper | Supporting responsible forestry
FSC® C016245

ECW's office is situated on land that was the traditional territory of many nations including the Wendat, the Anishnaabeg, Haudenosaunee, Chippewa, Métis, and current treaty holders the Mississaugas of the Credit. In the 1880s, the land was developed as part of a growing community around St. Matthew's Anglican and other churches. Starting in the 1950s, our neighbourhood was transformed by immigrants fleeing the Vietnam War and Chinese Canadians dispossessed by the building of Nathan Phillips Square and the subsequent rise in real estate value in other Chinatowns. We are grateful to those who cared for the land before us and are proud to be working amidst this mix of cultures.

ecwpress.com